"Frankly, Mr. Rider, I'm not convinced you're able to provide a stable environment for the children without a wife...."

The color drained from Jon's face as he stared at the social worker.

"My children are not leaving this ranch!" His shout echoed off the walls, the effect of his words clear from the small, pale faces of his children.

The eight-year-old girl looked boldly at Kaycee, her expression determined despite the apprehension imprinted there. She grabbed Kaycee's hand and pulled her down to eye level. "I'm Michele. What's your name?"

Startled, she replied, "Kaycee Calloway."

"Hurry!" Michele dragged Kaycee until she stumbled forward—right into the fray. Jon jerked toward them in surprise. The social worker eyed Kaycee over the rim of her glasses.

"This is her," Michele announced. "This is our new mother. We don't need a housekeeper anymore."

Dear Reader,

How did an only child from Alabama get tangled up with a widowed rancher, his seven children and a spirited lady vet? All I can say is, I didn't find them, they found me, clamoring to get their story on paper. But I grew to love them before the book was finished.

The loss of a family member is always heartbreaking, but it's especially traumatic for children. What if a child can't get past her mother's death? How does she cope? How does she deal with another woman threatening to take her mother's place?

And what will a father do to keep his young children safe from his in-laws when they're seeking custody? Anything, including faking an engagement to a woman he's just met.

But Kaycee Calloway has been hurt before, and getting roped into a pretend engagement is the last thing she wants. Besides she's got a demanding veterinary practice, which doesn't mesh with Jon's expectation of a wife and mother. Can she extricate herself from this predicament before she loses her heart to this sexy rancher and his lovable brood?

I hope you'll enjoy the ride as Jon, Kaycee and the kids learn that love is what defines a family—and no two are alike.

I love hearing from readers, so keep in touch! Write me at eygrant@aol.com or at 14241 Coursey Boulevard, Suite A-12 #212, Baton Rouge, LA 70817, or visit www.elainegrant.com or www.superauthors.com.

Elaine Grant

MAKE-BELIEVE MOM
Elaine Grant

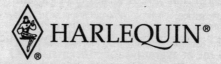

HARLEQUIN®

TORONTO • NEW YORK • LONDON
AMSTERDAM • PARIS • SYDNEY • HAMBURG
STOCKHOLM • ATHENS • TOKYO • MILAN • MADRID
PRAGUE • WARSAW • BUDAPEST • AUCKLAND

ISBN-13: 978-0-373-71445-2
ISBN-10:   0-373-71445-9

MAKE-BELIEVE MOM

This edition published by arrangement with Harlequin Books S.A.

® and TM are trademarks of the publisher. Trademarks indicated with
® are registered in the United States Patent and Trademark Office, the
Canadian Trade Marks Office and in other countries.

www.eHarlequin.com

Printed in U.S.A.

ABOUT THE AUTHOR

If you could own any horse it would be... son of the Black Stallion, named Satan. **Zane Grey or Louis L'Amour?** Both. **Did you have Breyer model horses growing up?** Oh, yes. **Do you still have your stable?** Yes, but most of the horses have broken and reglued legs because I rode my toy horses hard! **Who was your favorite?** My favorite was my rearing white stallion—or maybe his foal. (Can you tell I'm Pisces? One choice is not an option.) **Best cowboy name ever?** Bronco Lane. **Cowboys are your weakness because...** I admire their quiet toughness. "Talk low, talk slow and don't say too much."—John Wayne **Favorite hurtin' song?** "(Ghost) Riders in the Sky" (by anybody who does it). **What makes the cowboy?** Attitude—but a low-ridin' hat doesn't hurt.

This book is lovingly dedicated to my husband, Tony, and son, Justin, for their constant love and support in spite of my obsession with made-up worlds; my mother, Julia, who patiently read and reread the different versions; and my Aunt Grace, whose faith in me never wavers.

ACKNOWLEDGMENT

I would like to thank the following people for their knowledge, support, willingness to help, encouragement and input. Any misinterpretations or errors belong to me, not them.

My critique partners: Eleanor, Sylvia and Kris, who know this story backward and forward.

Barb McCritty, an extremely knowledgeable rancher from Wyoming, who gave me invaluable insights; Sandra Cahill of 63 Ranch near Livingston, Montana, who answered my questions about Kaycee and made her look good. Also, Noelle in Big Sky for pointing me to the ambience of Rainbow Ranch for that special date.

Bora Sunseri, who answered question after question about Child Protection Services and how a good social worker would interact with a family. Flavia Wright, science teacher, for input on school disciplinary issues.

Wally Lind and all the folks on his Crimescenewriter group, who answered many technical questions on child abuse, law enforcement and search and rescue.

Dr. C. J. Lyons, pediatric emergency physician, for emergency medical procedures.

CHAPTER ONE

TOMORROW HAD TO be better—if only he could make it through today. In weary frustration, Jon Rider wiped the sweat off his forehead with his upper arm. The anxious mother-to-be in front of him, held immobile by the headgate of the calving pen, lowed in distress and kicked at her swollen belly.

"Yeah, I don't blame you," Jon muttered. "I wouldn't want to be in your position."

His own position wasn't ideal, up past the elbow in the slippery birth canal of a first-year heifer. His hand measured the breadth of the two hooves stuck in the pelvic opening with little room for them to push through, and none for the calf's head. Jon's bare chest gleamed with sweat, blood and sticky amniotic fluid. For most of an hour, he'd been trying to turn the big calf so he and Clint could pull it, but he had resolved himself to the hard truth. This baby wasn't coming out the back door any way you looked at it, and a C-section was out of his league. If he didn't get help soon, he stood to lose both mother and calf—something he couldn't afford just now.

"No luck, huh," Clint said, striding loose-jointed down the aisle of the calving barn.

Jon extricated his arm and got up. "Not a bit. Is the vet coming?"

"Got the answering service." He raked his tousled sandy hair back and reset his hat. "Said she'd send out somebody named Dr. K. C. Calloway soon as she could."

"Great," Jon said. "Must be the young vet that took over old Doc Adams's practice. Know anything about him?"

"Naw, no reason to." Clint Ford had been foreman at the R-Bar-R ranch for thirty years. The veteran cowhand held to the old way of doing things, hands on and without outside help.

K. C. Calloway. Sounded like an outlaw's name. Hopefully the new vet could handle the job. Having learned from the best—his dad and Clint—Jon prided himself in rarely needing a vet. Birth was a natural progression on a ranch, as was death. Repositioning and pulling a calf was routine. But this narrow heifer needed help he couldn't give her. He had an excellent calving setup, so a C-section on the premises wouldn't be a problem—if the vet ever arrived.

"I'll finish feeding in the other barn unless you need me for something here," Clint said.

"I don't know anything we can do right now. Go ahead."

In the washroom, Jon lathered his chest and arms, toweled off, then slipped his flannel shirt on, letting it hang loose over his jeans. Pacing to the end of the barn, he scowled down the empty road leading to the ranch, then glanced toward the house.

Hopefully, things were going better there than with the heifer lowing behind him. Jon still expected Alison to walk out, waving for him to come in for breakfast. He shook his head. Impossible. She was gone.

And so was the last housekeeper. So, maybe the twins *had* locked her in the cellar and maybe they *had* threatened to burn her at the stake if she didn't bake cookies. Was that really a good reason to walk out on him? They were five years old—they couldn't even reach the matches. A smile twitched at his lips. They were just boys.

Clint joined him at the door, restless, shuffling his six-foot-four frame from foot to foot.

"Aren't you supposed to be somewhere with Claire this afternoon?" Jon asked.

"Some kinda music recital she's in. Don't matter. You need me here….".

"And what are you going to do if you stay? You can't get that calf out any better than I can." He knew how much it meant to Clint to make up for lost time with his daughter. She'd only come to live with him this year, to attend Montana State University in Bozeman. They'd been separated by distance since Clint's divorce when Claire was nine. "Once the vet comes, the section won't take but the two of us. Go on with Claire."

Gratitude and relief swept over Clint's leathery face. "You sure, Jon? You know I'll hang around."

"Claire's more important. Clean up and get out of here. If I need help, I'll pull somebody off another job."

Clint bobbed his head once and disappeared around the corner. Alone in the shadow of the barn, Jon's gaze drifted to the wild beauty of the high country, but even with the sun glinting off the snowcapped peaks, it didn't touch him today. Only hinted of early floods.

Everything about this winter had bitten him hard. Stunned into slow motion over the past year, he'd inadvertently let some things slip between the cracks—important things, things he'd never been careless of before. This heifer for example.

He always bred a first-year heifer for a small calf, but during breeding season, his in-laws hit him with that lawsuit over custody of the kids....

Jon pivoted on his heel toward the suffering heifer, his jaw clenched so hard the muscles ached. He couldn't absorb many more losses.

Where the hell was that vet! He strode to the phone on the post and was punching in the number when the crunch of tires on gravel followed by the slam of a door caught his attention.

"Well, finally," he said, hanging up. Silhouetted against the bright sunshine outside, the vet walked into the dark barn holding a large metal case in either hand. Jon couldn't make out any features but he noticed the vet's frail frame. Somehow he had a hard time picturing this guy pulling an obstinate calf out of a cow's backside or manhandling an irate bull.

As the vet approached, Jon's gaze traveled slowly upward, taking in coveralls tucked into Justin boots, shapely legs and sleeves rolled to the elbows displaying smooth, well-muscled forearms. A baseball cap shaded one of the prettiest faces he'd ever seen.

A woman?

Just showed how much he got into town these days, else he'd have heard about this. The new vet was a woman. And she was watching him with intense green eyes. Her light brown hair was swept back into a ponytail and looped through the hole in back of her cap, but a few curling tendrils had escaped.

She smiled as she put down one of the medical cases and held out her hand. "Hi, I'm Katherine Calloway, Kaycee for short. I believe you're Mr. Rider?"

"Yes. Jon Rider. Glad you're here." Impressed with her firm, confident handshake and enthralled by her soft-spoken Southern drawl, Jon reserved judgment about her vetting ability.

Kaycee cocked her head slightly. "Yes, I'm a woman. Yes, I'm a vet. Yes, I can pull a calf."

Jon hoped the dim light hid the embarrassment he felt. She smiled again, released his hand and picked up the metal box.

"Let's see what we can do for you."

Jon cleared his throat and tried to clear his head as he led the way. "Pretty sure she needs a C-section. Calf's huge, she's not." He stepped aside when they reached the heifer.

Kaycee didn't look around, but she could sense Jon Rider watching her every move as she opened her cases. She'd learned to get on with the job before the ranchers had time to object to her being a woman. Generally, once she successfully treated their animals, they grudgingly accepted her.

Although he hid it well, she sensed Jon's skepticism, but to his credit, he hadn't been rude to her like some had. No snide comments, no come-on for a date or worse—at least not yet. Whatever he might think of a young female vet, he was keeping it to himself and Kaycee appreciated that.

Or maybe he was just worried about his livestock. With good reason, Kaycee saw at once, as the heifer strained. Kaycee slipped on a shoulder-length OB glove and did a quick exam. This calf was locked solidly behind the mother's pelvic bone.

"You're right, she needs a Caesar. Let's prep her." Kaycee pulled a pair of electric clippers from her equipment chest. "Where can I plug these in?"

"I can shave her while you wash up," Jon said. He pointed out the washroom across the aisle.

"I'm going to give her a sedative to calm her, then a paravertebral block on the left side. Shave along her spine and from here to here and down her side." Kaycee indicated with her hands the area from the heifer's top midline to low on the flank.

By the time she returned, Jon had done an expert job of shaving the cow. Kaycee prepped the area, injected lidocaine along the edges of the vertebrae to block the nerves and laid out her instruments beside Jon's pulling chains. By now, the barn smelled strongly of antiseptic mingled with warm animal hide, sweet hay and human tension, the familiar scent of the career Kaycee had chosen long ago. Clean hay had been spread around the calving area.

Kaycee cast a glance at Jon. "Nice spread. How many head do you run?"

"Thousand to fifteen hundred, year to year."

Kaycee raised her eyebrows as she calculated the range necessary to graze that big a herd. Forty or fifty thousand acres. And this was the first time she'd been called out here.

Kaycee's scalpel sliced smoothly just behind the ribs, through thick hide and muscle. The anesthetized heifer munched contentedly on a sheaf of hay, unconcerned that her side now lay open under the surgical drape. "How long has she been in labor?"

"Couple of hours before I called you, maybe. We had her on close watch since yesterday. She was fine through the night, started showing signs of trouble this morning," Jon said, his voice edged with concern. "Calf locked up. I tried to turn it, but she was pushing too hard. Couldn't budge it."

"It's way too big. Sometimes Mother Nature plays tricks like that."

A careful second cut opened the peritoneum. Kaycee gently moved the rumen aside, then reached into the heat of the heifer's body, searching by feel for a foot to use as a guide to cut into the uterus. Finding it, she made a precise incision and extended the opening enough to deliver the calf without tearing. As she drew the foot out, Jon passed her a pulling chain, which she popped over the calf's leg above the fetlock adding a half hitch below to give surer purchase on the slippery legs. Handing the first chain off to Jon, Kaycee groped through the warm blood until she found the calf's other hind leg and attached the second pulling chain. Once the uterus was open, there was precious little time to get the calf out alive.

She worked quickly, with deft, practiced hands, ignoring the trickle of sweat down her forehead. She didn't want to admit that this baby's life might already be beyond saving. She sensed that same dread in Jon Rider, as he watched in silence.

Kaycee nodded. "Okay, let's get it out."

Jon set his full weight against the chains. She grabbed the calf's slippery hindquarters. Together they struggled to tug the sodden calf out of the steaming security of its mother's body.

"Daddy! Oh, yuck, what are you doing?"

Startled, Kaycee hazarded a quick glance at the breathless little girl pushing long, sun-streaked hair out of her eyes and staring in disgust at the cow's bloody side.

"Not now, Michele."

"But, Daddy, you have to come in—"

"Not now," Jon said in a sterner voice.

"But, Daddy, Rachel says—"

"Is Bo worse?"

"No, sir."

"Is anybody hurt?"

"No, sir."

"Is the house on fire?" Jon shot the questions at her in staccato succession, his voice choked from the effort to free the calf.

"No. But—"

"Then it can wait. Go back in the house."

"*Dad*-dy."

"Go!" Jon ordered, repositioning his weight, subtly changing the direction of the leverage.

"Good," Kaycee said. "It's coming. Just slow."

The wide-eyed girl turned and ran. Kaycee concentrated on her work, but it worried her that the child had seemed frightened. Maybe it was just the shock of coming upon a cow with her belly slit and a calf hanging half out.

Jon made no further comment as he strained harder against the chains.

"We need somebody else to pull," Kaycee said, her knuckles white as she gripped the slippery skin.

"I don't have anybody else around right now," Jon muttered between clenched teeth. "Stubborn little fellow."

Kaycee dug her heels in, knowing her strength would fail soon. Stinging sweat trickled into her eyes. Jon braced a booted foot against a support post and widened his stance. Sweat streamed down his face, too, veins popped out in his neck and his hard thigh muscles swelled beneath his jeans as he grunted with the effort. The chains inched back, digging into his leather gloves.

The calf's body shifted and the suction of the uterus gave way with a soft whoosh. The massive black calf squirted into Kaycee's arms, its weight staggering her backward. Jon caught her against his chest. He reached around her, grasped the big calf by the hind legs and hauled it out of her grip, gently shaking it to clear the mucus.

"Take care of my heifer," Jon said. "I'll see to this one."

Kaycee jerked her head toward one of her cases. "There's a resuscitator in there. Looks like you might need it."

Finding no postpartum problems, Kaycee cleaned and sutured the incision layer by layer. Behind her she heard Jon working feverishly with the calf, talking softly, urging it to live. All the while the mother stood patiently, her pain relieved by the anesthetic. She tried once or twice to look around for her calf, but the headgate restricted her. After a penicillin shot to waylay infection, Kaycee gathered her equipment.

She flicked a glance at Jon. He sat on the floor of the barn, his broad shoulders hunched over the black calf gathered in his arms like a child. He'd given up on the artificial resuscitator and was blowing his own breath into the calf, determined to force life into it. He jumped when Kaycee stooped beside him and put her hand on his shoulder.

"It's too late. He was probably dead before we pulled him."

"It's not too late." Jon blew another stubborn breath into the calf's nostrils.

"Use the resuscitator."

"Tried it," Jon said between breaths. "This is better."

Kaycee ran her fingers up and down the limp calf's sides, encouraging circulation. Still the baby didn't move. She watched Jon's desperate attempt to infuse life where there wasn't any.

"Jon," Kaycee said. "It's too—"

A tiny hoof quivered. Jon blew gently into the baby's nose again. A shiver ran down the slick black body. Jon grinned. "Told you."

Another five minutes of nurturing and the newborn was breathing without help. Gently Jon carried it to a box stall and laid it in the corner. He took off the soiled leather gloves and pulled his shirt collar over to wipe his mouth.

"I'll milk the heifer and get a first meal down this little one," he told Kaycee. "Then hope Mom takes over."

While Jon coaxed colostrum from the heifer's udder and made up a bottle, Kaycee removed the chains from the slender hind legs and laid them across the top of the stall door. Jon gave her the bottle to feed while he steadied the newborn calf. When the bottle was empty, he released the heifer into the stall.

"Maybe there's enough afterbirth left for her to recognize her baby. Never should have happened this way, but looks like it turned out okay."

"Looks like," Kaycee said with a smile. "Really big calf, though. Over a hundred pounds, I'd guess."

"Yep, felt that way. My fault, too. I should have had my mind on my business when I bred her, but I—" Jon stared at the confined heifer nosing her calf. "I just didn't," he said finally.

He studied Kaycee with eyes as deep blue as the Montana sky. His dark good looks overshadowed his somber, drawn expression. As tall as she was at five foot ten, she still had to look up to meet his gaze.

"You did a good job," he said. "I'm impressed."

"Thank you. I'm glad I could help." Warmth spread through Kaycee's midsection. Why did it thrill her that this particular rancher was pleased with her work? Before this, she'd only felt a satisfying triumph when she proved one more cowboy wrong about her.

They reached for the chains at the same time. Jon's hand accidentally closed over hers. A frisson of electricity crackled through her body. He tightened his grip and lifted her hand off the chains, so he could pick them up.

"I guess we need to clean up," he said, in a deep, low voice that resonated through her.

Kaycee cleared her throat and nodded. The barn was suddenly awfully close and overly warm.

"Urmmmm!"

Jon and Kaycee jerked apart at the sound of the accusatory grumble. A woman wearing a severely cut gray business suit glinted a hard look at them from a few feet away. No doubt they were a pretty sight, covered as they were with the drying remnants of new life.

Jon frowned at the newcomer. "Can I help you?"

Michele, along with another girl about her age and identical twin boys about five years old darted around the woman and regrouped behind Jon.

"I'm Nancy Hawthorn, the county social worker. Are you Jonathan Rider?"

"Yes," Jon said with a hesitant nod.

The woman approached, clutching a writing pad to her chest. Her eyes darted to the pool of blood and fluid on the floor, then to the cow and calf in the stall.

"May I speak to you alone, Mr. Rider?"

Jon indicated for her to follow him, detouring briefly to the washroom to wash his hands and arms and roll his shirtsleeves down. They stopped to talk in the doorway of the barn. Kaycee couldn't quite make out the conversation from where she stood with the children.

Before Kaycee could make a move to collect her things, she saw Jon's face suffuse with anger and he clenched his fists.

"Child neglect? What in hell are you talking about?"

Kaycee wasn't sure what to do. To get to her truck, she'd have to pass close enough to Jon and the social worker to eavesdrop. Although she'd always been a bit nosy, this conversation seemed too personal for idle curiosity. The four children, however, had no such qualms. Little by little they inched closer to the adults. Kaycee crossed the aisle to clean up. She slipped out of the soiled coveralls, rolled them into a ball and tucked them into a plastic bag in one of her medical cases, then washed her hands again. Wiping her boots clean in the thick hay, she glanced around for another way out of the barn.

She spied a back door, but couldn't be sure if she could get to her truck that way. The voices at the end of the barn grew louder, more strident. She turned, staring at the two dark figures against the bright light, so focused on each other that Kaycee doubted they would notice if she made a discreet escape around them.

Hoisting her cases, she edged down the aisle, stopping when she reached the tight cluster of wide-eyed children hanging on every word of the argument.

"Mr. Rider," Mrs. Hawthorn said, holding the notepad to her chest, "I'm here for your children's welfare."

"By scaring them out of their minds?" Jon snapped.

Kaycee wanted to tell him to calm down. He wouldn't do himself any good by losing his temper.

"I have no intention of frightening them. But, I must advise you that Montana law gives me full authority to speak to your children, without your consent and without your being present. Now, if you'll just answer a few questions, perhaps we can resolve this quickly."

Jon's jaw muscle ticked. He took a couple of breaths before he spoke again. "I'm sorry. You took me by surprise. Who made this accusation?"

"By state law, I can't reveal that information."

"Wait a minute," Jon said, his voice growing harsh again. "You can come into my house—harass my children, interrogate me—because of somebody's unsubstantiated accusation? And you won't tell me who made it?"

"*Can't,* Mr. Rider. I am not allowed to give you that information."

"I don't believe this." Jon raked a hand through his already disheveled hair. "How am I supposedly neglecting my children?"

Mrs. Hawthorn consulted her notes. "According to the report I received you do not have proper supervision for your seven…?"

Mrs. Hawthorn cocked an inquisitive eyebrow at Jon. Kaycee automatically raised her eyebrows, too. Seven?

Jon nodded and Mrs. Hawthorn went on, "Seven children. That the younger children may be suffering from neglect. That there is a scarcity of food in the house, that the kids are not being fed, clothed or tended properly."

"That's not true. I have two freezers full of food

in there. Who around here would say something like—" Jon's eyes narrowed. "My in-laws! That's who it is, isn't it? The Arants from San Francisco."

"I'm sorry, I can't—"

"Yeah, I know, you can't give me that information. You don't have to. All right, ask your questions."

"Your children are Rachel, aged twelve, Samantha, eleven, Wendy, nine, Michele, eight, twins Tyler and Zachary, five, and Bowie, two. Is that correct?"

"Yes."

"Your wife Alison passed away last year?"

"Fourteen months, five days, three hours and I can give you the minutes if you need that, too," Jon said, hiding whatever emotion he might be feeling.

Kaycee's lips parted slightly at the startling revelation and she looked at the motherless children through new eyes.

Mrs. Hawthorn's expression was a mix of sympathy and impatience as she jotted a note. "And you make your living by ranching alone?"

"Yes."

"Who supervises your children when you're busy?"

"I keep a full-time housekeeper."

"It's my understanding she quit."

"What makes you think that?"

"A report was filed, as I said. Judging by the condition of your house and children—"

"I've got seven kids, lady. It doesn't take long for the house to get cluttered, even with a housekeeper."

"So you do have a housekeeper?"

"I just said so, didn't I?"

"Good, that will help matters. May I meet her?"

"She's not here today."

"Why?"

Kaycee watched Jon fidget. She'd bet her next year's profit he did not have a housekeeper at the moment. Lying to a social worker was definitely a bad idea.

"Everybody needs a day off, Mrs. Hawthorn. Even my housekeeper."

"Your son has a fever. I assume you know that."

"Yes, I know that."

"He's had medical attention?" She looked at him for confirmation.

Jon took a deep breath. "Children's Tylenol every four to six hours," he said patiently as if quoting from the back of the medicine bottle.

"Why didn't you take him to the doctor?"

"He didn't need to go. It's just a low fever. Could be catching a cold."

Mrs. Hawthorn continued to stare at him expectantly.

"Okay, okay. If he's not better by tomorrow I'll take him to the doctor, all right?"

"As I understand this is not the first time you've been without proper supervision for the young children. Nor the first time you've failed to get medical attention when the children were ill. Can you defend these accusations?"

"Look, I don't take my children to the doctor for every sniffle. Neither did my wife. And yes, I've had housekeepers quit. I've also had ranch hands quit. People move on. It's a fact of life. Have you checked up on any other ranch families in the area? How many of them have someone to watch their kids? Probably none. Rachel's old enough—"

"Frankly, Mr. Rider, I'm not convinced that you're able to provide a stable environment for the children without a wife."

"Without a wife…?" Jon looked bewildered. "I can't help it if my wife died. I'm taking care of my kids."

Listening to the heated exchange, Kaycee was hesitant to leave until she knew what was going on. Even though Jon's personal matters were none of her business, she had a soft spot for children and wondered if a man who had doggedly brought a stillborn calf to life would neglect his family. .

"I don't see evidence that you're caring for the children today."

"It's calving season. Life around here gets hectic. It's got nothing to do with wife or no wife."

"Nonetheless, your children should be your first priority—"

"They are my first priority!" Jon practically shouted. "I am taking care of them. How dare you—"

"Do you have an anger management problem we need to address? I'm beginning to consider removing the children from your home until a hearing can be arranged."

The color drained from Jon's face as he stared at the social worker.

"Like hell you will."

"Mr. Rider, profanity and anger won't help. Now, you can calm down or I'll take measures to remove the children today."

In front of Kaycee, the children looked at one another with wide eyes and gaping mouths.

"What's she talking about, Wendy?" Michele asked in a low voice.

"She said we need a mother or she's going to take us away from Daddy," the sister said in disbelief.

"That's what I thought." Warily, Michele glanced up at Kaycee. She leaned and whispered in Wendy's ear.

Wendy shook her head fiercely, her straight blond hair whipping back and forth. "That won't work," she whispered back loud enough that Kaycee heard.

"Well, it might. You got any better ideas?" Michele's eyes locked on the arguing adults as Jon grew more upset with everything Mrs. Hawthorn said.

Kaycee didn't know Jon other than the few hours she'd spent with him, but she felt the urge to help him—she just didn't know how. There was a lull in the argument, and Kaycee heard Wendy's agitated voice. Tears welled in the girl's brown eyes as she clutched her sister's arm.

"You're going to get in trouble, Michele. I just want Mama back."

"Get real, Wendy," Michele said. "You know she's not coming back."

"My children are not leaving this ranch!" Jon's shout echoed off the walls, the effect of his words clear on the small, pale faces and eyes dark with fear.

Mrs. Hawthorn took a step backward and pulled a cell phone out of her briefcase. "If I have to call the authorities and have you arrested, I will, Mr. Rider." Her voice left no room for doubt that she would follow through on her threat.

"Make 'em stop fighting," sobbed one of the twin boys. "I don't want to go away. Make 'em stop, Michele!"

Michele looked boldly at Kaycee, her face determined despite the apprehension imprinted there. She grabbed Kaycee's hand and pulled her down to eye level. "I'm Michele. What's your name?"

Startled, Kaycee replied, "Kaycee Calloway."

"Hurry!" Michele dragged Kaycee until she stumbled forward—straight into the fray. Jon jerked toward them in surprise. Mrs. Hawthorn eyed her over the rim of her glasses. Kaycee's sudden intrusion shut them both up instantly.

"This is her," Michele announced firmly. "This is our new mother. We don't need a housekeeper anymore."

CHAPTER TWO

"MICHELE!" JON SAID.

"Kaycee's shy like Wendy," Michele rushed on. "But Mrs. Hawthorn needs to know we have a mother so you can take care of us. Well, here she is and now you can."

Mrs. Hawthorn narrowed her eyes and looked suspiciously from Kaycee to Jon and back to Kaycee. "Aren't you the veterinarian?"

"Well, I…I…yes, I am a vet."

"And you're married to Mr. Rider?"

Jon looked at his four kids with a stricken expression. Kaycee recognized sheer desperation when she saw it. He grabbed her by the waist and pulled her to his side, his strong arm squeezing the breath out of her so that she had no chance to speak. She could feel his body humming like a strand of barbed wire pulled too tight. Dangerous.

"We're not married yet," Jon said without hesitation. "But we soon will be."

"Why didn't you say so earlier?" Mrs. Hawthorn pressed, her skepticism obvious.

"You didn't give me much chance," he answered, then gazed down at Kaycee with adoring eyes that melted her to his side in spite of the tenuous situation—and the fact that the look was faked.

On her other side, Michele squeezed Kaycee's hand so hard it hurt. There was no way she should involve herself in this family's problems, whatever they were.… But there were three more little kids panicking behind her.

Kaycee held out her right hand—thank goodness she'd washed it already. "I'm Katherine Calloway."

Hesitantly, Mrs. Hawthorn took it as if it might be contaminated, pulling away as quickly as she could. "And you plan to marry Mr. Rider?"

Kaycee swallowed hard. "We've been seriously discussing it lately. The children do need a mother, I agree. Everything will be back to normal before you know it." Kaycee spoke carefully. She wasn't exactly lying. She was only filling the role for a few minutes, until this social worker left. Then Jon Rider would have to figure out his problems on his own.

"I see. When?"

"When?"

"We have to get calving season behind us," Jon said quickly. "But as you can see, Kaycee's here today and between the two of us, the housekeeper and my oldest girls, we'll make out until the wedding."

Good line, Kaycee thought, but was the social worker buying it? She didn't seem to have much of a case against Jon. If he'd kept his temper, the woman might have been gone by now. Kaycee's gut feeling told her the children weren't in danger of anything other than a messy house and a missing nanny, but she would make sure before she left.

"If you'll excuse me, I need to fix lunch for these hungry mouths." Mostly, Kaycee wanted to escape before she said something wrong to cause Jon more trouble. And get the kids away from here.

Jon released her with a twitch of his lips before turning back to the social worker. "Now, if you're satisfied, you can leave."

Mrs. Hawthorn made a long note on her pad before looking up at Jon. "I'm not satisfied, but I'm going to give you the benefit of the doubt since you have help. I am going to need four or five collateral references, Mr. Rider. People who can vouch for your character and fitness as a father."

Jon shook his head in disbelief. "It's bad enough you're nosing around here. Now you're wanting to spread this nonsense all over the community? Embarrass my children? Start some ugly rumor you can't prove? I don't think so."

Kaycee gathered the children around her. Michele kept a tight grip on her hand. Wendy watched her warily, but the twin boys fought to grab her other hand. Mrs. Hawthorne took a business card from her notebook and handed it to Jon. "You really don't have a choice. It could be a close relative. Dr. Calloway can be a reference. I'm not closing this case yet. I want to meet with you next week. Call to give me those references and make an appointment."

One of the boys tugged on Kaycee's hand. "We're hungry. Come on."

As they crossed the barnyard to the large ranch house, Wendy ran ahead and disappeared inside.

Michele looked up at Kaycee and said, "Thank you so much."

"You're welcome. But what we did wasn't exactly honest, was it?"

Michele shrugged, tears in her eyes. "We don't want to leave Daddy. Daddy loves us. Why would that woman take us away?"

"I don't know," Kaycee said.

Behind them, an engine started and the social worker's compact car eased down the road. Jon caught up to them.

"Michele," he said, taking the child by the arm and pulling her aside. "You didn't have any business dragging Dr. Calloway into our family problems."

"I didn't want that lady to take us, Daddy. I couldn't think what else to do."

"I'll handle things next time. Go on in with the boys. I want to talk to Dr. Calloway alone."

"But, Daddy," one of the twins whined, refusing to relinquish Kaycee's hand. "She just said she'd make us something to eat and I'm starvin'. Rachel's been too busy to feed us since breakfast."

"I'll feed you in a minute."

The look of disappointment on the boy's face was more than Kaycee could take. "How about we all go fix a sandwich together?"

"Yeah, Daddy, please!"

Jon gave Kaycee a lingering look. "You don't have to. I know you're busy."

"No problem, I need lunch, too. Y'all lead the way. I'm right behind."

The children's faces brightened.

"What's 'y'all' mean?" the boy asked.

"That's the way we say 'you' or 'you all' where I come from. You've never heard that before, huh?"

The kids shook their heads.

"Southern girl," Jon commented, bringing up the rear.

"South Carolina, born and bred."

"You're pretty far from home. Like it out here?"

"It's cold. But yes, I like it. I suppose you've always lived here."

"Yep, grew up in this house. Went away to college because my dad insisted, did some bull riding on the rodeo circuit. He passed away fifteen years ago and most of the ranch came to me."

Kaycee followed the brood through the back door into a utility area. Coats, caps and all sizes of shoes and boots were piled up in the corner nearest the entryway on the tile floor, scuffed and tracked with mud. Soiled clothes formed mountains on the washing machine and dryer. A rustic wooden bench stretched along one wall and floor-to-ceiling cabinets occupied another.

A doorway on the opposite wall opened into a great room. Action figures, toy animals, game pieces, coloring books and crayons, dolls and miniature clothing carpeted the floor of the sitting area. Broad windows across one wall framed snow-topped mountains and greening bottomland in pristine, orderly contrast to the shambles inside. Over the stone and wood mantel hung a large oil painting of the family. In a flower-strewn meadow, a youthful blond woman sat on the ground next to Jon, surrounded by the kids. As she gathered her brood close around her, her natural beauty and loving expression made her face radiant. Kaycee studied the picture for a long moment before moving on.

Wendy was already clearing the center island of plastic cups, plates crusted with dried food and a baby's sipper cup. An only child, Kaycee grew up in a serene, immaculate home, but she felt sure seven kids could easily make this big a mess in a day.

"Excuse me a minute," Jon said to Kaycee. "I need to wash up and make a phone call."

He disappeared down a hallway. The twins scrambled to claim their stools from the assortment scattered around the large island. A copper hood encased in a brick wall covered a gourmet cooktop. Two ovens were set into the adjacent wall, with a microwave built in nearby. Michele opened what looked like a double-doored pantry, but turned out to be a restaurant-quality refrigerator with doors custom-made to match the kitchen cabinetry.

This kitchen was designed for somebody who loved to cook, but from the few items in the refrigerator, it hadn't been overused lately. Kaycee looked around the island at the faces staring at her. Were these children being ignored, like the house? She hoped she'd done right by helping send off the social worker. If they were being neglected, she'd never forgive herself.

"Are you really going to be our mom now?" one of the twins asked eagerly.

Kaycee hesitated. "I think you'd better ask your dad about that."

"Okay, I will," he said with a decisive nod then tilted his head. "Can you bake cookies?"

"I can," Kaycee assured him. "Why?"

"Just wondering," he said innocently enough, but the look he gave his brother made Kaycee smile.

"I'm at a disadvantage here," Kaycee said to the two boys as she worked. "Y'all know my name, but I don't know yours. You look so much alike, I'm not sure I'll be able to tell you apart."

"I'm Zach," the talkative one piped up. "This is my brother Tyler. We're twins. But I've got a scar right here where I fell when I was learning to walk." He pointed to a tiny blemish on his chin.

They were robust, cheerful, with curling dark hair and their father's deep blue eyes. And identical other than Zach's inconspicuous scar.

"We're five years old," Tyler offered. "Both of us. 'Cept Zach's three minutes older than me. My daddy said so."

"And you're Wendy." Kaycee spoke to the quiet girl with straight blondish hair and somber brown eyes who nodded once then ducked her head.

"She's shy," Michele explained. "She doesn't like to talk. She likes to read."

"I see," Kaycee said, smiling at the bashful girl. Wendy ignored her.

Michele put turkey, ham, mustard, mayonnaise, peanut butter and jelly on the counter. Then Kaycee made sandwiches according to the instructions from the girls. Wendy slid a paper plate in front of her for each one. Michele then took it, dropped a handful of chips onto it and passed it along the counter for distribution with the timed precision of an assembly line worker.

Jon came into the kitchen, looking and smelling much better than when he left. His dark hair was still damp from a shower, ridged with comb marks, and he wore clean jeans and a long-sleeved, thermal knit shirt that hugged his fit body like a glove.

"Thanks for getting started," he said with a grin. "And for helping me out."

"I'm not sure if I helped or made things worse in the long run. Mrs. Hawthorn won't be happy when she learns the truth."

"Well, maybe we can keep her in the dark for the moment, if that's okay with you."

"I don't know. This worries me. We're not playing a game. The ramifications could be serious."

"Far from a game. I just need some time."

Kaycee didn't mind giving him time if it would help, but the thought of even a mock engagement didn't set well with her at all. She'd been there, done the real thing in South Carolina. And then there was the question of the kids' well-being. She wanted hard evidence that they were being cared for.

"Mrs. Hawthorn mentioned a baby with a fever."

"Bo." Jon put a gallon jug of milk on the table. "He's almost three. Rachel and Samantha are upstairs with him. That woman was overreacting. Babies run a fever sometimes. If I thought for a minute it was serious, I'd have already taken him to the doctor. A little medicine, keep him quiet today. He'll be fine tomorrow."

Seven children, Kaycee mused. She took in his broad shoulders, the chiseled planes of his well-muscled chest under the shirt, his easy smile and dark good looks. Yes, Kaycee could see the lure of making multiple babies with Jon Rider. He might talk like a mother hanging around the carpool line exchanging fever remedies, but he sure didn't look like one.

"Our mama's gone," Zach said. "Daddy takes care of us now."

"I guess you heard, she passed away last year." Jon's words were matter-of-fact, but Kaycee detected the underlying grief in his voice. The loss of their mother reflected in the children's eyes as they watched their father.

"I'm sorry," Kaycee managed, not knowing what else to say. "You must be pretty self-sufficient," she said to the children.

"We can take care of ourselves, 'cept that old Mrs. Hawthorn won't believe us," Michele said. "She can't take us, can she, Daddy?"

"Don't worry about that. We'll talk about it later." Jon pointed to a cabinet beside the refrigerator and said to Kaycee, "Would you pour the milk? Plastic cups are up there."

Meanwhile, he parceled out the loaded paper plates to each child. He put a couple of plates on a tray along with a peanut butter and jelly sandwich for Bo, plastic cups, Bo's washed sipper cup and the partial jug of milk. "Wendy, run this upstairs. Tell Rachel I'll be there in a few minutes to check on them."

"Yes, sir." Wendy picked up the tray carefully and left.

Kaycee made a sandwich for herself and a couple for Jon with the remaining meat and bread. What would they eat tomorrow, she wondered, noting the pitifully empty refrigerator.

"No more milk," Kaycee said to Jon. "How about water for us?"

"Sure. Let's go in the other room," Jon suggested.

They settled at a round table in an adjacent room. Quaint mullioned bay windows looked out over expansive grazing land running up the mountains. Jon sat back in his chair and exhaled a long sigh, contemplating Kaycee with a thoughtful expression.

"So, you're to be my new wife, are you? And not a minute too soon."

"Sorry, no mail-order bride here," she replied. "Not my style. But I would like an explanation. I feel like I walked into the middle of a war zone."

"So do I," Jon said. "Talk about being blindsided. But, thanks for what you did. My live-in housekeeper left without notice and I need to find a new one."

"No notice?" Kaycee said, between bites of her sandwich. "That's not very professional."

Jon shrugged a shoulder. "It happens. Seven kids are more than most housekeepers bargain for. I called everybody I knew yesterday, but no luck. Even called an agency in Bozeman, but from the way the woman snorted, I doubt they'll be sending anybody my way. With that heifer calving, I didn't have a chance to look this morning. Then, that damned social worker… I guess I should have expected something like this sooner or later."

"Under the circumstances, I think I'm entitled to know why a social worker would be checking on the children. Are some of them stepchildren?" The twins' eyes were a perfect match for the dark blue ones studying her now, but Michele and Wendy's were chocolate-brown.

"No, they're all mine. After my wife died, I let the children visit their grandparents in San Francisco, and my lovely in-laws tried to keep them. Filed a custody suit."

"You've got to be kidding. Why would they do that?"

"They think I'm not capable of raising the kids without Alison. They say I can't take care of the little ones or give the girls a proper social life out here 'in the wilderness,' as Alison's father calls it." Jon's face hardened, the light gone from his eyes. "Wouldn't allow me near the house to even talk to my kids. Took me a month to get them home again, and a hell of a lot of money to fight that lawsuit."

"It must be difficult managing with so many small children and a ranch to run," Kaycee ventured. She didn't want to make a judgment until she understood the situation.

Jon frowned and set his water glass down. "It is hard, damn near impossible sometimes. So what? Life's hard. I'm supposed to give up my children because of that? Alison would turn over in her grave if I let somebody take those babies away from me. Never going to happen." He leaned forward in his chair toward her, his jaw set. "And if you're thinking they might be better off with their rich grandparents, living in the city, you're wrong. They might be better dressed, they might have fancier food, they might be kept squeaky clean all the time—"

"Sorry, I didn't mean—"

"Let me tell you what they wouldn't have," he went on as if she hadn't spoken. "They wouldn't get the love that I give them. They wouldn't have one another to depend on for support and attention because their grandparents are firm believers in boarding schools and au pairs. Alison would tell you horror stories of her life growing up…" Jon clenched the water glass with both hands and looked away, blinking.

Kaycee's appetite gone, she laid the unfinished sandwich on her plate.

In the uneasy silence, he cleared his throat. "I won't sentence my own children to that fate. She wouldn't have wanted it and I won't allow it. It's as simple as that."

But Kaycee knew better. "It's not, is it? You're still worried."

He shoved his plate aside and leaned back in his chair. "The Arants are too wealthy for their own good. After their lawsuit failed, anytime I let the kids talk to them, they tried to use their money to lure them away from me. So I cut off communication."

Only Kaycee's paternal grandmother had survived long enough to be part of her life and she was dead now. Kaycee still missed her terribly. How empty her life would have been without Granny. No doubt Jon's children were feeling a similar loss.

"Do you mean they can't see their grandparents?"

"Can't see them, can't talk to them. Phone's off limits to San Francisco."

"Jon, that's severe. How do the kids feel about it?"

Jon shrugged slightly. "I'm sure they miss Hal and Marjorie. As far as the kids are concerned, their grandparents are wonderful. But it doesn't change what they tried to do to my family."

"The children might not understand—"

"Daddy," Michele said from the doorway, "we're finished eating and the twins want to go out to play."

Kaycee wondered how long she'd been standing there listening.

"Did you clean up," Jon asked.

"Yes, sir, but the trash can is full."

"I'll take care of it. You and Wendy watch the boys for a few minutes."

When Michele was gone, Jon nodded toward Kaycee's plate. "You didn't finish your sandwich."

"I'm not very hungry." She hesitated before asking, "Jon, don't you think you could find some common ground? For the sake of the kids?"

"Not anymore." He wiped his hands on his napkin then stood abruptly and picked up his plate. "Finished?" he asked, reaching for Kaycee's.

"Yes, thanks. I've got it." She took her glass and plate and followed him into the kitchen. "So what now?"

"I'm sure Hal turned in this complaint, and now I have my very own personal social worker. I wonder if he's got a private eye watching me and knew the housekeeper quit or just lucked out on his timing?"

Jon put her half-eaten sandwich on a paper towel then forced their plates into the stuffed trash can under the sink.

"I called my lawyer earlier," he said, transferring the trash to a large black garbage bag and tying the top. "Frank said he would try to get this case closed as unfounded. He strongly advised me to hold my temper next time, that Hawthorn could snatch the kids in a heartbeat, if she wanted to…and it could take months to get them back. That scares the hell out of me."

"I wanted to tell you the same thing—about the temper," Kaycee said, running hot water to wash the dishes. The girls had cleared the center island, but left the glasses and utensils in the sink. "My granny always said you catch more flies with honey than vinegar."

Jon arched an eyebrow. "Well, I'll try to remember that sage advice next time I see Mrs. Hawthorn. Be right back."

He took the garbage and her uneaten sandwich outside, and Kaycee heard him whistle. Through the open back door she watched him divide the food between the two dogs. He came back and washed his hands.

"You don't have to do the dishes," he said. "I'll put the girls to work later."

"There are only a few left. Did you tell the lawyer we're engaged now?"

He chuckled softly and snapped his fingers, then shot her a playful grin as he picked up a dishtowel and began to dry the glasses. "Darn, I forgot to mention that."

"Come on, Jon, be serious. Maybe you should come clean and beg Mrs. Hawthorn's forgiveness."

"I haven't done anything to be forgiven of—well, maybe dragging you into this. But that's for you to forgive, not her."

Kaycee shook her head doubtfully. "I don't know. I don't want to be party to you losing custody of your children when she catches us lying."

"Why does it have to be a lie?"

She jerked her head toward him in surprise. "I'm sorry...come again?"

"I mean, if we agree we're engaged, it's not for her to say we're not. And if we decide to break it off later, that's our business, too. Another one of those bad breaks in life that happen all the time."

All the time, Kaycee thought, rinsing the last fork and drying her hands. Through the window above the sink, she stared at the distant mountains, the snow-blanketed peaks sparkling like a glittering postcard. She didn't want to be reminded of those bad breaks—those reversals of fortune, as her ex-fiancé Brett had called them. The bastard. She hoped he and his new bride were happy. She sure didn't want to go through that again, not here, when she'd just begun to feel at home. Not even make-believe.

"I don't think it's the best idea," Kaycee said, her gut churning. "If news of this so-called engagement gets around town and you break it off as soon as you find a new housekeeper, I'll be in an awkward position."

Jon considered that for a moment. "Don't worry about it. When the time comes, you can jilt me in Little

Lobo, in the middle of Main Street at high noon. That way there'll be no doubt who dumped whom."

Kaycee still didn't like the deceit. And a public breakup would be embarrassing for both of them.

"I really hate that I got caught off guard and let this happen," he continued, drying the utensils as he talked. "But, will you just go along until I can call off my in-laws? I know it's an imposition, but you don't have to do anything physical." Jon fumbled for an explanation. "I mean…"

Kaycee cocked her head, waiting for him to extricate himself. He wouldn't look her way.

"I mean like coming out here or anything. We'll manage fine." He cleared his throat self-consciously. Still avoiding her gaze, he began to drop the forks and knives into the drawer beside the sink. "I don't think it will get around Little Lobo anyway and we can let it die a natural death, this lie. I'll tell the kids not to say anything. I'm sorry to put you in this position." He gave her a quick, frustrated look. "I wouldn't want you to…to…"

Kaycee bit the inside of her cheek to keep from smiling. He was trying hard. Finally she let him off the hook. "I guess I'll let it ride—for the time being anyway. Just hurry and get a housekeeper before we're caught."

Relief transformed the tension in his face to a smile that crinkled the corners of his eyes. "Thanks, Kaycee. I guess we both have to get back to work and I need to check on Bo."

"Um, if you don't mind, I'd like to see Bo, since I

vouched for him being okay to Mrs. Hawthorn. And I guess I need to know all my future children, just in case I'm questioned."

"Sure, come on."

The upstairs nursery was in much better order. The two preteen girls finishing their lunch looked up when Kaycee followed Jon into the room. One, a blonde with brown eyes, reminded Kaycee of the woman in the painting in the den; the other, a lanky girl with an unruly tomboyish, brown bob had her father's eyes.

"Rachel, Samantha, this is Dr. Calloway, the new vet."

The girls smiled at her and Rachel, the blond one, said, "Michele told us. Thanks for rescuing Dad. Is that nosy old biddy coming back?"

"Probably. If she does, don't be rude to her. Understand?" Jon said.

Both girls nodded.

"How's Bo?" Jon asked, moving to the side of the crib against the wall.

"He's better," Rachel said. "The fever broke a few minutes ago."

Kaycee looked into the crib. A beautiful, chubby little boy slept peacefully, his thumb stuck in his mouth. Kaycee gently laid her hand against his cool cheek. "He's a sweetie."

"He's a handful," Jon said.

Jon brought the empty tray as they returned to the kitchen. Kaycee took the liberty of opening the refrigerator to examine the almost bare shelves.

"Jon, I have to ask, as the children's pretend mother, what do you intend to feed them?"

"Well, let's see." Jon came to stand directly behind her, his nearness making her appreciate the cold air. "Hmm, that could be a problem. I swear I've gotten behind the past couple of days. Yesterday would have been the day the housekeeper bought groceries, but she quit on Thursday."

He reached around Kaycee and opened the meat drawer. Empty. A few eggs were stashed in the door compartment, along with a small chunk of cheese. Jon scratched his head. "Well, I have stew frozen that I can heat for tonight. Peanut butter and jelly sandwiches for tomorrow, until I can get to the store. And we can get eggs from the henhouse in the morning."

"We finished the loaf of bread. And no milk, either."

Jon pulled a face. "Guess we'll have eggs and stew for breakfast, too. I'll pick up groceries while they're in Sunday school."

"What about the cook in the bunkhouse? Maybe you could borrow some bread."

Jon chuckled. "Obviously you've watched too many reruns of *Bonanza.* Not many ranches have bunkhouses and cooks these days. Two of my hands are married and live in houses on the ranch. The three single men are bunked in another house closer to the grazing land. My foreman, Clint, lives a few miles from here. Don't worry, we'll manage on stew for breakfast. Some people have worse."

"How about this. I'll treat y'all to breakfast in the morning—Southern style at my place."

"You're kidding. All of us? You don't know what you're getting into."

"I'll take my chances. I have plenty of room and I scramble eggs like a pro. Then you can go on with your plans afterward."

"Kaycee, you don't have to—"

"No, but I want to. Look, you need help right now. And I'm offering."

From the surprised look on Jon's face, Kaycee wondered if she had insulted him. Men could be like that. Then he smiled and nodded.

"Okay, then. We'll be there. What time?"

"Around eight."

On the way back to town, Kaycee had time to think about Jon's predicament. She could see the grandparents' position in a way. Seven kids, no mother, a harried father with a ranch to run and now nobody to look after the children. Of course they would worry. It should be none of her concern, Kaycee knew, but she couldn't get the family out of her mind…. She couldn't shut out Jon Rider's rugged face and deep, smooth voice, either, as much as she tried.

And that surprised her. Brett's unfaithfulness had left her with a bitterness and distrust toward men. What a rude awakening she'd had on the day of their wedding. Five years loving Brett—and her heart had been obliterated in two seconds, two sentences: "I don't love you anymore. I'm going to marry Marissa."

Since then, although she worked almost exclusively with men, she maintained a wide emotional distance from them, especially the wild cowboys she'd come across since she'd been out west. But something about Jon touched her…the concern he showed for the newborn calf he resuscitated…the love and pride in his eyes when he looked at his children.

In spite of that—or maybe because of it—Kaycee knew she should stay away from him. Jon Rider was trouble on the hoof.

AFTER KAYCEE LEFT, Jon called all the children except the napping Bo to the long table in the dining room where they once held family meetings. This would be their first one since Alison died. Staring for a long minute at the chair at the end of the table where she used to sit, he wished he could conjure her spirit to help him out.

"Okay, kids, I'm going to lay it on the line. We've got a problem and you need to know about it."

"That social worker?" Michele said.

"Yes. Do all of you know what a social worker is?"

The older girls nodded.

Tyler shook his head.

"Mean," Zach offered.

"A social worker is somebody who makes sure children are safe from harm."

"Then why was she here? We're safe. You wouldn't let anybody hurt us," Sam said. "Did you tell her that?"

"I tried. But, honey, the problem is that somebody else has told her I might hurt you." He saw their surprise register. "I'm sure she doesn't believe I would hit you, not that kind of hurt. But by not having a housekeeper to watch over you all the time, she thinks I might not be able to take care of you."

"But Rachel takes care of us when you can't," Tyler said.

"I know, and she does a wonderful job, but she's not a grown-up and the social worker thinks we need a grown-up."

"I don't mind, Daddy," Rachel said.

"I know you don't. But you have school and you need time to do things you like to do, not just do chores and take care of your brothers and sisters every day."

"It doesn't have to be Rachel all the time," Sam said. "I know perfectly well how to babysit."

"Fact is, in a couple of years, when Bo and the twins are older, we'll be able to make do without a housekeeper. But right now, we need an adult here when the boys are home. I'll find another housekeeper soon."

Zach pouted. "I like Rachel better than any old housekeeper."

"And…" Jon's tone silenced Zach, but the boy crossed his arms across his chest in protest "…this time we're going to keep her. There'll be no pranks played and no backtalk. Absolutely no locking her in the basement." Jon leveled a severe look at the twins. "Understand?"

The twins squirmed and exchanged worried looks. Everybody nodded.

"Then will everything be okay? When we get a new housekeeper?" Wendy whispered, on the verge of tears.

"Don't cry, sweetie," Jon said, holding out his hand. Wendy ran into his arms. He pulled her into his lap then addressed the others watching him intently. "Everything will work out. But this lady, Mrs. Hawthorn, may show up at school wanting to talk to you. It's all right if you talk to her. If she asks questions, tell her the truth."

"I don't want to talk to her," Zach said.

"Me, neither," echoed Tyler.

"Listen, guys," Jon said. "If you don't talk to her, she might think something really is wrong and we don't want that. Don't let her upset you. I'm not going to allow anybody to separate us."

"But, Daddy," Michele ventured, "I heard her tell you she can take us away from you and make us live somewhere else if we don't have a mother. Is that true?"

Jon tried never to deceive his children. In fact, being caught up in the charade about marrying Kaycee pricked at him. He should have shot that down when Michele started it—but the look on the kids' faces, that fear deep in their eyes…. At that moment, he'd have done anything to protect them.

Quietly, he said, "Yes, it's true. She has the authority to do that if she decides you would be better off somewhere else."

"Where would she take us, Daddy?" Wendy sobbed.

"Maybe to a place like a hotel where other kids would be. Or maybe to stay with nice people in their homes until I could come get you. It wouldn't be for long," Jon said, careful to keep his own anxiety out of his voice. "But it's not going to happen, okay? We're going to convince her that we don't need her anymore and she'll go away."

"I wish Mommy hadn't died," Wendy whispered.

"So do I, darling," Jon said, lightly kissing the top of her head. He had never seen a paler bunch of kids and his heart hurt to see his children so frightened. "I know this scares all of you, but we can't run from everything that scares us. We have to face our problems. We'll make it though and we'll be a stronger family in the end." He wiped the tears from Wendy's cheeks and kissed her forehead.

"But, Daddy, Dr. Kaycee said she'd be our mom. She said so," Michele said, tugging at his sleeve. "Just get her to do it."

"No, we tricked her into saying that. I don't want you to tell anybody she's going to be your mother. Not the social worker or your teacher or your friends. Do you all understand that? Until Dr. Kaycee decides for herself what she wants to do, you're not to mention her name. If the social worker asks, tell her she has to talk to me about grown-up things. Everybody promise me you'll do what I say."

All around heads nodded, although Michele's agreement was reluctant.

"I think we need to clean up the house, too," Rachel suggested, "so the social worker knows we can take care of ourselves."

"That's a good idea," Jon agreed. "From now on, we pick up our own things, every one of us. Bring dirty clothes to the laundry room. Put the toys away when you finish playing. Don't leave wet towels on the floor in the bathrooms. Agreed?"

The kids bobbed their heads in unison.

"Good. Now who wants ice cream?"

Six hands shot up amid a chorus of "Me! Me! Me!" Jon set Wendy down and pulled the last two ice-cream containers from the freezer while Sam put bowls on the table. Rachel pulled out the drawer for spoons, but suddenly turned to Jon and threw her arms around his waist.

"It'll be all right, Daddy. I love you."

"Me, too!" Zach cried, flinging his arms around Jon's legs.

Tyler did the same. "Me, three!"

Wendy, Michele and Sam came running and Jon sank to the kitchen floor amid a flurry of arms, legs and wet little mouths kissing his face. Which was good because that way they didn't notice the tears in his eyes as he gathered them close and sent a silent prayer heavenward to help him keep his family together.

CHAPTER THREE

SUNDAY DAWNED like fireworks when the sun crested the mountaintops. Brilliant white rays exploded across the sky, igniting streaks of scarlet in the scattered clouds. Jon poured the last of the morning's feed into the trough then stood in reverent appreciation of nature's beauty.

His soul thrived in these mountains, where he and his family had worked the land for three generations. This was his heritage, his children's heritage—the wisdom gained by witnessing the cycle of life on the ranch, the respect instilled by experiencing firsthand the awesome power of God and nature. How dare a bitter old man threaten to steal that from them?

Under his breath, Jon swore for the thousandth time that he would not let that happen. But he couldn't quell the gnawing worry in the pit of his stomach. Not since talking to his lawyer, Frank Thompson. Hal could do serious damage without ever proving a thing, just by convincing the social worker or local law enforcement Jon *might* have done something wrong.

"Daddy," Michele called, running toward him, so pretty in her simple blue dress, her tawny, beribboned hair streaming out behind her. "Rachel said to tell you we're all finished with our chores and dressed for Sunday school."

The young girl leapt toward him and he caught her in midair. "Let's go, then." He swung her in circles until she giggled hysterically.

Michele wrapped her arms tightly around his neck as he carried her toward the house. "Daddy, you look worried this morning. Because of that social worker?"

Jon smiled. "Everything is going to be all right. I'll see to it." He hoped he was right. Knowing his in-laws' controlling mentality, he couldn't afford a misstep. He intended to call Mrs. Hawthorn to try to mend his fences with her, hopefully get her off his back, but he needed to have a full-time housekeeper in place before then.

"Hey, Jon," Clint called, catching up to them. "Anything in particular you need me to do today other than what we've already scheduled?"

"Check on that C-section heifer and calf. They looked good this morning, but I don't want to take any chances."

"Gotcha. Thought I'd get Rory and Cal to keep an eye out for any calving problems among the herd so I can spend some time with Claire later this afternoon, if that's okay."

"Sounds like a plan. I'll be around this afternoon."

Clint chucked Michele under the chin. "You're off to church mighty early. You been extra bad?"

"Has she ever," Jon said, giving the girl a mock frown.

"What'd you do?" Clint asked her.

"I'm not supposed to say," she said, looking up at Jon through her lashes.

"She's trying to get me married off again," Jon said. Clint was like family and would need to know what was going on with the social worker, but Jon was proud of Michele for not mentioning Kaycee.

"If Daddy will just cooperate," Michele said with a lopsided smile.

"Wha…?" Clint stopped, agape.

Jon laughed and kept walking.

"You're kidding me, right?"

Jon looked around at his foreman in amusement. "Not if Mish has her way. I'll fill you in later. Right now we're off to breakfast with my pretend fiancée."

A few minutes later the family piled into the four-wheel-drive Suburban that the kids had dubbed "Mom's Limo" and headed for town. During the half-hour drive into Little Lobo, Jon avoided glancing toward the passenger seat. Alison's seat. Now occupied by Rachel, tall and willowy for her age, who looked more like her mother than any of the girls. Right now, he didn't want to imagine Alison so close, yet not there at all.

The last time he saw her alive she'd been sitting beside him in his truck, laughing about some silly thing the twins had done. Out of the corner of his eye Jon had caught a glimpse of her beautiful face turned toward him and in that same instant saw the elk bound out of nowhere…directly into the truck's path. He couldn't dodge it, couldn't stop on the black ice. It was an accident. Nothing he could do…. A cold sweat popped out on Jon's body.

Stop thinking about it. How long would it take for the pain to ease? How long would he have to do penance for being behind the wheel that day?

In town, the children barreled out of the Suburban and, before Jon could stop them, the young ones blasted into Kaycee's clinic like a hurricane. Kaycee met them in the waiting room, bundling all that energy into her arms without missing a beat. Tyler and Zach went headlong. Bo hung back, wary of the woman he'd never seen before, until jealousy of the hugs and attention bestowed on his brothers got the better of him and he shouldered his way in. Kaycee gave him a hug, too. Michele stood close, beaming at Kaycee, already in love with her, Jon realized. The two older girls found a middle ground, waiting to take over the little ones by habit. Wendy stayed firmly behind Jon, her small hand in his, watching, but not participating.

Kaycee already had biscuits and toast prepared along with a huge bowl of scrambled eggs, crumbled bacon and cheese. Toasted cheese sandwiches cut into triangles waited on a warming plate on the counter. A bowl of fresh fruit sat in the center of the table. She produced a high chair for Bo stamped with the logo from the café next door. Amid the lively chatter, Rachel set Bo in the chair and gave him a plate with a piece of toasted cheese sandwich, slices of banana and poured juice in his sipper cup. The other girls helped Kaycee distribute orange juice and milk.

Soon the room was filled with the familiar bantering and squabbling of the kids. Jon watched Kaycee meld into his family so seamlessly that he had a hard time believing they'd met only the one time. If they were an imposition, she didn't show it. She appeared to enjoy them.

Her sun-burnished brown hair fell loose around her shoulders. A trace of makeup enhanced her large green eyes, and up close Jon noticed the gold flecks that made them sparkle. The yellow sweater she wore over tweed slacks molded to her curves.

Battling a blaze that started in his groin and worked its way up, Jon forced himself to look somewhere else. A sense of melancholy settled heavily in his chest as he realized how badly he missed his wife, missed the rapport of planning out their schedule each morning, of raising these children together. He hadn't allowed himself to admit how lonely he was until this moment.

Kaycee caught Jon's eye and smiled over the sea of heads. He answered with one of sincere gratitude and tried to shake off his gloom as she offered him a plate full of food and sat beside him. Jon mediated the minor disagreements between the children when necessary, kept up his end of the conversation with Kaycee and pondered how to manage the rest of the day. Sunday school and church for the children—he hadn't been since Alison's funeral—grocery shopping, getting everybody home and settled again so he could work the ranch. Call Hal. Somehow he had to find a compromise with his in-laws before this dangerous game irreparably damaged his family.

Jon checked his watch. "Let's move, kids. We don't want to be late for Sunday school."

In a flurry of activity, the children scurried to help Kaycee put the dishes in the sink.

"You want to come with us, Dr. Kaycee?" Michele asked hopefully.

"Michele," Jon admonished. This child would have Kaycee living with them if she could.

"Just asking, Daddy."

Unflappable Michele. Jon had to smile.

"I don't think I can dress in time for Sunday school. Suppose I join you for church?" Kaycee suggested, looking at Jon. "Are you going?"

Everybody in the room, Kaycee included, seemed to be waiting for his answer. Michele gazed up at him hopefully. Jon ran a hand through his hair. Truth was, he wasn't ready. He still had some differences to work out with his Maker before he could set foot in church.

"I can't buy groceries for all of us in an hour's time. Maybe next week."

"Will you come anyway?" Michele said to Kaycee.

"Sure, I'd love to. I'll meet y'all there."

Michele beamed as she climbed into the SUV with the others.

"You'd better stop that, Michele," Wendy said, buckling into the seat beside her sister.

Jon settled into the driver's seat, listening.

"What?" Michele said evasively.

"You know what. Trying to get her to be our mother. Just stop it."

"You can't make me. I want her to be our mom. Don't you think she's nice, Daddy?"

"I'd say she's real nice considering how you roped her into being mommy-for-a-day. How about leaving the mother-finding to me."

"But you're not doing too good," Zach piped up. "We gots to have somebody!"

Jon grimaced. "The fact is, she's busy and has a job of her own to do. She may not be in the market for a ready-made family. But don't worry, I'm going to find another housekeeper as soon as I can." Jon stopped in front of the church. "Now out you go. I'll be back for you."

He took a deep breath as he pulled away from the curb. The sudden silence in the car was unnerving. *This is how the world will sound if Hal gets the kids.* Sweat beaded on his upper lip. He almost turned around to go back for them. Gripping the wheel, he forced himself to keep going, to buy the food they needed and try to keep life normal for them.

Later that night, when everybody else was in bed, he poured himself a strong drink, something he rarely did— but then he rarely called his father-in-law, either. The worst call had been to tell him his only child, his baby girl, had been killed in an accident. That he'd never see her again or hear her voice, never make amends for the way he'd treated her since she married. Jon held himself responsible for her death. And so did his father-in-law.

Jon nursed the drink until he felt the soothing heat spread through his muscles and calm his overactive brain. He closed the door to his office and sat behind the massive oak desk. Beyond the open drapes, the black night spread into infinity.

Ten o'clock. Nine in San Francisco. He couldn't put off the call. In another half hour Hal would be in bed. Slowly he picked up the phone, punching in the numbers with agonizing deliberateness. He hated this phone number. Hated it.

"Hello."

He hated that voice more. Jon flinched at the sound. He gripped the receiver until his hand hurt. Fighting the urge to hang up, Jon forced himself to speak.

"Hal."

There was a long silence on the other end, then Hal said, "What do you want?"

"Call off this social worker."

Jon waited, listening to Hal's accelerated breathing.

"I don't know what you mean."

"Yes, hell, you do. You filed that complaint. Don't bother denying it."

Hal grunted, sounding pleased with himself. Funny, Jon had never really hated Hal until after Alison died, when he attempted to take custody of the kids. Before that he'd tried to tolerate the man in spite of his treatment of Alison—for her sake.

"Do you realize what you're doing to my children? That woman came here and terrified them. Is that what you want?"

"I want the children in a good home. You can't take care of them. You don't even have someone to watch them while you work. No food for them to eat. And you claim to be a good father?"

"What are you doing, spying on us? A private investigator?"

Hal laughed. "You'd like to know, wouldn't you? I have my ways. You should know that by now."

"Call them off, Hal. Leave my family alone."

"Not until I'm satisfied the children are being cared for."

"Then let me satisfy you. We do have food in the house. Did yesterday, too. A freezer full of it. These kids have never gone hungry a day in their lives. As for a housekeeper, that's a luxury I indulge to keep you happy. Ranch children learn young how to take care of themselves. But I'm going to have someone here so you don't have any excuse to say they're neglected again. I still can't believe you reported me to Child Protection Services," Jon said, amazed that Hal would have stooped so low.

"I didn't have any other way of checking on them since you cut us out of their lives. You forced me to take drastic action."

"Come off it, Hal. What did you do when I let them visit you after Alison died? Took out a restraining order against me, then had the gall to challenge me in court for custody. Why would I trust you to even talk to them, the way you bribe them? You tried to steal them from me once, but it won't happen again."

"You didn't have any qualms about stealing my child from me."

Jon closed his eyes and took a deep breath, frustrated at the old man's stubborn refusal to admit the truth after all these years. "Alison was a woman, not a child. Perfectly capable of making her own decisions."

"You lured her out there to that hinterland and then you killed her."

The venom in Hal's words was palpable, but the truth in them hurt Jon more.

Hal obviously understood Jon's prolonged silence. "Yes, you know you're to blame, don't you? No wonder

Marjorie and I are worried about the safety of our grand-children after what happened to their mother. We want them off that ranch and in a civilized environment."

Jon's body went rigid. "My children are where they belong. Don't pull this stunt with CPS again, Hal. It's not a game and you don't have any idea what that social worker might decide to do with the kids."

"No, I'm not playing around. I'm dead serious. I'll do whatever it takes to make sure my grandchildren are safe. Even if it means proving you an unfit father so we can get custody."

Jon slammed the receiver down. He'd planned to offer Hal some compromise. Laying his head against the back of the chair, he stared at the ceiling. How had life ever come to this? What the hell was Alison thinking, leaving him this way? Jon blinked back tears.

He had to come up with some way to stop Hal. The idea of calling Kaycee crossed his mind, but he decided against it. No need pulling her any farther into this. He threw back the rest of his drink and went out to make night rounds.

KAYCEE SAT DAYDREAMING AT THE desk in her office, the only room with lights on in the building. Her door was propped open, as was the door across the hall leading into the waiting area. She liked the arrangement—her living quarters were attached to the back of the veterinary clinic with access from the interior of the office complex, as well as from the outside. Several of the businesses along this strip of Little Lobo were built that old-fashioned way. Whoever popularized the idea of living in the suburbs and commuting had to be nuts.

She forced herself to concentrate on the form on her desk. She'd been trying to fill out the report on her visit to the Rider ranch for the past half hour. She couldn't get beyond Jon's name without becoming distracted. Hopefully he could call off his in-laws and they could break off their so-called engagement.

Like you really want to.

"Sure I do," Kaycee muttered.

In truth, maybe not yet. She'd enjoyed spending the morning with Jon and the kids. Even church had been an adventure, keeping the restless little ones from disturbing the sermon. Rachel and Sam did an exemplary job of mothering them. However, with the extra hour of church, they couldn't repress some squirming. Michele had then wanted to stay the rest of the afternoon at the clinic, but Jon wouldn't let her. So Kaycee had promised she could come back to visit soon, and invited the other girls, too.

She blew out a frustrated breath when she looked at the paper under her hand. *Name: Jon Rider.* As if on command, his face materialized, his troubled smile touching her heart.

Kaycee forced her pen to the next blank. *Phone number:* she copied the number from her notepad then picked up the phone almost without thinking. Just a short call to check on her new surrogate family. Jon wouldn't be in bed this early. But a tap at the glass of the outer door interrupted her.

Sarah James peered through, waving exuberantly, her curly hair bouncing like shiny red springs. Sarah owned the café and coffee shop next door, aptly named the Little Lobo Eatery and Daily Grind, and was trying to restore the huge rambling house behind it to open as a bed-and-breakfast. She was always in the kitchen by 4:00 a.m. to start the morning's fresh-baked pastries and biscuits and worked in her spare time on the renovation. Always on the lookout for extra money for her pet project, Sarah had offered to take the clinic's phone calls and do the day-to-day filing until Kaycee established her practice.

Sarah let herself in with her key. Kaycee had never had time for a close girlfriend before, but Sarah was so friendly and happy to have a neighbor other than Doc Adams, that Kaycee had already grown fond of her.

"Saw your light on," Sarah said. "Do you need help?"

"No, just catching up on paperwork. Come on back."

"Interesting day today, huh?" Sarah wiggled her eyebrows.

"Only if you enjoy driving forty miles to find out the rancher's already taken care of the problem and didn't bother to call back. Mr. Caldwell didn't call again, did he?"

"Nope. Those were the only calls after you left." Sarah pointed to the yellow slips on Kaycee's desk, then picked up the paperwork in the outbox and began to place the reports into their folders in the filing cabinet. "That's not exactly what I was talking about, and you know it."

Kaycee gave a little shrug. "What?"

"This morning?" Sarah motioned with her hand. "Come on. Come clean. I didn't miss Jon Rider's SUV at your place this morning. Neither did the rest of Little Lobo, I'd wager. So that's why you wanted to borrow a high chair."

The warmth crept up Kaycee's neck. No way this fake engagement would stay secret. "He brought the kids into town for Sunday school. How's the painting coming in the house?"

"Don't change the subject—but not so well. And Jon Rider just happened to stop by your vet clinic on a Sunday with his whole brood?"

"I fixed breakfast for them."

Sarah's face lit up. "Wait a minute! Have I missed something? Didn't I just see you the day before yesterday? You didn't let on you'd ever met Jon. When did you start cooking for his family?"

Kaycee wouldn't be able to put Sarah off for long. If she didn't fill her in, Sarah would pick at her mercilessly. One good thing, Sarah was no gossip. Kaycee would never tell Jon's business, but whatever she did say wouldn't be repeated. If all of Little Lobo was watching, she might do well to have Sarah as an ally to waylay rumors. So she briefly touched on her visit to the ranch and the subsequent invitation to breakfast. She skipped the parts about the social worker's visit and the fake engagement.

"And then there was church…sitting with his kids," Sarah prodded.

"Boy, you were everywhere today, weren't you?"

"You know, Jon would be hot property if he'd lighten up."

"Really?" Although hearsay wasn't necessary. Kaycee had been close enough to feel that heat firsthand.

"He's got a big ranch, made some good money from bull riding when he was young so he's better off than a lot of the ranchers around here. And he's a genuinely nice guy. Yep, even with all those kids, he wouldn't have trouble finding another wife. But he doesn't want one." Sarah leaned on the filing cabinet, staring outside. "All he wants is to have Alison back."

"How do you know all this?"

"Small town. There are no secrets around here."

That was exactly what Kaycee feared. And how long before her own private life was spread out for the town's scrutiny?

"What happened to his wife?"

"A tragic accident. The way I heard it, the girls missed the school bus that morning. Jon and Alison took the girls to school and were on their way to Bozeman to shop. An elk ran into the road, smashed through the windshield on Alison's side. She died in Jon's arms."

"Oh, no," Kaycee whispered, recalling Jon's determination to save the newborn calf yesterday. An unbidden image formed of him desperately trying to save his dying wife. "How horrible."

"Thank goodness they'd already dropped off the kids."

"Was Jon hurt?"

"Nothing major. They say he blames himself."

"Still wounded then." Kaycee recalled the sadness in Jon's ice-blue eyes.

"Well, there you go. You're a doctor—you can heal him."

Kaycee laughed and shook her head. "I'm a vet, Sarah, not a physician."

"Well, looks like you're doing pretty well after just one visit. Maybe the way to a rancher's heart is through a cow C-section."

"Oh, stop it, Sarah. There's nothing going on."

"Knowing Jon, I don't doubt that. Still, he did bring his brood over for breakfast. That's got to mean something."

"Means they were hungry. Any luck on getting a restorer for the house?"

"No," Sarah said, the frustration evident in her voice as she resumed filing. "Nobody wants to touch it. I've put ads in papers as far away as Denver, but no bites. But, thanks for this job. The extra money means I can move faster."

"Then it works for both of us. Full-time help's out of the question until I get more business. And don't worry about the restoration. Somebody will come along. Just the right person at the right time. You'll see. What all did you get done tonight?"

As she finished her work, Sarah rattled on about her favorite subject. By the time Sarah left, Kaycee decided it was too late to call Jon. She went to bed, but lay awake a long time thinking about his predicament. She fell asleep wondering what more she could do to help.

CHAPTER FOUR

"THERE'S THE BUS, everybody out!"

Jon watched the last of the girls' backpacks disappear into the yellow bus, then turned the SUV around and headed down the long lane to the house with the three boys. The twins normally attended preschool half the day, but for today, they would stay home because Jon didn't want to lose the time driving them to town only to have to pick them up a few hours later.

Glancing in his rearview mirror, Jon smiled broadly, his day already better. His pretend fiancée barreled down the gravel road behind him in her red pickup truck. At the house, Kaycee pulled up and parked, hopped out and was around the front of the SUV by the time Jon opened the door, so full of life Jon felt sluggish in comparison.

"Hi," she said. "I was out this way and thought I'd check on our little bull and his mama."

"They're doing well. We put them outside this morning. He's gaining weight and frisking around. I hate that you drove all the way out here for that." The increased thrumming of his heartbeat told him he really didn't hate it. Not at all.

"I like to see my patients when I can. Besides I was curious whether you resolved your housekeeper problem."

"Afraid not."

She peered into the Suburban. "So I see."

Jon pulled Zach and Tyler out of their toddler seats while Kaycee unfastened Bo's baby seat and lifted him out. She bounced him on her hip as naturally as if she did it every day, talking to him, making him giggle.

The sunshine brought out the gold in the wispy curls fluttering around her face in the early morning breeze. Her thick ponytail flipped back and forth as she played with Bo. Jon loved ponytails. Had since he pulled Maisey Gibson's long blond one every day in third grade to hear her squeal.

"You like kids, I see," Jon observed.

"I do," she said. "I was an only child, but I always loved babies—cousins, neighbors, strangers, it didn't matter."

A sudden longing for the companionship he'd lost hit Jon like a thunderbolt as she entertained his youngest child. Over the past year, he'd been so immersed in grief and the stress of keeping his family going that the thought of being attracted to another woman never entered his mind. So why was he thinking about it now? All he needed was a competent housekeeper, not a replacement for Alison.

And not with this woman who had a fledgling veterinary practice. She certainly wouldn't have the time to give the children the attention they needed.

"Stop," Jon snapped.

"What?" Kaycee looked startled. "Did I do something wrong?"

"No, nothing. Sorry." Regaining his composure, he said, "Come on, we'll check out that heifer so you can get to work."

Jon reached to take Bo from her. To his surprise, Bo pushed his hand away. "No, no, no!" The toddler clung to Kaycee with his other hand. "I stay here."

"I guess you've made a friend," Jon said with a laugh.

"Good." She gave Bo's round tummy a tickle with her knuckles, doubling him over with laughter. "I like him, too."

"Come on," Zach yelled. "We'll show you where the corrals are."

He and Tyler, in their clunky cowboy boots, ran ahead to the calf pens. Jon set the twins on the top fence rail on either side of him to watch the solitary heifer with the bull calf by her side. Other spindly legged calves played in an adjacent pen with their mothers. Kaycee agreed that the heifer and calf were thriving and could probably go out with the others soon.

"I can rope them calves, you know," Zach said, puffing out his chest with pride.

"That so?" Kaycee asked.

"Yep. My brother can, too. But he's not good as me."

"Am, too," Tyler protested.

Zach shook his head, and whispered loudly, "Really, he ain't, cause he's younger than me."

"A big three minutes," Jon said, with a wink to Tyler. "That's not a whole lot, is it, buckaroo?"

Tyler shook his head vigorously. "I'm bigger, anyway. And I know how to steer wrassle."

"Me, too," Zach shot back.

"Okay, enough. Both of you." Jon lifted the arguing boys down. "Run along to the house. I'm right behind you."

"We could show you, Dr. Kaycee," Zach persisted. "We could rope and wrassle some calves for you right now."

Kaycee laughed at the eagerness in their ruddy little faces. "Like a rodeo?"

"Yeah, a rodeo! You want us to?"

Kaycee slanted a look at Jon and smiled. "I don't think this is the best time. Your dad has other things to do and I have to be going shortly. Maybe another day. I'd want to see everything you can do."

"Oh, boy! Daddy, can we have a rodeo for Dr. Kaycee? Like we used to?"

"Like she said, another day," Jon responded.

"How about Saturday?" Zach suggested.

"Rachel and Sam can barrel race, and Michele's a trick rider on her horse, Dusty," Tyler said.

"And guess who's the rodeo clown?"

The boys jumped around like little kangaroos, talking at once to her, to Jon, to themselves, to the two herd dogs also getting rowdy at the excitement in the air.

"Bo?" Kaycee guessed.

"No. He's too little," Zach said.

"Am not," squealed Bo, wriggling to get out of Kaycee's arms and on the ground with his brothers, who seemed to be having more fun than he was.

"Who, then?"

"Wendy," Zach said.

"Wendy? The shy one?"

"Uh-huh. She's funny when she's gots on clown paint." Zach screwed up his face to mimic his sister's. "And we dress up Tilly and Chloe like clowns, too."

"The dogs," Jon clarified.

"That sounds like lots of fun. I'll look forward to it."

"Saturday, Daddy?" Zach pressed.

"We'll see," Jon said. "Now get along like I told you."

The twins took off running for the back door of the ranch house and Bo toddled behind without complaint as fast as his chubby legs would carry him.

Jon and Kaycee drifted toward her truck as they talked. "I was going to put on another pot of coffee after I settled the kids to play," Jon said. "Do you have time?"

Kaycee smiled, as if she had been hoping he'd ask. Just his imagination, Jon figured, but he didn't care.

"I'd love a cup."

"Good, come on in." Jon noticed that Kaycee glanced around when they went into the house. "Looks better than when you were here before, I hope."

"Much."

"We had a family powwow and reassigned some chores," Jon said, as he filled the coffeemaker and turned it on to brew. "The kids will do whatever it takes to stay together, just like I will. Let me settle these boys down to play. Be right back."

A few minutes later, Jon returned. Kaycee's gaze followed him as he moved about the kitchen, bringing mugs, sugar and cream to the island where she sat. With his spare muscular build, the easy grace of a rodeo rider and his no-nonsense outlook on life, Jon was Brett's opposite. Her ex, the lawyer, had been well-practiced in hiding and disguising his feelings.

"A penny for your thoughts," Jon said. He brought over the steaming coffee and poured, then set the carafe back on the warmer before settling down near Kaycee.

Kaycee laughed self-consciously. "Not worth your money, I promise you."

In the silence that fell between them, Kaycee wondered if staying for coffee had been a good idea. She had an excuse for leaving on the tip of her tongue when Jon shifted in his seat and cleared his throat.

"I phoned my father-in-law last night."

Kaycee settled back and focused on Jon, hoping to hear news of a truce. "Did he admit calling the social worker?"

"Yes, but I didn't need his confession to know that."

"Have you two never gotten along?"

"Not really. Bull rider was not the profession of choice for Hal Arant's son-in-law. Neither was rancher."

"Seems like a perfectly legitimate occupation to me—well, rancher, at least."

"Not if you're San Francisco aristocracy. Alison's father is a wealthy businessman. Her mother's family is upper crust. They had lofty goals for her. I'm far from destitute, but I made a lot more money bull-riding those few years than I made the past fifteen years ranching. You ranch because you love it, not for the money."

"That's hard to deal with," Kaycee said, having had a taste of it herself. Brett's father liked Kaycee because he loved horses. However, his mother, being a social climber extraordinaire, was thrilled with Brett's new status as Marissa's husband. She'd viewed Kaycee's career as an albatross around her son's neck as he ascended the ladder toward a judge's robes, maybe politics later. Hard as it was at the time, things had turned out for the best. That seemed especially true right now in Jon Rider's kitchen.

"You can say that again," Jon said.

For a startled moment, Kaycee thought he was reading her mind.

"Even though we never saw eye to eye," he went on, "Hal and I managed to live and let live. Until Alison died, when he tried to take my kids away. I'm not letting him near my children again."

Kaycee frowned. "How do they feel about that. Surely they love their grandparents. And obviously the Arants love them, or else they wouldn't be so concerned about their welfare."

Jon cocked a cynical eyebrow, but before he could respond, an outcry came from the room where the boys played. Jon went to the door.

"What's going on in here?" he asked.

"It's my turn to play with the big GI Joe, but Tyler won't give it to me!" Zach yelled.

"He wouldn't let me have it back last time. He kept it way too long," Tyler said.

"I gave it back," Zach retorted, "and now it's my turn again. Daddy—"

"Listen, both of you," Jon said sharply, silencing

them. "Either you work things out without all this fighting, or I'll take it away."

"But—" Zach began.

"Did you hear me?"

"Yes, sir."

"Yes, sir," Tyler repeated.

"And watch Bo with those toy soldiers. Don't let him put anything in his mouth."

"We know," Zach said. "He might choke. We don't have the little pieces out."

"Okay. Now keep it down," Jon said. He came back to the table bringing the coffee pot to refresh their cups, setting it on a trivet on the table.

"Did you ever think about buying two big GI Joe's?" Kaycee asked with a smile. "Minimize the arguing?"

Jon stirred cream into his coffee then shook his head. "Nope. I can't afford to buy two of every toy when they break within a few weeks. Anyway, they need to learn to work out their problems."

"Just a thought," Kaycee said. "We were talking about the kids and their grandparents."

"And I agree with you, they do love the children, but they show it in the wrong way. I know I'd never see my kids again, if they manage to spirit them away from me. Hal said some awful things last night."

"Like what?"

"Like he'll do whatever he thinks necessary to protect his grandchildren." His eyes grew dark with worry. "I don't know what he's cooking up, but I'm sure I'll find out soon enough. I can't even imagine life without my kids."

"Surely, you can work things out."

Jon stared at the spoon as he slowly twirled it with his fingertips. "With Alison gone," he said quietly, "I don't know how to heal the breach between Hal and me, but I'm not going to let him take my children, no matter what I have to do."

Kaycee studied the swirls of steam rising from her cup, Jon's anxiety palpable and suffocating.

That he still suffered from the loss of his wife was stamped on his face, clear in his every word. But losing his children...? She didn't need this unexpected sense of connection to Jon Rider. The constriction in her chest threatened to trigger tears.

To her relief, her cell phone rang and she grabbed for it. Sarah relayed an emergency call that had just come in.

"I'm at the Rider ranch right now, so it should take me about an hour to get there. Call back and tell them when to expect me," Kaycee replied and hung up. "Guess I'd better go."

Jon nodded, rising from the table along with her. "I need to get busy, too. I'll walk out with you."

When she was in the truck, Jon closed her door and leaned in the open window. "Thanks for stopping by to see the heifer."

"No problem."

Their eyes met for a long moment, and the unbidden exchange scared Kaycee silly. She started the engine. Jon pushed away. She eased down the gravel drive to the highway then shot away from the Rider ranch like a rabbit running for its life.

A sense of unexpected loneliness followed Kaycee as she drove the ten miles to the Bullock ranch, leaving her depressed and confused.

Get him off your mind, Kaycee. You've got a job to do.

She found the turnoff, coming to a stop in the graveled area outside the main barn. She sat in the truck for a few seconds, gathering her thoughts, trying to clear her head.

A bay quarter horse stood in crossties in the barn aisle with a pool of blood between his front feet. Two men pressed pads against the wounds to stifle the bleeding. The older man eyed Kaycee suspiciously, with that look she'd grown to expect.

"I'm Dr. Calloway," Kaycee said, setting her case down and holding out a hand.

"Harvey Bullock," the older man said, shaking her hand timidly, as if he might hurt her. "Hoss here spooked, went through a barb fence."

"Sorry to hear that," Kaycee murmured, moving to the horse's side and soothing him for a moment before bending to examine the wounds.

Two jagged gashes crisscrossed the muscular chest. Although the cuts were deep, the muscle was intact. Had the muscle tissue been shredded, Kaycee would have suggested a different treatment. But she could safely close these and reduce the scarring on this gorgeous animal.

After prepping the horse, Kaycee sat beside him on a bale of hay, suturing the wounds layer by layer. She tried to ignore Harvey's critical observation so she could concentrate on the tiny sutures. She'd learned this part of her trade well on the expensive purebred race and show horses in South Carolina, where an obvious blemish could knock thousands off the animal's value.

She placed a drain in the wound to circumvent infection, then injected an antibiotic. Pulling off the surgical gloves, she turned to the older man.

"Do you have a neck cradle to keep him from chewing the stitches? If you don't, I have one in my truck that—"

"Naw, I don't need no store-bought contraption. I know how to make one."

"I'm not kidding, put one on him before you turn him loose in the stall. Otherwise he may do damage that can't be repaired."

Kaycee cleaned up and put her instruments away, snapped shut her medic case. As she reached for the handle, Harvey's hand beat her to it. He hoisted the case, carried it out and put in the truck for her.

"Thanks," Kaycee said, opening her door.

The crusty old rancher nodded. "You did a fine job on that hoss."

Kaycee smiled. "Appreciate it. Well, I'd better be going. More calls to make."

She phoned Sarah for any new messages and learned of a couple of nonemergencies. Good. She needed to fill the day, rather than dwell on Jon's problems.

Even though she was primarily a large-animal vet, she was the only vet of any kind within a twenty-mile radius of Little Lobo and some of her work involved house pets. She didn't mind. The little critters had unique personalities, as did their owners.

Since she worked alone, however, her clinic hours

were sporadic, which was why she couldn't afford a full-time receptionist yet. She wasn't staffed for surgery, either, and had to refer that work for the moment. She hoped to change that soon.

Her last call, late in the afternoon, was for Joey Barker's lame Shetland pony. She showed Joey and his mom how to make a poultice for the swollen fetlock and promised to check back the next day. Joey ran to get a bucket of feed for the pony.

"I noticed you sittin' with the Rider gang in church yesterday," Mrs. Barker said, with a twinkle in her eyes.

Kaycee wanted to roll her eyes. Was there no escaping small-town gossip?

"Yes, they asked me to sit with them. Nice bunch of kids."

"I didn't see anybody come in with them. Has he lost another sitter?"

"Is that a regular occurrence?"

"Oh, yes. He's had everybody in Little Lobo and the surrounds since his wife was killed. Not that they're bad kids, just that there are so many of them and most people simply aren't up to the job."

"I only knew the last one quit rather suddenly. He's having trouble finding another."

"I figured that. That's why I brought it up. My sister-in-law Rosie's widowed. She's been living with us since she sold her house, looking for a job and an apartment. She might jump at that job."

"Even with so many kids?"

"I can't answer that for her, but she and her husband ran a day-care center in Helena for decades. She's not here right now, or I'd introduce you. For all I know, she might be tired of dealing with kids after all these years."

Disappointment dampened Kaycee's hope.

"But I don't think it was the children that got to Rosie as much as the red tape and paperwork that her husband always took care of," Mrs. Barker went on. "Rosie struggled for a couple of years after he died then decided to close it and find something else to do."

What a catch, Kaycee thought, if Jon hired Rosie. "Could be her own little day care without the paperwork," she said.

"Exactly what I was thinking."

"I'm pretty sure it's live-in. Would she mind that?"

"Between you and me, I think Rosie would be real lonesome living alone in an apartment. Probably why she hasn't been too anxious to move away from us."

"Can I give Jon your phone number and have him call Rosie?"

"Do that. Sounds like it might work out all around."

Back at the clinic that night, Kaycee picked up the phone and dialed Jon's number, wondering how his day had gone and eager to tell him about Rosie.

"Hello?" The voice on the other end was definitely not Jon's.

"This is Dr. Kaycee. Who's speaking?"

"Hi, Dr. Kaycee, it's Michele. Zach told us about the rodeo Saturday. We're going to have a blast." She hesitated. "You are coming, aren't you?"

"Sure, unless an emergency comes up."

"Great! We're going to do so many things. Bo is even going to ride the barrel bull."

"Sounds like fun. Is there anything I can do to help?"

"Nope. You just come. We'll have everything ready. We girls are going to make food and after the rodeo we're going to get Uncle Clint—he's our foreman—to give us a hayride to the lower meadow for a picnic."

"Sounds like a great time. I'm looking forward to it."

In the background, Kaycee heard Jon's voice. "Who's on the phone, Mish?"

"Dr. Kaycee. I was telling her about the rodeo on Saturday." Into the receiver Michele said, "Here's Daddy. See you Saturday."

"See you." Kaycee heard the phone being transferred.

"Hello," Jon said.

"Hi. Sounds like the children are excited about Saturday."

"That's all I've heard since this morning. We haven't had one since…well, in a while." He paused then asked, "How was your day?"

"Busy. I was wondering if you found anybody to take care of the kids?"

"I have a couple of maybes. Neither of them could commit to more than a week, but at least that gives me some breathing room."

"I may have good news, then. Mrs. Barker's sister-in-law Rosie might be interested. I've got her number if you want it."

"I know Mrs. Barker. I trust her recommendation. Thanks."

Kaycee gave him the number and heard him scribbling it down. She pictured him on the other end of the phone line, his tanned face stubbled with the shadow of a beard, hair still tousled from the wind. A strong, handsome cowboy, who from the sound of the gurgles coming over the phone, had a baby on his hip and maybe even an apron around his waist. The image stole Kaycee's heart and made her wish she were there.

"Do you have somebody to watch the boys tomorrow?" she asked.

"My foreman's daughter is taking a half day off from college to stay with them. She's been a lifesaver in emergencies, but she can't keep skipping or she'll jeopardize her grades."

The baby began to fret.

"Sounds like you need to go. I'll see you on Saturday."

JON HUNG UP THE PHONE, bouncing Bo to pacify him. His mind reeled with thoughts of Kaycee Calloway. Her materialization in his life had him off balance. He found himself thinking about her more than he should and he couldn't deny that he was looking forward to seeing her again on Saturday.

Saturday. The kids' rodeo. They'd never held a rodeo without Alison. Jon didn't know how he'd get through it, but the children were too excited for him to dampen their enthusiasm.

He'd just manage, that was all. Somehow, he'd manage.

CHAPTER FIVE

WEDNESDAY MORNING, Kaycee unlocked the door of her clinic and walked out to get the newspaper. The sign on the small brick building near the end of Main Street still read Doc Adams's Large Animal Clinic, but the shingle hanging beside the front door displayed her name.

An architectural facade gave a modern look to the front of the building housing her office, the examining rooms and a two-bedroom apartment. Kennels for sick animals and the occasional boarder were in back. Vacant land flanked her office on one side, a good spot for evaluating motor problems with large patients. On the other side, Sarah ran the Little Lobo Eatery and Daily Grind.

As her gaze swept the building, she felt a surge of pride knowing that this building, this practice, was hers now, bought with the hard-earned money she'd saved since college. Money she had intended to use to begin a practice in South Carolina after she and Brett married.

So much for that. But this small, independent operation was a perfect fit. Many of the large animal vets worked solely out of their pickup trucks, taking calls on their cell phones, with no clinic to maintain. Kaycee wanted more.

In time, when she was established, she was determined to expand to include small animals as well.

In spite of the gossip, which she'd endured back home, too, Kaycee loved this tiny town, nestled in the cradle of a long narrow valley, with the Bridger Mountain Range to the north, the Gallatins to the south and skirted by the Little Lobo River. It was home to her now, the place she wanted to settle.

Kaycee resisted the urge to follow the aromas to Sarah's café. She needed to get moving. Checking the appointment book, she noted a noon call to a nearby ranch to worm and vaccinate calves.

"Hey, you busy?"

Kaycee jerked her head up as Jon punctuated his words with a couple of light raps on the doorframe.

"I invited myself in. Hope you don't mind."

Mind? His smile brought an answering one to her face immediately. *Mind? Far from it.*

"No…no, I'm glad to see you. I was just thinking…"

Kaycee caught herself before she finished the sentence. Almost every waking thought she'd had for the past two days connected in some way to Jon Rider and his youngsters. Yesterday she'd almost called him to tell him they should stop pretending and he needed to find another way to solve his problems, but she hadn't.

"I was just wondering if you called Rosie," she said.

"She moved in yesterday. Took over like she'd lived with us for years. There'll be some rough spots, I'm sure, but I think she'll work out."

"I'm so glad," Kaycee said. "How do the kids like her?"

Jon laughed easily, much more relaxed than he had been the last time she saw him. When his face lit up that way, Kaycee's insides caught fire.

"The girls love having her so far. Less for them to do," he said. "Rosie thinks the girls stay up too late, so they might not like her as well when she announces their new bedtime tonight. The twins are still taking stock. She's got their number and they know it. Just don't know what to do about it."

Kaycee chuckled, imagining the twins' resistance to having their reins drawn in.

Jon's smile faded. "She didn't like the idea that the kids can't talk to their grandparents, but she'll have to live with it. Anyway…" he tipped his hat to Kaycee "…thank you for finding her. In the long run, I think we'll all adjust."

"Glad to be of help."

Jon looked around. "Nice facilities."

"You've never seen them?" Kaycee asked in surprise.

"Doc built this right before that heart attack forced him to retire. We rarely need to bring an animal in. Rarely need a vet at all," Jon said, then cocked an eyebrow. "Well, didn't used to need one."

To hide the blush rising up her neck, Kaycee turned to pick up her keys from the desk. "Want a tour?" she managed.

"Love one."

"Follow me."

Jon complimented the immaculate examination

rooms, the sterile surgery and the holding pens for stock outside. They compared modern veterinary medicine to the age-old treatments favored by seasoned cowhands, who thought vets were for city people. Jon's extensive knowledge of animal husbandry and veterinary medicine impressed Kaycee and she marveled at their easy camaraderie, chatting like old friends as they strolled through the pens toward the back door of the building.

"I plan to expand as soon as I have the means. I hope to be able to invite my cousin Daniel to join my practice next year. He's specializing in small animal work and he could man the clinic while I'm on calls." Kaycee saw the busy clinic in her mind's eye, every detail of it. "Sarah answers the phones for me now and does some filing."

"I wouldn't think Sarah had time to turn around, much less work in the clinic."

"She's got more energy than anybody I've ever seen. When she found I was about to hire an answering service, she wanted the job to earn more money for her bed-and-breakfast project."

"Hadn't heard about that. You don't mean the old house behind the café?"

"The very one. She thinks it can be restored. She doesn't have to spend much time over here. I forward the calls to her phone at the café when I'm gone, and she files at night. It's only temporary, anyway. Someday, I'll have a full-time staff. A receptionist and maybe a vet tech to assist Daniel. In the summer I'll take on a couple of pre-vet students to give them experience."

Jon studied her seriously. "Wow. Sounds like you've got life mapped out. No plans to marry, raise a family in there anywhere?"

The way he said it pricked like somebody had stuck a pin in her balloon.

Kaycee shrugged. "Maybe someday. Right now, I've got too much going on to think about that."

Jon propped a boot on the bottom rung of the fence and crossed his arms on the top rail, scrutinizing the distant mountains. "This is demanding work, Kaycee. Dangerous sometimes. Not to mention the erratic call outs and emergencies all times of the day and night. Takes a special breed to hack it."

His skepticism took Kaycee by surprise and made her defensive.

"Sure, it is, but I love the challenge. You do the same thing on the ranch, don't you? If something comes up, you have to take care of it. Even in the middle of the night. You can't wait until it's convenient to deal with an emergency."

Kaycee saw his jaw muscle tighten.

"True, but it's right there at my doorstep. Worst scenario, I have to ride up in the mountains a few miles. Besides, I can delegate to my cowhands when I need to. You don't have anybody to fall back on."

And I'm a man and you're a woman. He had the good sense not to say so outright.

Kaycee set her hands on her hips and glared at him. "I don't need anybody. At least not right now. I've been able to hack everything, as you put it. Like I said, I plan to expand, take on help when I can afford it."

He faced her, eyes glinting in the sunshine. "What about Saturday? My kids are counting on you being there for their rodeo. They're putting it on just for you, you know. They'll be terribly disappointed if you don't show."

"I know that," Kaycee said, opening the door and stepping into the room housing the kennels. Jon's words stung, but she tried not to show it. "I made arrangements with another vet to take any calls on Saturday."

Jon followed. "Good. I think you'll enjoy it."

Good for him, Kaycee thought, but if it weren't for the kids, she'd be a no-show, considering his attitude toward her work. Jon didn't seem to notice her irritation.

A lone puppy whined from the kennel, his tail furiously thumping the sides of the enclosure and Jon stooped to poke a finger through the wire to scratch its muzzle. He smiled as the dog licked his finger and leaned against the wire door to get more attention.

"Is he sick?" Jon asked.

"No," Kaycee said, calming down somewhat. Why should Jon be any more accepting of her job than the other ranchers she'd met? "Somebody dropped him on my doorstep. That happens a lot. They expect a vet to take care of abandoned animals and find them a home. But I haven't had time with this one yet. Michele and Wendy wanted to spend an afternoon here, so I thought playing with the puppy would give them something to do. You don't mind if they come, do you?"

Jon straightened. "No, I don't mind. Wendy's no trouble, but Michele's a live wire, I have to warn you."

"Oh, I've seen her in action."

Jon gave her a wry smile. "So you have. When do you want them?"

"Next Wednesday's good for me. I stay here for appointments anyway and I can pick them up after school."

"That's okay with me. By the way, I've invited my favorite social worker to the ranch to meet Rosie. I hope that gets her off my case."

"So do I. When is she coming?"

"I'm not sure. She's supposed to get back to me. Want to join us?"

Kaycee rubbed her hands along her upper arms as she considered the invitation.

"I don't know about that. The fewer questions we have to answer the better."

He fell silent for a moment, then shrugged. "You're probably right, but just so you know, if she asks about our engagement, I'm going to tell her it's still on, if that's okay with you."

"Is that a good idea? Maybe we should let this engagement thing drop now that you've got Rosie."

Jon shook his head. "Not just yet. Suppose Rosie doesn't work out? And if we move too fast, Mrs. Hawthorn might get suspicious. Let's consider it a safety net."

"What about the kids?"

"What do you mean?"

"Don't they believe we're getting married? How will this affect them when they find out we've been lying to them?"

"They know you were tricked into saying you'd be their mother. I think they understand it's not real."

"I hope so. I don't want them to be hurt."

Jon furrowed his brow. "Don't worry, I'll take care of my kids. I just want to keep up the pretense until I'm sure everything is settled." They made their way outside to Jon's truck. Jon leaned against the fender and crossed his arms.

"Just remember we're still engaged for the time being. No running around on me." Jon's eyes twinkled with mischief.

"Umm, I hadn't thought about that restriction. As a matter of fact—" Kaycee waggled her eyebrows "—I was thinking it was high time I picked up my wild and crazy social life again."

"Really?"

That irked Kaycee. She might have had a wild, crazy social life at some point. Not that she had, but he didn't know that.

"I guess you're going to have to put that notion on hold a while longer, then," Jon continued. "Wild and crazy's not my style and it won't impress Mrs. Hawthorn."

Kaycee pulled a pout. "Okay, I'll try to behave. Goes both ways, you know. You have to be on good behavior, too."

Some of the light went out of Jon's eyes and Kaycee wished she'd kept her mouth shut.

"Believe me, I'm on good behavior all the time." He sniffed the air. "Sarah's cooking something good today. Can I buy you lunch?"

"Sorry, I can't. I have thirty calves to worm and vaccinate at noon."

"Another time then." Jon checked his watch. "Guess I'd better get on the road."

He swung up onto the seat, slammed the door and leaned out with his arm propped on the window frame. "See you Saturday."

"I'll be there."

As Jon drove home after finishing his errands in town, his mind lingered on Kaycee. He'd had no real reason to go by the clinic, just wanted to see her. The look on her face when he surprised her gratified him. Maybe she harbored a little interest in him.…As for him, he couldn't keep his mind off her. He found himself lost in fantasies he had no business indulging. As if their engagement were real. As if some day he'd have the privilege of kissing those satin-soft lips, running his hand over her—

"Whoa, slow down," he growled out loud, as the pressure in his jeans grew uncomfortable. "You're acting like a damn rutting buck."

It should be enough that she was going out of her way to help him with the social worker. But it wasn't. For the first time in over a year, somebody aroused not only his libido, but a longing for the companionship of a woman. Somebody who would share all that was important to him. Maybe that somebody was Kaycee Calloway. Or maybe not. She had big talk about expanding her vet practice. Life with Kaycee would not be the same as life with Alison, for him or the children. *Don't fall in love with somebody you can't live with.*

He pulled up in front of the house and saw the social worker's car.

"What the—"

In the foyer, Jon eased the door closed behind him, listening. Low voices drifted from the kitchen. He glanced into the clean, orderly den as he passed. Zach and Tyler sat in the far corner, intent on creating something big out of Legos and building blocks. From the dining room, he could see the two women in the kitchen. Mrs. Hawthorn sat at the bar, her back to him, with her notepad open in front of her, pen in hand. Rosie sat on an adjacent stool, her light brown hair pulled back into a tight bun, her face ruddy from baking. The kitchen smelled of cookies and hot coffee. Bo snuggled in Rosie's lap, his cheeks puffed out from the teacake he munched, crumbs spilling on the counter, his shirt, Rosie's apron.

"How long do you expect to stay in this position?" Mrs. Hawthorn asked.

Rosie's pleasant expression put Jon at ease. She didn't seem the least perturbed. "Oh, I'll stay as long as Mr. Rider needs me."

"Mr. Rider has had a problem keeping housekeepers in the past, I've learned. This is a hard job. Seven children."

Rosie laughed, her merriment causing Bo to look up at her and smile. "Mrs. Hawthorn, I ran a day care for fifteen years. Just me and my late husband. I've had as many as twelve at a time under my care at different times, from newborn through preteen. I loved them all, but some could be a trial. These sweet children are like a breath of fresh air. Well-raised, well-behaved. Good-hearted. They're spirited, there's no doubt of that, but there's only seven of them. No, I'll not be giving up this job until Mr. Rider runs me off."

"I suppose since he's getting married, that could change. Have you met his fiancée?"

Jon grimaced. He hadn't mentioned the fake engagement to Rosie.

Without skipping a beat, Rosie looked directly at Mrs. Hawthorn and said, "I don't believe in discussing my employer's private life, if you don't mind. Besides, a lot of married folks have housekeepers."

Jon exhaled in relief.

"Yes, they do," he said, stepping into the room. "There's been a full-time housekeeper here since Samantha was born. Don't worry about your position, Rosie. As long as you want it, you've got a place here."

Mrs. Hawthorn twisted on her stool toward him. "Mr. Rider, I was hoping you'd get back before I left."

"I'll bet."

Rosie slanted him a warning look. She eased Bo into his high chair and gave him a plastic bowl filled with Cheerios. "Mr. Rider, would you like a cup of tea? Or coffee? Mrs. Hawthorn? Maybe a cup now?"

"No thank you, I'm fine," Mrs. Hawthorn said.

Jon took Rosie's hint along with a deep breath. *Play nice. It's important.*

"Coffee, please," he said and turned to Mrs. Hawthorn. "I didn't expect you today or I'd have stayed home."

She leveled her gaze at him and said, "Sometimes it's best to show up unannounced."

"Do you think I'm covering up something?" Jon said, forcing a calm he didn't feel.

"I don't know. Are you?"

"I'm trying to protect my children, that's all. You know by now those charges my father-in-law brought are bogus. I have a housekeeper, like I said I did."

She pursed her lips and stared at him for a moment. "Not the same one that quit, though. Her name wasn't Rosie. I don't believe for a minute you had anybody the day I was here."

Jon glanced at Rosie, fixing his coffee nearby. She was getting an earful, but she acted as if she heard nothing. A bonus was in order for that woman.

"Think what you want to. I always have somebody to supervise my kids. I don't neglect them. I don't abuse them. And I won't stand for anybody else doing it, either. Anybody."

"Meaning me?" Mrs. Hawthorn asked sharply.

"Meaning my father-in-law, who's responsible for you being here."

"I haven't said who filed the complaint."

"You don't have to. I talked to him the other night. He as much as admitted it." Jon hesitated, wondering how open he should be with this woman. He wanted her on his side, not Hal's, and he'd gotten off on the wrong foot with her. He was going to do his best to remedy that. "I want to apologize again for flying off the handle with you Saturday. You caught me by surprise with those charges."

"Thank you for the apology. I have to do my job, even when it's unpleasant. We never want to take a chance with a child's life. You do understand that?"

"But what happens when the charges are false? My father-in-law threatened to file more if you close this one."

"We don't look kindly on false charges."

A pat answer—one Jon wasn't sure he believed.

"I'm glad to hear that. So you can stop Hal from filing more?"

"No, we don't have the authority to do that. And I have to warn you, we would have to investigate any new charges. We can't make an arbitrary decision that a report is false. We need proof. You think I'm persecuting you, but I'm only doing my job."

Jon lifted his hands, exasperated. "Isn't there some way to keep him from filing charges? It's a waste of your time and mine."

"There are legal incriminations if we prove somebody is deliberately filing false charges, but most of the time even if they're reported, the D.A. doesn't have time to follow up."

"That's encouraging," Jon said, unable to keep the sarcasm out of his voice.

He settled on a bar stool as Rosie brought his coffee. Then she went to the utility room for an armload of folded towels, which she took upstairs, leaving them alone to talk.

"So, what will it take to close this case?"

"I'd like to know more about your home life on a day-to-day basis. How do you manage to take care of this large ranch and still give your children attention?"

"I employ several full-time ranch hands. Besides, this is a family operation. Ranch kids grow up fast and learn to carry their share of responsibility. I don't go out and work all day while my kids sit in the house and watch TV. They all have chores. Even with a house-keeper."

"Give me an example of what they have to do."

Jon stirred his coffee, giving the request some thought before responding.

"Okay. Well, Rachel and Sam help take care of Bo and the twins. They bathe them, help them dress, play with them. Three of the girls have a horse apiece, and are expected to feed and check them every day, rain or shine. Michele and Wendy feed the dogs and the poultry and gather eggs every morning before school. Tyler and Zach have pet rabbits, which they feed and care for and they help feed the other horses. Bo has to help put his toys away along with the others. They're all expected to pick up after themselves and keep their rooms clean. Of course, none of us is perfect. There are days like last week when you were here that things slip by the wayside, but we get along."

"When do you spend time with them one on one?"

"I grab any chance I get," Jon said truthfully. "If they're doing their chores or playing, I see them off and on. When they come home from school, I take a few minutes to ask how their day went, if they have any problems or notes from school. The older girls help the younger ones with homework in the afternoon. If the girls need help, I work with them at night."

Jon took a sip of coffee and set the cup down. "Are you sure you don't want something to drink?"

"No, thank you. Go on. Do you have a bedtime routine?"

"After the children are bathed and ready for bed, we have reading time together. Granted, my wife used to do most of that, but now it's up to me."

"Who bathes the children?" she asked.

A red flag shot up in Jon's mind. Just when he started to relax, she threw him another curve ball. *Stay calm, answer the question.*

"Except for Bo, they're all old enough to bathe themselves. The twins still need some supervision," Jon said cautiously.

To his relief, she seemed satisfied with his answer. "Do you read to them?" she asked.

"When they want me to. Otherwise, I listen. Whoever wants to read gets a turn. Even the twins can manage beginner books. Sometimes that's all they want. Somebody to listen to them."

As Jon talked Mrs. Hawthorn took notes.

"How do you handle dating and introducing the women in your life?"

Jon frowned and took a swallow of coffee. This prying into his private affairs didn't set well. But, if that's what it took to satisfy her, so be it. "There haven't been any women in my life since my wife died, so that's easy enough."

"Really?" she said, arching an eyebrow. "I thought you were engaged to Dr. Calloway."

Good job, Jon! Get yourself out of this one.

"Well, I meant until her. And actually my daughter got us together."

"How did your daughter know her?"

"Michele loves animals. Wants to be a vet someday.

Kaycee goes to our church." None of it was a lie. It wasn't the truth, either, which stung Jon's conscience. Just as Kaycee feared, the web was getting more tangled. One deception covered by another one. Sooner or later, somebody would slip up and Mrs. Hawthorn would figure things out. Or Hal would.

"When is the wedding date?"

"Sometime after calving season, like I said. We both have to be flexible since we can't control nature or set our schedules in stone."

Bo, having scattered his Cheerios across the high chair tray, began to kick his feet against the legs of the chair, making an awful racket.

"Bo, stop," Jon admonished.

The baby grinned and kicked harder, stretching his arms toward his daddy.

"Out, peez," he demanded.

Jon sat the child on his knee.

"How old are you, Bo?" Mrs. Hawthorn asked.

Bo looked at her with round blue eyes.

"Tell her how old you are," Jon encouraged. "Show her on your fingers."

With his left hand, Bo manipulated his right until only two fingers stuck up. "This many."

"Two years old. Do you go to school?"

Jon wondered if she was just making conversation or if this was part of her agenda.

"My b'others do. An' Rwachel."

"You stay home with your daddy then?"

Bo nodded and grinned broadly up at Jon. "My daddy. We p'ay horsey."

He squirmed around and crawled up Jon's lap, putting his chubby arms around Jon's neck, hugging him hard. Jon could have cried at his son's innocently well-timed show of affection. He squeezed back, his senses flooded with the sweet smell of the child's clean hair and the touch of sticky lips planting a kiss on his jaw. He glanced up to find Mrs. Hawthorn studying them intently. She had a nice smile. Too bad she didn't use it more often.

"Well, Mr. Rider, I'm going to recommend we close this case as unfounded. But I'd like to have a follow-up meeting with you and your fiancée soon. All right?"

"Sure, but give me notice so I can check with Kaycee. She never knows from day to day where she'll be working."

"Certainly. I understand that." She chucked Bo under the chin as she rose. "Go play horsey with your daddy."

Rosie came down in time to see Mrs. Hawthorn out, and Jon suspected she'd been listening for a cue. As the front door closed, Jon breathed a deep sigh of relief. Maybe now life could get back to normal. Without thinking, he rocked Bo gently in his arms, his lips resting on top of the baby's silky head. He should get going. He was far enough behind at the ranch already.

Instead, Jon tightened his embrace. The quiet spell of this moment, the peacefulness of the house, was too reverent to break. The love he felt for this child nestled against his chest, for all his children, rose like a cresting river through him. He closed his eyes to hold in the tears. He would never give up these precious children. No matter what he had to do.

CHAPTER SIX

KAYCEE DROVE THROUGH the tall, iron entrance with the brand for the R-Bar-R Ranch welded into the overhead arch. She breathed in the sweet morning air whistling through her truck and her gaze swept the expanse of green land stretching up the lower slopes of the surrounding mountains. There wasn't a cloud in the silver-blue sky—perfect for a pint-sized rodeo.

A small herd of boisterous children and two Australian shepherds greeted her truck. As she got out, the kids surrounded her, talking all at once, each striving to be heard over the others.

"Calf roping..."

"Barrel racing..."

"Apple dunking..."

"Barrel-bull riding..."

The dogs joined in the excitement, whining and wriggling their stub tails vigorously. Kaycee took in the well-scrubbed faces of the kids, overflowing with eagerness, and she had an uncanny feeling that she'd just come home. Zach grabbed her hand and started tugging her along toward the barn.

"Come on, the grandstand's ready and everybody's waiting."

The spirit of the day filled Kaycee as one of the taller girls plunked a well-worn cowboy hat on her head. Red, white and blue bunting ran the length of the makeshift grandstand set up along one side of the paddock beside the barn. A few cowboys sat scattered across the bleachers alongside a middle-aged woman whom the girls introduced as Rosie.

"Nice to meet you," Kaycee said, shaking Rosie's hand. "I'm glad you took the job."

Rosie smiled pleasantly. "So am I. I appreciate you giving Mr. Rider my number."

Jon was nowhere to be seen as the kids offered Kaycee the seat of honor next to Rosie with an excellent view of the entire arena. As if on cue, there was a terrible racket as Bo banged mightily on an overturned galvanized washtub in his version of a drumroll.

A gaudy rodeo clown in absurdly large cowboy boots bounded to the center of the arena, his tattered clothing a cacophony of color. A huge white painted grin outlined his mouth, black line crosses accented each eye and he sported a pair of red circle cheeks. An explosion of white hair escaped from under a crumpled straw hat.

"Ladies and gentlemen, welcome to the R-Bar-R Rodeo!"

Kaycee laughed aloud hearing Jon's voice. The twins giggled, too.

"We betted you wouldn't know who Daddy was all dressed up in his gear. He used to be a rodeo clown sometimes," Zach announced, then grabbed Tyler by the shirtsleeve. "Come on, we gotta go." The boys took off toward the end of the area.

"I thought he was a bull rider."

"He was when he was young," Michele said, "but he helps out with the junior rodeos in the area and he's a clown for them sometimes."

Kaycee pondered this facet of Jon. He was usually so serious. Yet, he played the clown for kids. She decided then and there that she wanted to hear Jon Rider laugh. A free, unburdened laugh.

"And now, for our first performance," Jon called loudly, "those two pint-sized, potbellied, precociously proficient ropesters extraordinaire—Zach and Tyler Rider!"

The twins ran into the arena, their round faces ruddy beneath the oversized Resistol hats on their heads. Each boy held a coiled lariat in hand. In the center of the corral stood a wooden barrel on stick legs, with a spindly neck and a bucket with large google-eyes for a head. With wild whoops and yee-haws the little boys scampered around the wooden calf, unfurling their ropes and twirling the loops haphazardly over their heads. Tyler slung his lariat toward the calf and missed. Zach moved closer and landed his throw on top of the bucket head. After a few more throws, Zach won the event and earned a blue ribbon, while Tyler got a red one for second place.

"Did you see us?" Zach asked when the twins climbed the grandstand a few minutes later. "Weren't we good?"

"You were great! You must practice a lot," Kaycee said, examining each boy's ribbon with great interest.

"My rope slipped," Tyler said, in defense of his red ribbon.

"Daddy says you can't win every time. You just have to try again," Zach said, reaching across to pat his brother's knee.

Kaycee smiled at the earnestness of Zach's voice and the determination in Tyler's as he replied, "Yeah, I'm going to win next time."

In the arena, the cowboys marked the perimeter of a large triangle with fifty-five-gallon drums, measuring off the distance in long strides.

"And now, my barrel babes!" Jon called from center stage. "Sam riding Rampage and Rachel on Sweetie Pie."

The gate swung wide. Jon pulled a stopwatch from his pocket, held a red bandanna high overhead, then dropped his arm. A thunder of hooves threw up a cloud of dust at the end of the arena.

A wild-eyed black-and-white paint exploded from the center of the maelstrom with Sam bent over the saddle urging him on. Rampage was a good name for this horse, Kaycee thought, as he pounded around the barrels. Sam flapped the long ends of the reins from side to side as the horse rounded the last barrel cleanly and raced for the finish line.

Jon clicked the stopwatch and relayed the time to the cowhand next to him. A few moments later, he raised the bandanna and lowered it again. This time a compact bay quarter horse tore out of the gate. Rachel rode lower and quieter in the saddle than her sister. The horse knew its business and moved with efficiency and grace. Racing toward the finish, Rachel urged her horse with voice alone.

Afterward, Jon jogged to the center of the arena and announced, "And the winner is…by two tenths of a second…Miss Rachel Rider and Sweetie Pie."

Kaycee and the other onlookers clapped heartily for the winner. Sam looked crestfallen for a moment then she rallied and high-fived her sister.

Distracted by the commotion at the end of the arena, Kaycee was startled to hear Jon's voice close at hand.

"Hope we're not boring you." His mawkish painted grin made Kaycee smile.

"Not in the least. It's great fun. Your children are very competitive."

"Sometimes too competitive, but today they're on good behavior or else."

"For my sake?"

"And my sanity." Jon laughed. "You're staying for the hayride and picnic, aren't you?"

"Oh, yes. I'm looking forward to it."

"Good." Jon looked toward the gate. "Well, back to work. I see my next rider is ready."

A beautiful palomino with a soft golden cream coat pranced into the arena.

"Now a demonstration of trick riding by Michele the Magnificent on Gold Dust Dreams, better known around here as Dusty."

The mare's flaxen tail flowed like a satin banner as she trotted with a high showy motion that belied the smoothness of her gait. Michele sat small and still in an ornately tooled trick saddle, appearing far too young and frail to control such a large creature. Yet the horse obeyed every nudge and flick of the reins.

Jon stood in the center of the circle Dusty and Michele were describing, turning slowly, always facing the horse as his daughter put Dusty into a slow canter, laid the continuous reins across the horse's neck and dropped her feet from the stirrups. In a graceful movement, she hoisted herself into the saddle and stood, holding a short rope hooked over the saddle horn with one hand and waving her hat over her head with the other. Dusty's ears flicked back and forth, aware of the least sound from Michele or Jon, who gave low commands to horse and rider as he pivoted with them.

Michele dropped lightly back into the saddle, then immediately slid out of sight. As she passed the grandstand, Kaycee saw her hanging off the side of the horse, one foot hooked behind the saddle and hands clinging to the saddle horn and breast strap like Kaycee had seen riders do in the Westerns to hide from the enemy. The children on the bleachers clapped and cheered as their sister came by and exited the corral.

"And now, ladies and gentlemen, while we set up for bull riding, here are wacky Wendy and her wondrous woofers."

A miniature, come-to-life Raggedy Ann flounced into the ring, followed by the two dogs with colorful bandannas around their necks. Wendy tripped on her huge shoes and rolled around on the ground before getting up again and dusting off her butt with great exaggeration. The little children giggled wildly. Wendy gave them a stern look and shook her finger at them. They giggled harder. She whistled up the dogs and put them through their tricks, which included the standard sit, stay, roll over and shake, then progressed to crawls, flips, leaps over each other and Wendy. It was an impressive display of obeying hand signals.

By the time Wendy took her bow, the cowboys had positioned an odd contraption in the center of the arena. It looked like a barrel topped by a tiny saddle with stirrups, suspended a few inches from the ground by long ropes tied to opposite fence rails. A leather handle attached in front of the saddle provided a handhold. A beginner's bull for a baby bull rider. Deep sand had been heaped beneath the low-slung barrel while Bo waited on the sidelines wearing a helmet under his over-large cowboy hat.

"And now the one and only—Bo the bullrider!" Jon called as one of the cowhands set Bo on top of the barrel and tucked his tiny cowboy boots into the stirrups. Grinning from ear to ear, Bo took firm hold of the grip on the front of the barrel and raised his other hand high overhead.

"Ready?" Jon called.

Bo nodded.

"Open the chute!"

Ranch hands positioned at the ends of the ropes began to tug gently and the bull bounced erratically up and down as Jon counted, "One…two…three…four…"

A sudden jerk of the bull barrel sent Bo flying off with a shriek. His bottom hit the sand with a soft plunk. He jumped up with a giggle and brushed off his jeans.

"Again," he pronounced, scrambling back into the saddle with help from the cowboy nearest him. Bo's chubby fingers tightened like a clamp on the handle.

With his other hand, he pushed his hat down snugly, curly blond hair sticking out on all sides. He nodded that he was ready.

One of the cowboys manning the ropes winked at the other and they started tugging, gentler this time.

"Don't let up," Jon ordered. "He'll do it on his own, not because you guys are pushovers."

This time Bo hung on for six seconds before landing in the sand again. The audience moaned in sympathy. Bo's face scrunched up as he was about to cry.

"Bo, what have I told you," Jon called sharply.

Bo ran his lip out, but held back the tears. "Bull riders don't cry," he said, his mouth twisted tight.

"That's right. You riding again or not?"

Bo narrowed his eyes. "I ride," he announced, and climbed back on.

The bull bucked and bounced. Bo clung to it for all he was worth, losing his balance once, but managing to recover.

"Six…seven…eight."

A cheer erupted from the kids on the sideline. "I dood it!" Bo shrieked. "I ride the bull!"

One of the cowboys lifted Bo off the barrel and hoisted the exuberant child onto his shoulders to parade him around the ring to the wild cheers of the onlookers. Bo's bright blue eyes shone.

As they passed by, Jon gave Bo a playful slap on the rump. "Good job, son. And that, ladies and gentlemen, concludes our show. We hope you've enjoyed it and will come again." Jon took off his hat and bowed to the bleachers, then trotted off.

Kaycee and the others applauded and whistled their approval. Then, before she could even get her breath, the youngsters grabbed her by the hands and led her to the waiting hay wagon.

"That's Uncle Clint," Zach announced, pointing to the man sitting on the driver's seat, reins in hand. "This is Dr. Kaycee."

"Ma'am," he said with a nod and tip of his hat. He raked back his sandy hair, which was receding at the temples, and set his hat in place while they piled onto the hay.

"Daddy said he'd give you a horse to ride, but we want you up here with us and Bo, okay?" Zach said, his wide eyes beseeching. "And Wendy always goes on the wagon, too. She'd rather read than ride."

"Sure, I like taking it easy on Saturdays." Kaycee climbed high up in the hay with the three little boys.

A few minutes later, Jon rode up on a tall Appaloosa. The rich chestnut color of its coat dissolved into a brilliant white blanket across the rump, sprinkled with a few golden spots. Muscles bunched and rippled as the horse fidgeted and bobbed his head, eager to be cut loose. Jon moved as if he grew out of the horse itself, reins held loosely in one gloved hand, the other hand resting easily on his thigh. He had managed to get most of the clown makeup off, but there were still traces of white along his hairline, and the black smudges around his eyes gave him a rakish look.

"You sure you don't mind riding in the hay? You can have your pick of horses. Wendy can watch the boys."

Kaycee smiled. "I was promised a hayride and I'm going to have one. This is fine." And really it was. She liked the solid little bodies pressed against her, as the boys jabbered to one another. Wendy climbed aboard with a book in her hand and made her way to the front of the wagon to lean against the seat.

"You were great, Wendy," Kaycee said. "Did you train the dogs yourself?"

Wendy smiled shyly. "Thanks. Mom helped me...." Her voice trailed off.

"Y'all did a good job."

Wendy stared down at her book without comment. The other three girls rode up beside Jon on different horses than the ones they'd ridden in the rodeo. The three prancing piebald mares could have been sisters, too, they were so similar in coloring.

As the wagon lurched forward along the dirt path Kaycee steadied the boys and settled back in the hay to listen to the banter among the kids, Jon and Clint. Too bad the social worker couldn't witness this.

Close to an hour later, they stopped on the edge of a small meadow. The grass was beginning to green and wildflowers budded in the sunshine, despite the snow lingering in the shade of the overhanging spruces. Kaycee's heavy jacket felt good in the nippy air. The twins jumped down. Jon rode up and took Bo from Kaycee's arms. Wendy hopped off the tailgate of the wagon, then held her hand up to help Kaycee down. Kaycee smiled as she took the fragile hand, pleased that the shy girl had reached out to her.

"What are you reading?" Kaycee asked as they walked toward the flat area where Clint was spreading out a large quilt for their picnic.

"Harry Potter."

"I read a couple of those. Who's your favorite character?"

"Hermione, of course," Wendy said with a giggle.

Rachel and Sam hefted the large picnic basket to the blanket and began to unload it while Jon dismounted and set Bo on the ground with his brothers. He dropped the reins, loosened the saddle girth and commanded, "Whoa." The big Appaloosa stood still, his head up, watching Jon. Kaycee had seen this ground-tying technique a lot since she'd been west. If the Appaloosa was as well-trained as he appeared to be, he would stand there until he dropped unless Jon released him from the command.

Jon helped Clint bring over a couple of large ice chests from the wagon before they loosened girths and unbridled all the horses, hobbling them so they could graze. That done, Clint climbed back on the wagon, tipped his hat in Kaycee's direction and clucked to the team, turning the wagon and heading back down the mountain. The patient Appaloosa stood the whole time, watching Jon, waiting. Finally, Jon went to him, released him with a low command, patted his neck, slid his hackamore off and turned him loose without hobbles.

They all gathered around to fill their plates with cold fried chicken, potato salad, deviled eggs or peanut butter and jelly sandwiches. Balancing plastic cups of tea and milk, everybody found their own spot to settle down to eat. When the twins clamored to join Kaycee and Jon, Rachel herded them off and made them eat with the other children.

"It's beautiful up here," Kaycee said, taking in the panoramic view of the mountain ranges rising on all sides of the meadow. "Big Sky Country is a fitting name."

"God's country," Jon said quietly. "I don't think I could live anywhere else."

"I never really believed anyplace could be so awe-inspiring until I moved out here. Of course, the winter was a lot harsher than I expected. We never have cold for this long back home. In fact, once when I was visiting cousins near New Orleans, we wore shorts at Christmas."

"You're kidding?"

Kaycee shook her head. "Nope, I'm not. I didn't like that. It's at least supposed to be cold at Christmas, even if it doesn't snow. You know, this was my first white Christmas."

"I've rarely had a Christmas that wasn't white. And I've never worn anything short in December." Jon talked between bites off the chicken leg he held. "By the way, I'm glad you came today."

"So am I. The rodeo was fun. Your children are real showmen."

"Show-offs." Jon grinned. "They're good kids. Keepers, every one."

Kaycee smiled at the pride in his voice.

"I heard the kids call Clint uncle. He's your brother?"

"No. He's just been foreman on the ranch for years. I used to call him Uncle Clint when I was a kid. He stayed on after my dad died. My younger brother is career navy stationed in the Middle East right now and I've got a couple of sisters who moved east after they married."

"Were you ever in the service?" Kaycee asked.

"No. Dad needed me on the ranch. I admire my brother a lot, though. He's a tough guy, very dedicated to his country and his beliefs."

Kaycee leaned back, letting the sunshine warm her face, enjoying the peaceful afternoon. Jon gazed from beneath the brim of his hat at his children now scattered around the meadow. The twins played a game of tag with Bo, their giggles ringing out across the valley. Wendy was propped against a broad tree trunk reading, while Rachel, Samantha and Michele sat nearby with heads together, deep in conversation.

The big Appaloosa snorted so close by that Kaycee jumped. The horse's grazing muzzle was almost within reach of her hand. When she held it out, he stretched his neck far enough to take a sniff then, uninterested, fell back to munching the fragrant new grass.

"He's beautiful," Kaycee murmured.

"Good horse, too. Smart, big heart. Great with the kids."

"What's his name?"

Jon laughed heartily as the horse snorted and shook his mane. Kaycee glanced at him in surprise. That was the laugh she'd wanted to hear, one that came from within and lit his face.

"Well, a fine horse like that should have a fine name, and right after he was born I was trying to think up one for the registration papers. Then my girls decided to make a pet out of the new baby. They had just learned what an Appaloosa was, so they started calling him Happy the Appy and the name stuck."

The sun turned the sleek horse's coat to burnished

copper and silver as he grazed, his tail swishing contentedly with each step. Kaycee thought the name fit, silly though it was.

"I invited Rosie to come today," Jon said, "but she begged off to catch up around the house. Thanks for finding her. The twins won't be locking her in the cellar because she doesn't bake cookies."

"Is that what happened to the other housekeeper?" Kaycee asked, her lips twitching. She recalled Zach's cookie question at lunch the first time they'd met. She could see the twins doing that.

Jon set his empty plate aside, pulled his hat low over his eyes and leaned back on his elbows.

"Yep, that was the last one. The one before that, Bo and the twins all came down with chicken pox, and Wendy got the flu the same week. The one before her... Well, you get the picture. But Rosie's different, she even handled Mrs. Hawthorn like a pro."

"Oh? And when was this?"

"She was at the house when I got home Wednesday, having a nice chat with Rosie."

"Hmm. Surprise visit again."

"Seems to be her style. She said she was closing the case as unfounded, but she wants to have a follow-up meeting next week. Wants you to be there, too."

Kaycee shifted toward Jon, wishing they had never started this charade. "Do you think I should go?"

"I hope you will. She asked about you more than once. As if she was trying to catch us in a lie."

"Maybe we need to straighten things out with her before that happens."

Jon stole a look at her out of the corner of his eye. "Maybe. I have to say, though, I'm thoroughly enjoying our engagement."

Kaycee smiled at him. "So am I, actually. I've almost come to think of the kids as mine."

Jon was quiet for a moment then said, "It's been a relief to have you to talk to. And I appreciate how you stuck your neck out for us with the social worker."

"I'm glad I could help. In a way, I'm flattered. I'm sure you must have a lot of people around Little Lobo who would go to bat for you."

"Funny, I thought about that, but…" He turned onto his side to face Kaycee, propping himself up on one elbow and sliding the hat up on his forehead. "I don't know, maybe it sounds strange, but I don't want to talk to somebody who's known my family for years, who's known me all my life. This is too personal and I want to keep it out of Lobo as much as I can."

"I understand." Kaycee knew the mortification of having something deeply personal aired to friends and family—much worse than having strangers know the intimate details. "And anytime you need to talk, call me. Even after we're not engaged anymore."

"Thanks," Jon said with a lopsided grin. "You know, I'm not sure how I'm going to like that. Takes away my excuse to see you now and then."

Kaycee nodded, but couldn't quite meet his eyes.

"Well, shoot, maybe we just ought to stay engage—"

A squeal caught their attention. The twins ran across the meadow toward them, waving their arms wildly and screaming at the top of their lungs.

CHAPTER SEVEN

"DADDY! DADDY! DAD-DEEE!" Both of the twins hit Jon full force, knocking him backward onto the ground and squirming on top of him until he caught them and flipped them over. They giggled and fought vigorously to get away, but he held fast.

"What do you wild things want?"

"We want to ride Happy. Can we? Can we?" They spoke almost in unison, their singsong voices like a chant.

"Happy is a mean, ornery bucking bronco and he'll pitch you right off."

"No, he's not," Zach chimed. "He's sweet."

"Don't call my horse 'sweet,'" Jon said, affronted. "Don't ever call my mean, ornery horse 'sweet.'" Jon tickled the two boys until they were silly then let them up. "Okay, come on. If you think you can stay on him."

He pushed up from the ground and the boys hopped to their feet. Jon turned back to Kaycee. "Coming?"

"I think I'll go over and talk to the girls."

Jon held his hand out and Kaycee took it, acutely aware of the warmth that flowed through her as his strong calloused fingers closed around her hand. He pulled her up easily and she was so close, their locked hands were the only thing separating them. Her breath quickened and her whole body tensed when it seemed he might kiss her. Right here in front of his children. Kaycee pulled back slightly. Jon caught himself and glanced around self-consciously.

"Daddy, come on!" Tyler called.

"Later," Jon said to Kaycee, his deep voice husky.

Kaycee stood there, breathless, for several long seconds after he walked away, the boys following him like puppies. She turned to find the eyes of all four girls riveted on her. Heat crept up her face and she bit her lip, wondering what they thought of her in their lives.

Jon gave a short two-note whistle. Every horse in the meadow lifted its head and looked, but Happy pricked his ears and walked toward Jon.

Jon slipped the braided hackamore over the horse's head and fastened it into place, then lifted Tyler and Zach into the saddle. "No trotting."

"Awwww," Zach said.

Jon frowned.

"Okay," Tyler quickly said.

The boys kept up a constant chatter as they rode away. Jon walked after the horse, keeping his distance, yet close enough to intervene in an emergency. Ramping up her courage, Kaycee joined the girls. Michele jumped up and caught her hand, pulling her into their circle. Neither of the older girls seemed bothered by what they'd just witnessed. Wendy buried her nose in her book again.

"Did you like the food?" Sam asked.

"Yes, it was very good. Did you make it all?"

"Rosie fried the chicken for us, but we did the rest."

"How do you like Rosie?" Kaycee asked.

"She's really strict and she makes us go to bed earlier than Dad did, but that's okay," Rachel said. "It's better than having to do all the housework. Or being taken away from Daddy."

"Today has been fun," Kaycee said. "Do you have rodeos a lot?"

"We used to," Rachel said. "The last one was before…" Her voice trailed off and Rachel glanced toward her dad across the meadow.

"Before Mama died," Wendy finished. "Last time we came up here for a picnic was with Mama and Daddy, too."

Kaycee detected the hint of resentment in the small voice, but she thought it better to pretend she didn't notice. "Well, I've certainly enjoyed your hospitality today."

She gazed at Jon walking behind his sons, his stride long and easy, his bearing erect, hat cocked down over his eyes. Were his thoughts on his lost wife today?

Kaycee ran her hands up and down her arms to ward off the chill as the sun drifted down toward the mountain tops. "I'll bet it gets cold up here fast at night."

"It does," Sam said. The sprinkling of freckles across her nose and cheeks stood out after a day in the sun and wind. Her bobbed brown hair stood out around her face in charming disarray. "Real cold. We'll be heading back soon. Daddy always wants to be close to home by dark."

Happy and the twins approached slowly. Jon picked

up his pace until he walked even with the horse's head. A few feet away, he gave a soft command and the Appaloosa stopped. Just then Kaycee heard the rumble of the approaching wagon before it crested the ridge.

"I wanna ride, Daddy," Bo pleaded, holding his hands up. "I wanna ride Happy, too."

"Just a short one. Uncle Clint's here to take us home." Jon lowered the twins to the ground and put Bo up. His little legs stuck straight out on either side of the broad saddle. "Hold on tight," Jon told him. This time Jon kept the reins. "Tell him giddy-up."

"Giddy-up, Happy," Bo called, clapping his legs against the saddle.

Jon gave a cluck and Happy started walking. Bo held on to the saddle horn with the same concentration he'd given the barrel bull earlier. No way was he falling off. Kaycee also noticed that Jon kept a hand on the saddle beside Bo's leg, just in case.

"Bo likes to ride, doesn't he? He was determined to ride the barrel," Kaycee commented.

"I don't see why not," Sam said. "He's been in the saddle since he could sit up by himself. We all were."

Jon made a much smaller circle than with the twins, returning to where they started within only a few minutes.

"Whoa," Bo commanded. Happy stopped. Bo looked at the girls proudly. "I ride Happy."

"You sure did," Rachel said, holding out her arms for him to get down. She put him on her hip and gave him a loud smack on the cheek. "You're a good rider."

Bo beamed.

"Let's get the wagon loaded," Jon said. "We should be heading home."

"Told you," Sam said behind her hand as she winked at Kaycee.

When everything was packed away, the girls put the twins and Bo on the wagon and climbed up themselves. The horses were tied to the back.

"We all ride home in the wagon. Even Daddy. You're riding with us, too, aren't you, Dad?" Michele called.

"Not this time," Jon said, ready to mount up.

"Daddy, please!" the twins clamored.

The others chimed in.

"All right, all right. Make room." Jon looped the rope reins loosely around Happy's saddle horn and climbed up. The twins scooted over, leaving a space for him between them and Kaycee. As the wagon lurched into motion, the tethered horses came with it and Happy followed on his own.

"I can't believe that horse," Kaycee said. "He acts more like a dog."

"He's been like a pet most of his life. Maybe he thinks he is a dog." Jon looked around. "Girls, throw us a couple of blankets. Come here, Bo."

Bo scooted away from Rachel and crawled into Jon's lap. The twins snuggled close to him and he spread a blanket across all of them. He handed Kaycee one and she wrapped up, too. The girls settled in against the sides of the wagon, hunched under their blankets. The evening was quiet and peaceful as the sun set and a large, almost-full moon emerged beyond the distant peaks. In the half light, the wagon lumbered down the track toward the ranch and for a long while, nobody spoke.

"Daddy, let's sing 'Git Along Little Dogies,'" Zach finally said.

"Okay, you and Tyler start."

The twins took a deep breath and began: "Whoopee ti-yi-yo, git along, little dogies—"

"You sing, too, Daddy," Zach insisted.

Jon took up the song with them. "It's your misfortune and none of my own, whoopee ti-yi-yo, git along, little doggies. You know that Montana will be your new home."

Kaycee enjoyed the music as they all sang one cowboy song after another: "Home on the Range," "The Streets of Laredo," "Red River Valley," "Shenandoah."

"Daddy, sing 'Sweet Baby Bo,'" Sam said.

Kaycee didn't know that one, but when Jon began the slow, melancholy song, she recognized it as James Taylor's "Sweet Baby James" about a lonesome cowpoke, with Bo's name substituted. Nobody joined in this time and Jon sang alone.

In the fuzzy moonlight, Kaycee closed her eyes and listened to Jon's deep, rich voice in the still night air and thought how nice it would feel to be lulled to sleep every night by that pleasant sound. She felt the deepest peace she'd known since leaving South Carolina behind. Soon Bo's head lolled against his father's chest. The twins nestled deeper into their hay bed and appeared to drift off, too.

"Do Mama's song, Daddy," Wendy whispered from behind him. "The one you used to sing to her."

"Wendy…" he said reluctantly.

"Please. Just for me."

Jon hesitated a moment, looking up at the white moon overhead. Then in a low and lilting voice he began to sing "You Raise Me Up."

Tears stung Kaycee's eyes at the aching sadness in his voice. She thought she would have liked Alison. She certainly admired her choice in a man. Behind her, she heard Wendy murmur, "Good night, Mama."

When the wagon creaked to a stop in front of the house, Clint climbed down and took Bo out of Jon's arms, ferrying the child to the open doorway where Rosie waited. The girls woke up, scrambled across the hay to the end of the wagon and jumped down one by one. Michele and Sam untied the horses from the back of the wagon and led them into the barn. Clint unhitched the draft horses.

"I'll be back to take care of Happy," Clint said as he passed, leading the team to the pasture.

"Wendy and I'll put the boys to bed, Daddy," Rachel said, rousing them from the hay.

Jon dropped to the ground and reached around to help Kaycee. His hands encircled her waist and he lifted her down, holding on to her longer than he needed to. She looked up at him and thought again he might have kissed her if they were alone. Gently, she pulled back.

"It's late and you look sleepy. Why don't you stay the night?"

Taken off guard, Kaycee stammered, "No-o, no, I don't think that would be a good—"

"I didn't mean it that way. I have extra bedrooms."

"Of course not. I know you didn't." Kaycee hoped the darkness hid her blush. Certainly, he didn't mean it that way. What had made her give such a stupid answer. "I really need to be getting back to town."

She felt his reluctance to let go, but finally he did. Kaycee was almost to her truck when Michele's wail pierced the quiet night. Kaycee turned to see her run from the barn and grab Jon's hand.

"Daddy! It's Dusty! She's colicking. Come quick." She tugged at Jon and he went back with her.

Kaycee didn't wait to be asked to look at a colicky horse. Usually the intestinal blockage wasn't life-threatening, but it could be if not treated promptly. She lifted the cover of one of the toolboxes on her truck, pulled out her vet bag and headed after them. As she approached, she heard Jon's voice.

"Michele, go see if Dr. Calloway's already gone, then find Uncle Clint. He took Happy to the stallion barn."

Michele wheeled around and saw Kaycee in the doorway. "She's here, Dad," the girl said, clearly relieved.

Michele ran past Kaycee out the barn door. Jon glanced up at her when she reached Dusty's stall, then turned his attention back to the horse lying in the hay trying to roll. "Looks like a pretty sick horse."

"Can you get her up?"

"I think so."

When the horse kicked onto its side again, Jon moved swiftly to her head and grabbed her halter. He rocked against her gently, encouraging her with his voice. She groaned and lurched to her feet. Jon rubbed her neck and led her from the stall, while Sam stood by watching nervously. Michele joined her, out of breath, eyes filled with tears.

"Did I do something wrong, Dad?" Michele asked. "Did I make her sick?"

Jon shook his head as he held the horse for Kaycee. "I don't know, honey. Sometimes they just colic. Did you give her a lot of water after the rodeo?"

"No, sir. Just a little in a bucket and I took it away like you told me. Is she going to be okay?"

Kaycee examined the mare thoroughly, checking pulse and respiration. She pressed the gums for signs of a toxic reaction or dehydration.

"She's a little dehydrated," Kaycee said. "She may have been colicky for a few hours."

"Can you fix her, Dr. Kaycee," Sam asked. She took Michele's hand and held it tightly.

"I'll do my best."

"Have you bedded down the horses you rode today?" Jon asked the girls.

"Yes, sir," Sam said.

"I took care of Happy," Clint said, watching from the corridor, his arm around Michele's trembling shoulders.

"Good. Sam, you go on in the house."

"Do I have to? I want to help."

"Michele's the one who needs to stay. Dusty's her responsibility. Go on now and help Rachel."

Sam looked disappointed, but she gave Michele a hug and left. Kaycee moved to the rear of the horse, quickly wrapping the tail to keep it out of the way, and took the mare's temperature.

"Temperature's elevated, pulse is a little fast. Looks like an impaction. Let's get a tube in."

"Michele, go get the twitch from the tack room," Jon said.

Michele ran down the corridor to the back of the barn.

"Ordinarily I wouldn't twitch her, but she's not listening to me very well right now," Jon said. The mare kicked at her belly and moaned softly when she breathed. She kept jerking her head, trying to get away from Jon's grasp. Clint snapped a lead rope to the halter to help control her.

"She wants to roll again," Kaycee said. "Try to keep her up. Wouldn't want a twisted intestine to deal with. I'm going to get an IV in. I'll give her a mild dose of Banamine for the pain, then we'll see how she reacts to walking."

When the IV was in place, Kaycee pulled a nasogastric tube and lubricant from her bag. Jon set the twitch on Dusty's upper lip and Clint took hold of the halter from the other side. The horse stopped fidgeting long enough for Kaycee to slide the long, flexible tube down her nose and into her stomach. Quickly she began to administer the mineral oil, which she would alternate with water to help move the blockage in the horse's digestive system.

"Okay, let's walk her," Kaycee said when she was done.

"I'll do it, Daddy," Michele offered.

"I'll take the first shift. You can take over when she calms down," Jon said, removing the twitch and rubbing Dusty's nose and lip to soothe her.

She tossed her head and turned to look at her belly. Jon led her away, walking the length of the aisle and back, again and again. Finally, the horse began to settle.

Jon motioned to Michele and handed over the lead rope. "You go with her now. Just keep her moving. If she tries to roll, get out of her way."

Michele nodded and led the mare off.

"Thanks," Jon said to Kaycee.

"No problem. She's looking better already. I'll check her over after Michele walks her a little more."

"Good idea. I'm going to see how the girls are doing while I've got the chance. Clint, keep an eye on Michele and Dusty until I get back?"

"I don't mind staying the night if you need me," Clint said.

"Probably not necessary, but we'll see," he replied, on his way out.

Kaycee reorganized her bag, leaving the medicine and instruments she anticipated needing again on top. Clint puttered around the barn, doing small chores. After a while Jon returned, sent Clint home and ambled down the row of stalls checking each horse as he went. He walked back up the aisle with Michele and Dusty. Kaycee checked the horse's vital signs again. She pressed her stethoscope against Dusty's belly and listened.

"Still not much gut noise," she said. "I think we'd better dose her again and keep walking."

After doctoring the horse once more, Kaycee took the lead rope. "My turn."

"You're the doc. You don't have to do the grunt work," Jon said with a grin.

"Trust me, I've walked my share of colicky horses. I need to loosen up anyway." She stepped away and Dusty plodded passively beside her. The mare showed fewer signs of discomfort. Still, the bout of colic wasn't over yet. Kaycee felt sorry for Michele. Sometimes you just never knew the source of colic. But the child felt at fault.

As Kaycee made her third trip up the aisle, she noticed Michele curled up, eyes almost closed, on a blanket spread over a pile of hay in the end stall. She managed a little smile as Kaycee passed, and Kaycee smiled back. By the time she circled again, Michele was asleep. Jon walked quietly up behind Kaycee and whispered in her ear.

"I'm going to take Michele to the house and put her to bed. I'll be right back. Do you want me to call Clint to help you?"

"No, I'll be fine," Kaycee said, trying to sound more in control than she felt. The horse was no problem, but his closeness took her breath and she didn't want him to know that.

"I won't be long."

Jon gently scooped the slumbering girl into his arms and left Kaycee alone with her disturbing thoughts. She wasn't going to get involved with Jon Rider or anybody else. Sure, she liked him—a lot. His kids, too. She enjoyed being with them. She had her demanding career, while he had seven kids and an idealized vision of what a mother should be. Yet, the electricity that shot through her when his breath hit her neck was more than "like." Even more disconcerting was the heat rising in her at the sound of his footsteps coming back into the barn.

"How about a coffee? And I brought you an extra jacket, since it seems you may be staying the night after all." He cocked an eyebrow as he set a large mug of steaming coffee on the bench and laid a fleece-lined denim jacket beside it. "I always get my way."

He winked and his hand brushed hers as he took the lead rope. "Give me the horse for a while."

The warmth in her turned to licking fire as she watched the movement of his muscled butt and thighs in those Wrangler jeans, the breadth of his shoulders under the soft, faded jacket.

He caught her staring and grinned. Kaycee busied herself in her vet bag, the heat of lust suddenly becoming a flame of embarrassment.

When he drew close, she lifted her stethoscope and moved to the other side of the horse to listen. She pressed Dusty's gums and felt her pulse.

"Much better," she said, patting the coat, rough with dried sweat from the ordeal. "I think we can put her in the stall and just keep an eye on her the rest of the night."

"I'll direct you to the guest bedroom, if you want to go inside and get some sleep. I can watch her."

"No, I'm not sleepy. I'll stay."

Jon led the horse into the box stall and turned her

loose while Kaycee gathered her equipment and placed her bag near the door. Hopefully she wouldn't need it again tonight.

"We might as well get comfortable," Jon said.

He sat down on the blanket Michele had spread on the hay. Kaycee sat, too, as far from him as the blanket would allow. She was still bothered that he'd caught her staring at him.

"Something wrong?" he asked after a few minutes of silence.

"No." Kaycee nervously fingered the fringe on the blanket. Just being near this man made her tingle as if she were touching a live wire.

"You're quiet all of a sudden."

"A little tired, that's all."

He gave a curt nod. After a few minutes of uncomfortable silence, he said, "Do you miss South Carolina?"

"Sometimes. I miss my family, of course."

"Big family?"

Kaycee laughed. "Not at all. I'm an only child, but I have my parents, an aunt and uncle and my cousin, Daniel, who's like a brother to me."

"He's the one you're thinking about taking into your practice?"

"Yes. He's a good kid, hard worker. I hope he'll come."

"Were you in practice with him back there?"

Kaycee shook her head. "He's just graduating vet school. I worked for a large racing stable. Posh job for a young vet."

"And now you're out here on your own."

"I wanted a little excitement. A change in scenery." Kaycee's voice sounded harsh, even to her.

"Sorry, didn't mean to pry."

Kaycee felt a prick of guilt. He'd been open and forthcoming with her when she'd pried into his private life. Didn't he deserve the same courtesy?

"My long-time fiancé decided to marry my millionaire boss's daughter. I didn't think I could hack being around them constantly on the job, so I quit. After moving around for a while, working for other vets, I found this practice for sale."

There were things she still couldn't bear to tell—not to him or anybody. Kaycee wished she could blot out her wedding day altogether.

Instead of saying "I do" like he should have, Brett had whispered in her ear, "Sorry. Oh, and I'd like the engagement ring back."

"You loved him a lot?" Jon asked.

Kaycee hesitated before admitting, "Yes, I did. For a long time. Over five years. We met right after I graduated vet school when I went to work for his…his future wife's father. Brett was a legal advisor for the stable. He acted so proud of my accomplishments. My career. But in the end, I guess that wasn't the kind of wife he wanted."

Jon fell silent. After a moment, he said, "Five years. That's a long time. Sorry it didn't work out…. Well, maybe not too sorry."

Kaycee looked at him in surprise. He lifted an eyebrow slightly. "His loss," he explained. "I'm glad you're here. If he was stupid enough to let you go, he deserves what he gets."

"Yeah. Set for life with a drop-dead-gorgeous wife on his arm, not to mention her daddy's money."

Jon shook his head. "Poor dolt. I hope he enjoys it. Not for me, though. And there's no way she could be prettier than you."

Kaycee's mouth went slack at the offhand compliment. He moved closer and slid an arm around Kaycee's waist, pulling her to him against her halfhearted resistance.

"You married a rich girl," Kaycee pointed out, putting a hand against his chest.

Jon shook his head. "That was her parents' world."

He eased Kaycee backward onto the blanket. As he pressed his body along the length of her she felt his desire for her evident against her thigh.

His lips were soft, his mouth tasted of coffee and what…? Cinnamon maybe? Good, anyway. He intensified the kiss, his lips caressing hers, his tongue seeking, finding its way inside.

Her head cradled in the crook of his arm, Jon drew back to look at her, intense desire simmering in his eyes. "How could anybody give you up, Kaycee Calloway?"

Her own eyes widened at the tenderness in his voice, the earnestness in his face. Jon's lips brushed hers, trailed across her chin, along her throat. His warm hand slid under her coat, under her shirt, across her belly, his touch sending a quiver down her spine. Goose bumps rose on her flesh.

What was wrong with her? Hadn't she been kissed before? Yes, of course. But never like this. Not by a man like this. No wonder he had seven kids.

She arched her head backward, basking in the delirious sensations his kisses evoked. She pushed his hat off his head to lace her fingers through his hair as he moved down her body unbuttoning her shirt as he went.

The cold air in the barn hit her skin like a wake-up call. She sucked in a breath. At a rustle in the straw, Kaycee glanced to her left and gasped. Four round eyes, two blue, two brown, watched them curiously. Kaycee giggled.

Jon nuzzled her neck. "What?"

"We're being watched."

His head snapped around as if she'd slapped him.

Jon blew a relieved sigh and slumped against her. "I thought you meant the kids."

"Well, it very easily could've been."

He narrowed his eyes at the dogs. "What are you two doing? Spying on me, too? Voyeurs."

The dogs whined, their tongues hanging out. They clambered across the haystack and piled onto Jon. He dumped them back onto the floor.

"We need to check on Dusty anyway," Kaycee said, laughing as she buttoned her shirt.

Jon stopped her hand then drew his fingertips gently across her chest just above her bra. "You're right. This isn't the time or place, but I intend to take up where I left off later."

"Jon, I'm not…ready for this…at least not right now." Love had to be based on trust. And maybe these intense feelings she had for Jon were just a knee-jerk rebound from her broken relationship with Brett.

Jon pulled his hand back and let her finish buttoning.

"Yeah," he said softly. "Maybe it—"

He pushed off the hay and went into the stall, walking stiffly. Kaycee noticed him make an adjustment to his jeans that made her smile. This situation called for some deep consideration because her desire for Jon Rider had just busted out of the chute like a bronc with no reins. And it was a long way to the ground if he bucked her off.

CHAPTER EIGHT

JON BLEW OUT A quiet, controlled breath once he was inside the sheltering panels of Dusty's stall. He shifted, trying to relieve the uncomfortable pressure of his unrelenting arousal. He had almost done something he probably would have regretted. Probably.

His attraction to Kaycee was growing too fast. It was getting to the point all he wanted to do nowadays was be with her.

But he knew her commitment to her career. Besides, he couldn't go back out there and take her in his arms and beg her to feel the same way about him that he felt about her. Couldn't impose his life and his brood on her. She might never be ready and he'd have to accept that. Better start now, he thought, as she came to the door of the stall.

"Let's see how she's doing," Kaycee said, as calmly as if he'd never kissed her, never touched her. That irritated him. He picked up a curry brush from the ledge of the stall, moved to the opposite side of Dusty and began to smooth out the mare's bedraggled mane.

Kaycee examined Dusty and patted her neck. About that time, Dusty lifted her tail and deposited smelly evidence of her recovery on the stall floor.

Kaycee laughed. "Good girl. I think you're going to be fine. Give her a good bran mash this morning and tonight, then get her back on her regular schedule tomorrow."

"Yep, I know."

"Okay." Kaycee hesitated then dusted her hands off. "Well, I guess I'll get going."

"Yep." Jon wanted her to go. Just let her get out of sight so he could get his heart rate back to normal.

"Well, 'bye," she said.

"'Bye." Jon's hand stilled on the horse's neck. He was treating her badly because she'd been honest with him. That wasn't right. He came around the horse as she was leaving the barn. "Kaycee."

She turned, waiting for him to catch up.

"Kaycee, I'm sorry."

"It's all right. I understand."

He shook his head. "No, probably not. But I don't want to lose your friendship by being an ass. Thank you for taking care of Dusty. Send me the bill, so I can pay you."

"I will. Call me when we need to meet with Mrs. Hawthorn."

Jon nodded and watched her climb into her truck and drive off in the gray dawn light.

"You like her a lot, don't you, Daddy?"

Jon nearly jumped out of his skin. Michele and the twins stood just behind him. The boys had their hands over their mouths, trying to suppress giggles.

Jon cleared his throat and brushed a clump of hay off his sleeve. "What, uh, makes you say that?"

"Oh, just the way you look at her."

"We saw'd you kiss her in the hay," Tyler blurted.

"Shut *up!*" Michele snapped.

"Then Mish made us come back outside." Zach rolled his eyes and giggled. "Like we never saw'd you kiss Mommy or anything. I told Mish that's just what daddies do to grown-up women. Right, Daddy?"

Jon felt his neck flush. He'd better keep his hands off Kaycee, at least while at the ranch.

"Yeah, uh…look, guys, we'll talk about that later. Michele, Dusty needs a bran mash this morning and tonight. Get Clint to help you make it. Tomorrow back to normal feeding."

"You and Dr. Kaycee stayed up with her all night," Michele said, hugging him. "Thanks so much. I hope you marry Dr. Kaycee." Michele looked up. "We all do."

Jon disengaged her arms gently, suddenly feeling smothered by his conflicted feelings for Kaycee and what was best for his family. "Don't get your hopes up, sweetheart. Dr. Calloway isn't in the market for a family right now. Let's just be happy to have her as a friend."

"Maybe you need to take her on a date. And we'll be extra good when she's here."

"No need fooling the poor woman." Jon laughed. "At least give her a taste of what she'd be getting into."

"She likes us already," Zach said, with the confidence of a five-year-old.

"She does, does she?" Jon said, tickling the boy's ribs. "Why aren't you guys ready for Sunday school? Are your chores done?"

"Chores are done. Michele wanted to see about Dusty, and we did, too."

"Scoot then, go see Dusty and get dressed."

"Are you coming with us to Sunday school, Daddy?" Michele asked.

"I don't think so."

"You never do anymore. Please, come today. Please…?"

"We'll see. You go on with Rosie. I might make church."

Jon stared after the kids as they ran into the barn. He hadn't set foot in the church since Alison's funeral. Did he blame God for her death? No. He blamed himself for that. But his faith had faltered. Maybe the time had come to move forward. To forgive himself and get his life back on track.

Two hours later, Jon stopped inside the double doors of the sanctuary of the small church that his family had attended for generations. His children sat bunched together in the front pew, Rosie directly behind them. Clint sat next to her, a little closer than necessary. Well, well, what have we here? Clint and Rosie? Jon smiled. That ought to be an interesting matchup.

Then Rosie leaned forward to speak to the twins and Jon saw Kaycee sitting in the middle of the squirming mass of youngsters. He grimaced and stepped back, but it was too late. Rachel had turned around, saw him and waved. The other children began to gesture madly for him to come down. He had no choice now. The curious eyes of the congregation followed him to the front. He scooted the twins over so he could sit, but Michele immediately rearranged everybody. Bo settled on one side of him and his shoulder touched Kaycee's on the other.

"You just can't seem to get away from me, can you?" she whispered.

"Guess I'm not trying very hard. I'm surprised to see you. I'd expect you to be sleeping."

"Same with you. Besides, Michele said you don't come to church anymore."

"First time in a long time," Jon said.

The preacher ascended the pulpit. Michele reached over and squeezed Jon's hand hard. Leaning over Bo's head, she whispered in his ear, "Thanks, Daddy."

An hour later, Jon couldn't quote a word of the sermon, but he could describe perfectly Kaycee's subtle perfume, the silkiness of her shining brown hair, the exact shade of the blue dress she wore, the pitch of her voice when she stood next to him to sing. He also could have counted how many times he remembered Alison there beside him all those years and the constricting guilt he felt for enjoying being next to Kaycee.

"Now, friends, go out this week and battle temptation," Reverend Smith said, ending the sermon.

Right. Easy for you to say, Jon thought, when it's me sitting next to temptation.

A hand patted his arm. Bo held out the church program where his scribbling filled the blank spots. Jon rubbed the child's towhead and nodded his approval. When he lifted his gaze, he met Kaycee's warm green eyes. Whoa, he couldn't even look at her without wanting to kiss her. He quickly stood while the children filed into the aisle. As the congregation fanned out the church doors, Rosie gathered the children.

"I told them we'd go for ice cream, if it's all right with you, Mr. Rider."

"Please, Daddy," they begged.

"Sure, go ahead." Jon pulled out his wallet and handed Rosie a couple of twenties.

"You come, too, Dad," Rachel said.

"I need to get back to the ranch." In truth, he just wanted breathing room, away from the sight and scent and sound of Kaycee.

"Oh, Daddy, you've got to come," Michele wheedled. "We're buying Dr. Kaycee a banana split for curing Dusty last night. Come on, it's just a few minutes. One ice-cream cone. Double Dutch chocolate, your favorite. You owe Dr. Kaycee for helping Dusty, too."

"You're a little schemer, Mish," Jon said. "Besides, I'm sure Dr. Calloway would rather have money from me than ice cream."

"I'm a sucker for sugar," Kaycee said. "I might be persuaded to give you a break on my bill."

One look at Kaycee's sparkling eyes crumbled his resolve.

At the ice-cream parlor, Rosie ordered for the children and paid, then took Bo and the twins outside to sit. The girls gathered round a table by the window. The only seats left inside were at a table for two in the back corner. Jon followed Kaycee and took a chair across from her. They ate their ice cream in uncomfortable silence. The only thing Jon wanted to say to her, she wasn't ready to hear.

"You're going to drip," Jon said finally, indicating a

melting glob of ice cream running down the side of the cone she'd chosen over a banana split.

He watched, mesmerized, trying to ignore the pressure cooker threatening to explode inside him as she concentrated on catching it, her tongue running sensuously around the cone. She caught him staring and raised her eyebrows. Laughing, she laid her hand on his arm. "Oh, Jon, the look on your face is priceless. Men are so easy to read."

"You're heartless, Doc. You drive a man to distraction, then laugh at him." Jon's own ice cream had run unnoticed down the cone and onto his hand. He tossed the mess into a nearby waste receptacle. Drying his hand on a napkin, he started to get up. She caught his hand and coaxed him down into his seat.

"Please, don't go."

Looking over Kaycee's shoulder, Jon noticed all the children huddled outside at the table with Rosie. Trouble brewing for sure. Suddenly Zach broke away and ran inside, pulling Jon down to his level to whisper in his ear. "Mish says ask Dr. Kaycee for a date."

Taken by surprise, Jon involuntarily glanced at Kaycee. She cocked her head, watching. Jon turned Zach's head to the side and whispered, "Tell Michele I said no."

Zach frowned and ran back to his sister. A few minutes later, Tyler came with the same message. By now, Kaycee was smiling broadly. Neither five-year-old whispered very quietly. Jon gave the same answer to Tyler, only more sternly. Tyler pouted and ran outside. All was quiet on the kid front for several minutes then Michele held the door open for Bo.

When I get you home... Jon hoped his look relayed his thoughts to his mischievous daughter. She grinned at him. Instead of coming to Jon, Bo trotted up to Kaycee, tugged her down with his sticky hands and said in a raspy voice, "Ask for date." He giggled and ran away.

A smile twitched Kaycee's lips again. "I think I'm supposed to ask somebody for a date. Must be you."

Jon rolled his eyes. "Sorry. I'll have a talk with them."

"Well?"

"Well, what? I said I'd talk to them."

"But are you going to ask me for a date? Or do I have to do the asking."

"You want to go on a date with me?"

"Might be fun. I promise not to tease you."

"What about this morning?" Jon asked. "You said you weren't ready for—"

"I don't know if I'm ready for a serious relationship, but I didn't mean I want to sit home every weekend for the rest of my life."

"Ah, I see." Jon's spirits sank. He wanted a relationship; she wanted casual dating.

"Something wrong with that?"

He shrugged. "Guess not. I'm game. Would you like to go out on a date with me Friday night, Dr. Calloway?"

"Sure. Where?"

Jon considered his options. He could take her just anywhere or really romance her—but that entailed going to his and Alison's favorite spot. *Forgive me, Alison.*

"There's a nice place in Big Sky called the Rainbow Ranch Lodge. A five-star restaurant overlooking the Gallatin River with great food. Pick you up around six o'clock?"

"Wow, five-star? Sounds wonderful."

The kids were growing boisterous outside, and Jon could see Rosie's patience running out. He stood, pulled a few ones from his wallet and laid them on the table.

"I guess we'd better get out of here."

Kaycee rose. "I need to get going, too."

"Look, thanks for being so patient with my crazy youngsters."

"No problem. Don't forget. Michele and Wendy are spending Wednesday afternoon at the clinic. I'll pick them up from school and they can play with the puppy."

"Are you sure you still want them to come?"

"Of course I do. I promised. And I'll bring them home later."

"No need for you to make that long drive. I'll come for them and they can eat at Sarah's place. That's always a treat." Jon hesitated, then asked, "Would you like to join us?"

"I'd love to. See you then."

KAYCEE FELT LIKE A real mom parked in front of the school Wednesday, watching closely as a steady stream of children filed by. When the Rider girls came out, they spotted her truck immediately and came over, all four of them crowding the window to talk to her.

"I want to come help you one day, too," Sam said.

"You're welcome anytime. All of you."

Rachel grinned. "We'll come one day this summer when we can stay all day." She poked Sam. "Come on, we'll miss the bus."

They ran off, and Michele and Wendy climbed into the cab. An endless flow of chatter filled the truck during the mile ride to the clinic. Once there, Kaycee showed the two girls around and explained her work. Wendy proved surprisingly astute and observant when she could be persuaded to comment. Michele questioned everything. When would she have animals at the clinic? How were all the surgical instruments used? How long did Kaycee have to go to school to be a vet? In the boarding area, they spotted the lanky, big-footed stray puppy.

"His name's Red," Kaycee told them. "He needs somebody to take him outside to play. Any volunteers?"

Both hands shot up.

"Good," Kaycee said, releasing the exuberant pup whose tail was thumping the sides of the kennel as the girls called him. He lumbered after them into the fenced backyard.

Kaycee took the opportunity to take stock of her medical supplies, then sat at her desk to write an order to fax her supplier. Immediately, her mind drifted back to those moments in the hay stall with Jon. Her fingers curled at the thought of touching the honed muscles of his arms and chest. She ran her tongue over her lips, almost able to taste his mouth on hers.

Kaycee fanned herself with a sheaf of papers. "Wish you were here," she muttered.

"Who?" Wendy asked from the doorway.

Quickly, Kaycee put the papers down and cleaned up her thoughts. She smiled at the girl. "Uh, nobody. Y'all finished with Red?"

"No, ma'am. Michele wanted to know if you had any treats we can give him. We're training him."

"Ah, good idea. I think I can find something." Kaycee went to the storeroom and rambled around until she found a box of dog munchies. She handed it to Wendy, who shifted from foot to foot nervously, her eyes on the floor.

"What is it, Wendy?"

"Dr. Kaycee, please don't marry my daddy," Wendy said softly.

She clutched the box to her chest, spun and ran away before Kaycee could overcome her surprise. After waiting a couple of minutes, she went through the building to the back, standing just outside the open door where she could hear the girls talking in the other room.

"I told her not to marry Daddy," Wendy said, sitting cross-legged on the ground, hugging the squirming puppy, waiting for her sister's reaction.

"Wendy, you dodo! You're going to ruin everything."

Wendy narrowed her eyes. Michele thought she knew everything even though she was a year younger. "I don't think she ever meant to marry him anyway. You tricked her that day. Besides wouldn't you rather have our mama back?" Wendy buried her face in the dog's scruffy coat, fighting back the tears that threatened every time she thought about her mother.

Michele stamped her foot. "Listen to me, Wendy. Mama's not coming back. Not ever. I don't care how much we wish it or pray for it. She's just not going to come back to life."

Wendy's tears began to fall. She *knew* if she wished hard enough she could make her mother come back. How could she make Michele understand? "I don't want to give up hope yet."

"Well, you might as well. Have you ever seen anything at the ranch come back alive? No. Because it doesn't happen."

"But this is our mom, Michele. And Harry Potter saw his parents after they were dead—and he talked to them."

"That's a book. It's made up. You're too smart to believe all that stuff."

"It's magic." Wendy sniffled. "And I do believe in magic. I talk to Mama sometimes and—"

"What? You do what?" Michele's disbelief told Wendy she'd gone too far.

"Nothing. I mean I talk to her in heaven…at night, in my prayers."

That wasn't the whole truth, but Wendy didn't dare tell her sister what she'd been doing. Boy, would she be in trouble. But she had to keep believing. Even if Harry was a make-believe kid, he had powers that let him see his parents. And Wendy had conjured her mother's voice, so maybe, maybe like Harry, she could make her mother come back. She just needed time. And if her daddy married Dr. Kaycee… Well, it couldn't happen.

Michele watched her for a moment, then softened and stooped to put her arm around her shoulder. "Wendy, she already would have come back to us, if she could have. Don't you see that? And you heard that social worker say if we had a mother, everything would be okay. So see, if we had a mother, even a new one, nobody could take us away from Daddy. It's got to work. Now stop crying before Dr. Kaycee comes out here and sees you."

Wendy wiped her eyes and sniffed hard. "I wish all this hadn't happened. I want our real mama, not a new one."

"Well, I'm sorry, Wendy, but we can't have her back. Anyway, Daddy's lonesome. Don't you see how sad he is all the time? He needs somebody else to help with us. And he already likes Dr. Kaycee. He kissed her in the barn the other day. You're gonna have to get used to it. I know they're going to get married. Do you think Dr. Kaycee might let us have this puppy? I like him. Come on, Red." Michele clucked to the dog and offered him a treat. He clambered off Wendy's lap and galloped after Michele.

Wendy watched her sister for a minute, then buried her head in her arms and really cried. She just couldn't let her daddy marry again. Not until she was sure her mother was gone for good.

Her heart aching, Kaycee quietly backed away from the door and went to her office. So some kids had been watching her and Jon in the barn. Thank goodness they hadn't let their emotions get out of hand. They had to discuss this. On an adult level, their pretense of an engagement was bad enough, but had either of them thought through the consequences for the children when the truth came out? She didn't want to be hurt, but even more, she didn't want these children hurt.

The girls heard Jon's pickup before she did and they

went barreling outside to greet him, the clumsy puppy right behind them. Jon came through the front door with both of the girls hanging on him, begging.

"Please, Daddy, can we have him?" Michele said.

"His name's Red and he's so lonely here by himself," Wendy added.

"Dr. Kaycee said she can't find a home for him."

"Please, Daddy, please!"

"So this was your ulterior motive for having my girls over here," Jon said to Kaycee in a stern voice, but his eyes twinkled. "An easy way to unload a mutt."

"Best I could think of," Kaycee said, winking at the girls. "He does need a good home."

Jon stooped and the puppy scrambled to rear up on his knee, licking at Jon's hands as he scratched behind its long ears. "Friendly fellow, anyway."

"Can we have him?" Michele looked imploringly into Jon's eyes. "Chloe and Tilly, they're really your dogs. Wendy and I want a dog of our own. We've already started training him."

"Okay," Jon finally said, straightening, "but you two are going to take care of him, not Rosie or me, and not Rachel. Understood?"

"Yippee!" Michele whooped, grabbing Wendy and dancing her in circles. The puppy yapped with excitement, too, prancing on his hind legs, licking anything that came in range.

"Girls, take him outside for a few minutes so he can do his business," Kaycee said.

"Dinner next door still on?" Jon asked, after the girls left.

Kaycee nodded. "But we need to talk while the girls are gone."

Jon frowned. "This doesn't sound promising."

Kaycee quickly told him the conversation she'd overheard, and Wendy's wanting her not to marry him. "They think we really are planning to marry. Maybe not the older girls, but these two and probably the twins. You and I knew all along nothing would come of it in the end, but the children—"

Jon sat down in Kaycee's office, his expression serious. "They believe what they hear. They trust me to tell them the truth and I did try to explain we tricked you into saying you'd be their mom and the decision was up to you. But I guess that just confused them more." He blew out a long, weary breath. "I never thought about them not understanding. And Wendy…believing Alison's coming back? Where is she getting that?"

"We have to call it off now, Jon. Before they get too attached to me and I get too…" Kaycee felt the telltale sting behind her eyes. Too late. She was already attached. But they had to do what was best for the children.

Jon's lips parted as if he were going to speak, but instead he got up and crossed to her. Cupping her face in his hands, he drew it up so that she looked into his eyes. Kaycee's heart pounded violently against her rib cage.

"Kaycee," he said, then cleared his throat. "Kaycee, what if…"

Kaycee thought her chest might burst. *Don't ask me that, Jon. Not yet. I don't know the answer.*

"What if we…"

It's too soon, it's too soon! Only a few weeks. She'd known Brett for years and still misjudged him.

Jon cleared his throat again. "Maybe we could—"

She put her fingers against his lips. "Jon—"

"Okay, Red's wee-wee'd and poo-poo'd. He's good to go." Michele slid to a stop in the doorway. Wendy bumped into her.

Jon jumped at Michele's voice and dropped his hands.

"Oooo, Daddy," Michele sang out.

Over Jon's shoulder, Kaycee met Wendy's angry glare and stepped back. Jon turned to his children as if nothing was amiss. "Ready to eat? Who's going to order one of Sarah's famous milk shakes?"

"Me!" Michele said.

"I'm not hungry," Wendy said. "I'm going to stay here with Red."

"I don't think so. This is the only meal you're going to get before breakfast. Put the dog in the kennel and let's go."

Wendy's look could have frozen ice on the sun. "I'm not going to eat."

"At least you'll have the opportunity," Jon said. "Hurry up."

Grudgingly, Wendy put the puppy away and sulked behind them to the café. Kaycee had her doubts that going to Sarah's was the best idea and, when they all walked in together, she knew they should have gone somewhere else. Several diners eyed them curiously. Sarah's eyebrows shot almost to her hairline and she grinned openly at Kaycee. *Great.* On top of everything else, now there'd be a slew of questions from her friend that she couldn't answer, because she didn't know the answers herself.

"Right this way," Sarah said, smiling up at Jon. "Haven't seen you in here in quite a while, Jon. And look how your girls have grown."

"Like weeds," Jon said. "Smells good as usual. What's the special tonight?"

"Venison stew or rainbow trout."

"Sounds as good as it smells." Jon turned to Kaycee. "Excuse me while I wash my hands. Come on, girls, you need to wash yours, too, after playing with the puppy."

Jon exchanged greetings with the other diners as the three wound through the tables, ladder-back chairs and highly varnished support posts to disappear into the back of the café. Sarah seated Kaycee in one of the fanciful pink vinyl upholstered booths along the wall.

"You've been holding out on me," Sarah said in a low, teasing voice. "I warned you. In the morning you're going to tell me everything. Be in here by six. We have to go over some invoices anyway. I'll have your favorite coffee ready and I'm going to bake those berry tarts you crave."

"That's no fair. You know I can't resist those."

"Exactly. Six a.m."

The bell over the door tinkled and Sarah laid out the menus while Kaycee slid into the booth. "Be back in a jiff."

Sarah headed off as Michele sidled into the booth

across from Kaycee and motioned for Wendy. "Come on, sit here."

Kaycee saw through Michele's ploy to get her next to Jon again.

A moment later Jon eased in beside Kaycee and studied the menu. "What do you want, girls?"

The girls jumped in with their orders, Wendy's snit forgotten for the moment, but Kaycee sensed a change in Jon. He seemed quiet, almost brooding. She'd love to be a mind reader—or maybe not. His thoughts didn't look all that pleasant. If Michele and Wendy hadn't talked constantly as they played songs from the tableside minijukebox, the booth would have been more like a tomb.

As they walked back to the clinic later, she handed Wendy the key. "Go get Red. Look in the room where I got the treats today and grab a bag of dog food. Next week feed him half my dog food and half your dog food so he can adjust."

Wendy and Michele ran inside.

"You didn't speak two words all night," Kaycee said.

Jon shoved his hands in his back pockets and refused to look directly at her.

When he spoke, his voice was subdued, husky. "Just thinking about what we discussed earlier. About ending this charade for the children's sake. But, I...I don't—"

Kaycee shook her head. "We can't hurt these kids. They've gone through enough."

He touched her lips. "I appreciate what you did for us. Think about the way you want to end our little engagement so you aren't embarrassed. I know that bothered you from the start. Let me get my girls and get out of here."

The girls came flying out the door with the puppy. After a couple of minutes of chaos, they were gone, leaving Kaycee staring after them, wondering how, in a few weeks' time, her world had flipped upside down, and what she was going to do about it.

CHAPTER NINE

IN NO MOOD TO CARRY ON a conversation, Jon was grateful for the puppy as he drove home through the darkness. Red sat in the backseat between Michele and Wendy, whining and licking their faces as they talked to the dog.

Jon clenched the steering wheel. He didn't want to lose Kaycee. They'd known each other less than a month, but Jon already knew he needed her in his life *now;* she obviously needed more time.

At home, he left all the children in the den oohing and aahing over the new canine member of the family. Jon met Rosie and Clint in the kitchen doorway, coming to see what the commotion was about. Apparently they'd been sitting at the bar having a cup of coffee if the two half-empty cups and plate of biscuit crumbs on the island were any indication. Rosie must have already figured out that the way to Clint's heart was through homemade biscuits. Rosie waylaid Jon, her expression far too serious for his liking.

"You had a call from your father-in-law. He wants you to call him back no matter how late."

"Great," Jon mumbled. "Thanks, Rosie, I'll be in my office."

Perfect ending to a perfect day. Jon closed the door behind him and grabbed the Glenlivet bottle, poured a double Scotch straight up and drank it down.

He poured another double, sat down behind his desk, stared at the phone. Working up the resolve to deal with whatever Hal threw at him, Jon lifted the receiver and dialed the number.

Hal picked before the second ring. "Hello."

"Hal. You wanted me to call?"

"Yes. I spoke to your new housekeeper. How long do you think you'll be able to keep this one?"

"Is that why you called?"

"No. I want to know what the hell you're trying to pull."

"I don't know what you're talking about."

"Engaged, Jon? Who are you engaged to? Some slut off the streets there in Little Cowville?"

Jon ground his teeth to keep from snapping back what he wanted to say. "What makes you think I'm engaged?"

"That's what you told the social worker, isn't it?"

Jon narrowed his eyes. If the information on who filed charges against him were so confidential, why wasn't his information equally sacred? Damned social worker. "Kaycee's a very nice woman, Hal. And we're n—"

"I don't care what you think of her. You know how much value I put in your opinion. Don't you bring another woman into that house with my grandchildren."

"Be reasonable, will you? Alison's gone. We have to go on with our lives. Why can't you understand that?"

"Sure, go on with your life. Too bad my daughter can't do the same. If you want to remarry, fine. If we can judge by history, you'll have plenty more children. Give us our grandchildren so they're not neglected or pushed aside for your new family."

"No way in hell."

"Don't mess with me, Jon. You know I'll win."

"So you're telling me if I don't marry Kaycee, you won't harass me any more about my children."

Hal snorted. "No, I'm just warning you not to bring some other woman into my grandchildren's lives before I can get them out of there."

"You don't care how bad you hurt the children, do you? Alison would despise you for what you're doing."

The loud click in Jon's ear told him he'd hit a nerve. He leaned back in his chair clutching his glass hard enough he was afraid he might crack it. He quickly put it down. Hal's ultimatum infuriated him. The very idea that his family could be threatened was maddening. No way would he allow Hal to dictate his life, any part of it. He'd marry whomever he pleased and Hal be damned...but then there was Wendy, who thought her mother was coming back.

Jon went to the door and called Rosie. "Find Wendy for me and send her in here, please."

When Wendy appeared in the doorway, Jon motioned her in. "Close the door, sweetie."

Wendy came forward slowly, warily. "Have I done something, Daddy?"

"No, of course not. I just wanted to talk to you. We don't get much time together, just the two of us, do we?"

"No, sir." She climbed into his lap. "Thanks for the puppy."

"You're welcome. We'll have to introduce him to the other dogs tomorrow and to Bo. You girls have to watch Bo closely so he doesn't pull Red's tail or ears. I don't want him getting nipped."

"Okay. I'll tell Michele, too."

"Good. How are things going with you? School okay?"

"Sure. I like school. My teacher's fun."

"What are you reading these days?"

"Finishing another Harry Potter book. I love those books, Daddy. I wish I could do magic."

Wendy looked up at him with such wistfulness that Jon wished *he* could perform magic. At the same time, his emotions were at war—his loyalty to Alison versus his growing feelings for Kaycee. Kaycee would never take Alison's place, but Jon knew he had room in his heart for her.

"I guess magic would be nice sometimes. But that's just make-believe, you know that." Jon hugged her close, rocking her like he did when she was a baby. "What would you do if you could make magic?"

Wendy grew quiet in his arms. Finally in a small, almost babyish voice she said, "See Mommy again."

Jon cleared his throat. "We all need to go up to Mom's grave soon. Now that the snow's melting off."

"I don't mean that. I don't want to go up there. I won't like it."

"How do you know? You've never gone back with us since Mom was buried. You'll see how peaceful it is."

"I don't want to go, Daddy." She shrugged. "I just don't like to think about her up there all alone. And I'd see the line shack where we went all the time and know she's supposed to be inside painting, but if I open the door she won't be."

"No, she's not up there, Wendy." Jon struggled to find the right words—then struggled harder to get them out. "Not the way we knew her. Her spirit is in heaven. But we still feel her memory with us. I do. All the time. I feel her watching over us, wanting us to be happy. Her grave's just a memorial. A real place where we can honor her and take flowers to her. Maybe feel her presence a little stronger because that high meadow was her favorite place."

Wendy turned in his arms to look up at him. "Why can't she come back, Daddy? I want her to so much."

"I know. So do I. But she can't."

"Not ever?"

"No. We have to learn to accept death, sweetie. Someday we'll see her again, but not on earth. No matter how much we wish it."

Her small fingers twisted into Jon's shirt and she buried her face in his chest. But she didn't cry. Jon stroked her silky hair then gave her a tight hug. "Everything's going to be all right. I'm here and I'm not going anywhere, okay?"

Wendy nodded. *Now the hard part.*

"I love your mother, Wendy, and always will. I enjoyed being married to somebody I loved. There'll come a time when I fall in love again. And I'll want to marry the woman I love and make her a part of our family."

"No!" Wendy bolted upright. "No, I don't want another mother. I don't."

"She wouldn't take your mom's place. She'd be like a second mother, to take care of you and love you. There are some things I'm not going to be very good at when you girls get a little older. Rachel and Sam are already old enough to need a mother's advice, and soon you and Michele will be."

"We've got Rosie."

"It's not the same thing. And like I said, it'll be somebody I love and need in my life, too. Somebody I hope you and your brothers and sisters will love."

Now the tears came, running down Wendy's face as she pushed away from Jon. "I don't want another mother," she choked out. "I don't want you to marry Dr. Kaycee or anybody else."

She struggled away from him and ran out of the room.

"Wendy, come back," Jon called. But by the time he got to the door she'd disappeared upstairs. He leaned heavily against the door frame. Growing up on a ranch had taught him that life could be harsh, but he'd never expected this. He wanted more than anything to talk to Kaycee. Instead he turned off the light and left the room.

THE PHONE WOKE Kaycee the next morning after a long, restless night. She answered, half-hoping to hear Jon. Instead, Sarah's bright voice made her even more depressed.

"Kaycee!"

"What?" Kaycee mumbled, prying her eyes open to see the clock. "It's six o'clock, for goodness sake."

"And your coffee and pastries are waiting. Get up, girl. Come on over here."

"All right, all right. Give me a few minutes to wake up."

"Just hurry. The breakfast crowd'll be here in an hour and we have a lot to discuss."

Twenty minutes later, Kaycee stumbled into the café, still half-asleep. She needed to be up and moving, though. She had a couple of calls on the back side of nowhere this morning and a seminar in Bozeman in the afternoon.

A sprite of a woman, Sarah flitted behind the counter, readying the grill. With her shining red hair pulled back into a net and a bright-green-and-blue plaid shirt tucked into her jeans, she reminded Kaycee of a hummingbird, never still.

The sweet aroma filling the place made Kaycee's mouth water as she slid onto a high pink-and-silver swivel stool at the counter. Sarah placed a pink platter of berry tarts in front of her and poured a cup of Kaycee's favorite coffee, a rich New Orleans blend of Central American and French roast, laced with chicory.

Setting a pitcher of cream in front of her, Sarah laughed. "Go ahead, ruin my perfect coffee. I swear it must be a Southern tradition, pouring all that cream in."

"Café au lait," Kaycee said, adding cream until the coffee was a lovely butterscotch color. The first sip brought her wide awake.

"Much better," she murmured, taking a bite of one of the tarts. Blueberry—thick, sweet, rich—topped with cold clotted cream, which Sarah ordered direct from

England. Kaycee dabbed at her mouth with the pink striped linen napkin by her plate.

"Right, long enough for you to wake up. Here are the invoices that came in the mail yesterday. If you'll approve them, I'll print the checks and leave them on your desk to sign. Also, I'm doing the billing statements today. Do you want me to let Mrs. Norrington off for another month. She told me she'd have her doctor bill paid by then."

Kaycee listened to Sarah, as she flipped through the invoices, confirming everything she'd bought the past month for the practice. "These are okay to pay. Mrs. Norrington has the broken ankle? Yes, let's carry her bill over another month, give her a chance to catch up with her other expenses. I felt so sorry for her last time I checked on her dog. She was still hobbling around with a walker."

Sarah put the paperwork under the counter. "All right, enough business. Now tell all. We don't have much time," Sarah said. "Let's get straight to the good part. You definitely have something serious going on with Jon Rider."

A blush crept up Kaycee's neck as she recalled Jon's breath on her face, his lips covering hers.

"It's not serious."

"Oh, sure. I see that blush. I'd forgotten what a stud he was until he was in here last night. I don't care if he does have seven kids. Guess that just shows he can perform." The half-dozen silver bangles on Sarah's arm jangled as she gave her hand an "ooh-la-la" shake.

"Good Lord, Sarah. You're what's making me blush."

"Uh-huh. But you were sitting with him in church last Sunday and with his kids the Sunday before."

"The kids invited me to sit with them. They didn't think he was coming. Wait, why am I being interrogated?"

"You know that was the first time he's been in church since Alison's funeral."

"Really?" Kaycee pondered that interesting fact for a moment. "Well, there's nothing going on. I vetted his horse and fed his kids and that's the extent of it."

"You're not seeing him again?" Sarah looked Kaycee in the eye. "You *are*."

"I don't know. We were supposed to have a date tomorrow, but he may call it off."

"Why?"

Kaycee shrugged. "It's complicated—this…relationship."

"Why? You like him, he likes you. Bingo."

"It's more than that. I…I really don't know if I even want to talk about it."

Sarah pulled up a stool on the other side of the counter and laid her hand on Kaycee's arm.

"I know Brett jilted you, but he's one man. Jon's not that type."

"Lots of things worry me. He's still in love with Alison, for one."

Sarah nodded. "True, but if he's falling in love with you, that will fade in time. I mean he'll always love her, but she won't always be between you two like she is now."

"And I have my career. I've worked so hard to get

where I am and I just don't know if I'm ready to give it up."

"Why give it up?"

"He's used to a stay-at-home wife, a full-time mother always available to them. I can never be that kind of wife or that kind of woman."

"Has he said he wanted that?"

"No, but the other day he asked a lot of questions about my long hours and being on call. Speaking of which, I need to get on the road."

"But you do have a date Friday night?" Sarah pressed. "Where are you going? Did he say?"

"A restaurant in Big Sky. The Rainbow Ranch, I think."

"Oh, honey! That's a fine place. Have you got something to wear?"

"Well, sure. If we go."

"I know you don't mean that sad Southern Girl stuff you brought up here with you. I'm talking about some sassy cowgirl clothes. We have to go shopping this afternoon. I'll get Jack to cover for me."

"Really, Sarah, I don't have time for that. What I have will do."

"Oh, no, it won't. What time can you meet me?"

"Don't get your hopes up. I'm not ready for—"

"What time?"

When Kaycee saw she couldn't win the argument, they made plans to meet after the seminar that afternoon.

When she got home from Bozeman late that night, she saw a message on the answering machine. She stared at the blinking light for a long time, afraid it was Jon breaking their date. Finally, she pressed play.

"Kaycee—" Jon's deep voice "—I don't know how you feel about going out with me after the way I acted last night. If you want to break the date, I understand. But, if I don't hear from you, I'll pick you up at six."

Kaycee closed her eyes and took a deep breath. "Thank you."

FRIDAY NIGHT WHEN he arrived, she met him at the door. The appreciative expression on Jon's face as he looked her up and down made her glad she'd gone along on Sarah's shopping spree.

Saying that it brought out the green in Kaycee's eyes, Sarah had picked out the cropped turquoise silhouette jacket, with twisted fringe, black bone and silver beadwork. She wore it with a black turtleneck and split gaucho skirt.

Kaycee had balked at the pricey turquoise-and-black ostrich boots, but Sarah had insisted. Jon's eyes lingered on them and he arched an eyebrow.

"Nice boots."

Thanks, Sarah.

"You don't look so bad yourself," she said.

"Why, thank you, ma'am, I did put on my best hat just for you."

And a sexy hat it was, black as midnight, with a wicked dip just over his eyes. Below his shearling saddle coat and creased pants, she noticed he wore his own high-end cowboy boots—croc in a deep cherry-black. Since she'd been in Montana, Kaycee had learned to judge the cost of a cowboy's hat and boots, and Jon's were handmade and must have set him back a few bucks.

She held her own hat in her hand, another turquoise extravagance that matched her jacket and boots. Jon took it from her and placed it on her head at just the right angle, careful not to tangle her hair.

"There. Beautiful," he said. "Now we're ready to go."

Beautiful? She hadn't expected that. She smiled as she settled into Jon's Suburban. They were quiet for a while as the dark highway rolled by. Finally, Jon broke the silence.

"We need to talk about some things."

"All right. What's on your mind?"

"First off, I didn't mean to be so moody the other night."

"That's okay. I knew what I said about Wendy worried you."

"It's more than that. I've selfishly pulled you into a bad situation you don't need."

"Jon—"

"No, I've been totally self-centered and I apologize. But I need to ask you to bear with me a while longer." Jon slanted a look at her. "If you will."

"Mind telling me why?"

"Hal called Wednesday night. Somehow he got wind of our 'engagement' and called to warn me off."

"If you tell him we're not getting married, will he leave you alone?"

"No, I asked him that outright. He warned me not to

bring another woman into the children's lives before he gets custody. Like his getting custody is a given."

"Sounds like he doesn't want anybody else replacing Alison, either," Kaycee said.

"He's an arrogant, stubborn fool. Another reason to keep my children out of his control."

"So what's your plan?" Kaycee asked.

"I've called my lawyer. I have an appointment with the social worker Monday and I was hoping you'd still go along with me. I think Hawthorn likes the idea of us being engaged."

"Okay, if you think it's best for you and the children. I don't want to see the kids hurt, and this man scares me."

Jon nodded. "He scares the hell out of me, too."

"It's sad. Their grandparents could help them to find the closure they so badly need."

"If they would, instead of making it harder." He drove in silence for a few minutes before glancing over at Kaycee. "Then there's Wendy. I talked to her the other night. She's been holding in a lot of confusion. Where has my mind been these past months that I've missed the signs that my child was hurting so badly?"

"You've been grieving, too. It's only natural. And you've had to be there for all the children, to help them cope. That's a heavy load."

Jon closed his hand over hers on the seat, his strong callused fingers warm. "See why I'm looking for every excuse to keep you locked into this engagement?"

His words took Kaycee's breath. He wanted to keep her close. So many obstacles…which one would trip them up?

"When I was in Bozeman yesterday, I noticed a flyer

for the Montana State Rodeo this weekend. Maybe the children would like that," Kaycee said. "We could take them tomorrow night. Starts at seven."

"They'd love it. So would I, for that matter." Jon's grin was disarming. "I'm glad you didn't break this date. I haven't been out on the town in a long time and I was looking forward to it."

"So was I."

She turned her hand over and clasped his. They rode like that the rest of the way to the restaurant.

The Rainbow Ranch was all that Kaycee expected. Warm light spilled from a bank of windows across the front of the two-story log cabin that served as a lodge and restaurant. In the lobby, antler chandeliers hung over the supple dark brown leather sofa and chairs flanked a roaring fire. With his hand at the small of her back, Jon escorted her to the restaurant.

"Mr. Rider, how good to see you again. It's been a while," the maître d' said with a smile and a slight bow. "Ma'am."

"Too long," Jon said.

The maître d' led the way to a table overlooking the river and handed them menus. Kaycee gazed out the windows while Jon ordered wine. Although night had fallen, a full moon lit a long stretch of riverbank. Kaycee thought there might not be a more romantic spot in the world.

"This is lovely," she said when they were alone.

"One of my favorite places."

He'd brought her to one of his favorite places. He certainly knew how to make a woman feel special.

Their waiter decanted the wine, allowed Jon to approve, then filled two glasses. "An appetizer to begin, sir?"

Jon suggested a goat cheese ravioli and Kaycee agreed. For her entrée she had duck and Jon ordered grilled Black Angus tenderloin that looked as if it would melt in his mouth. He must've noticed her coveting gaze. Cutting a small bite, he held his fork across the table. She leaned forward, and he placed it carefully in her mouth and very slowly withdrew the fork.

His eyes lingered on her long after she swallowed the mouthwatering steak. With her heart racing, she thought if he asked her to marry him right now, she might just say yes and work everything out later.

Instead, he leaned back and cocked his head. "Good?"

She nodded.

"I thought so, too."

They took their time over dinner; Kaycee hated to have the meal end too soon. When both entrées finally disappeared, Jon asked, "Would you like dessert?"

"It's tempting, but no, thanks."

"Coffee or an after dinner drink?"

She shook her head and turned away from his pene-trating blue eyes to stare out the window before she went up in flames.

"It's not too cold yet tonight. How about a walk along the river? There's a wedding reception in the gazebo. We can steal a dance to their music."

"Sure. I'd love to see the river."

They skirted the wedding party as they crossed the

meadow to the river, but the clear voice of a female singer floated on the night air. A few feet away, the Gallatin River rushed by, its ripples flashing like tumbling diamonds in the moonlight.

The gurgling of the river blended with the music, filling Kaycee with a thrum of excitement. Jon's hand steadied her as they strolled along the uneven trail.

"It's so peaceful here," she murmured.

"We used to come here all—" Jon broke off. "Sorry."

"It's okay. I thought you must have. Everybody seems to know you. I feel honored that you invited me."

Jon stared at the dark water.

"Sometimes it helps to talk," Kaycee suggested.

Jon shrugged. "What's the point of talking about things you can't change?"

"I'd like to know more about Alison. She must have been a very special person."

He picked up a stone and flung it far out across the river. "She was and she loved it here. Montana, I mean. All of it—mountains, lakes, meadows, cold weather, spring thaws, falling leaves. Her children. She loved her life."

He was quiet for a while, and Kaycee didn't want to press him. She listened to the music and waited. When he spoke again, his voice was so low she had to strain to hear.

"You know, the accident was my fault. I have nightmares of her dying in my arms. Sometimes I can't remember her alive because all I can see is her dying and I hear myself begging her not to leave me."

Kaycee's heart broke as she saw a glint of tears in his eyes. He shoved his clenched fists into his jacket pockets and stared across the river, the rise and fall of his chest visible in the moonlight.

"It *was not* your fault. Just a terrible, unavoidable accident."

"God, I miss her." Jon swallowed hard and turned away. He flicked his thumb under his eyes then cleared his throat abruptly. "Sorry. Again."

Kaycee gently rubbed Jon's back. He grew very still and she saw that his eyes were closed.

"It's odd, the small things I miss most," he said after a while. "Like this. A touch of comfort. A smile at the right time. A look from across the room that says everything's okay." He fell silent for a long moment then turned to face her. "Not very good dating manners, is it, talking about another woman."

"She's not just another woman. Of course you should talk about her if you want to. And I understand what you're saying. I miss those things, too."

He stroked up and down her arms. "You do, don't you? You lost somebody, too."

Kaycee smiled wryly. "Yes, but I disliked him extremely by the time he was gone. Still, there are those little familiarities that a couple grows accustomed to. I miss picking up the phone and having somebody to call on a bad day or to share good news."

"I've got an idea. Let's swap. You rub my back when I'm down and I'll be on the other end of the phone when you want to blow off steam."

Kaycee smiled. "I like that deal."

Jon leaned close. "Seal it with a kiss," he murmured. "That needs to be part of the deal, too. Because I enjoyed kissing you the other night about as much as I've ever enjoyed anything."

Kaycee's breathing quickened and she stepped into his arms. "That makes two of us," she whispered.

Jon enfolded her in his warm arms. As her body molded to his, she succumbed to the music, the twinkling stars and the magic Jon awakened inside her.

The distant music grew mellow and slow. He kissed her and began to sway to the rhythm. On the grassy riverbank, they continued to slow dance long after the band stopped, with Jon's arms wrapped around her waist, hers looped around his neck and their lips so close between kisses that their frosty breath formed a mist around their faces. They only stopped when the lodge shut off the outside lights. The heat of his body felt good in the cold night.

"Guess we have to go," Jon said, his voice hoarse.

After a final long kiss, they strolled back in the dark to the Suburban. On the way home, Kaycee's tender lips could still feel Jon. Regardless of the consequences, she was falling in love with him.

He reached to take her hand and draw it to rest on his thigh. She thought of Alison and how her young life was cut short without notice. Nobody knew how much time was left on earth, and suddenly Kaycee didn't want to waste another minute not loving Jon. She ran her hand lightly up his thigh and saw him smile in the dim glow from the instrument panel.

"You'd better stop that before you get in trouble."

Kaycee shifted toward him in her seat. "I think I'm already in pretty deep."

"Come on over here and get in deeper then."

CHAPTER TEN

WHEN SHE THOUGHT ABOUT the night before in Jon's arms, Kaycee figured her cheeks turned about the color of the hot pink shirt she was wearing. The smoldering good-night kisses they'd shared at her door had left her shaky, crazy for more, reluctant to let him leave.

But he wouldn't come in so late at night—or rather so early in the morning. Little Lobo had too many prying eyes. And he was right, though last night Kaycee would have argued the point. He left her with vivid, erotic dreams that jolted her awake with a longing for him so powerful it hurt.

Even now she felt like a jittery schoolgirl as the Suburban pulled into her parking lot. She reminded herself she had to be on good behavior today whether she wanted to or not. She definitely did *not*.

She needn't have worried about temptation. To accommodate them all, Michele sat on the bench seat between her and Jon. Kaycee had no choice but to keep her hands to herself. Thank goodness, Michele's nonstop talking diverted her thoughts.

At Montana State, they found a parking place and Jon took the boys to the stockyards to check out the bulls while Kaycee bought the girls cotton candy. They were to meet at the bottom of the arena stands in the field house in half an hour.

As they neared the area where the horses were stabled, Rachel, Sam and Michele bounded ahead, looking through the slats of each stall they passed. Wendy stuck beside Kaycee, intent on her cotton candy.

When the other girls were out of earshot, Wendy looked up at Kaycee. "My daddy has another girlfriend, you know. In San Francisco."

Kaycee took another couple of steps before she responded, reminding herself that Wendy was still grieving for her mother. The child couldn't be blamed for resenting Kaycee. Kaycee felt sure Jon would have mentioned another woman, but the San Francisco connection piqued her interest.

"Really?" Kaycee asked. "What's her name?"

"Bailey," Wendy answered immediately, stuffing a wad of cotton candy in her mouth.

"Do you mean an old girlfriend before he married your mom?"

"No. He's known her a long time though and dated her since Mama died. She's really beautiful."

"Oh?"

"Yes, she is. She looks a lot like my mama and my grandparents just love her. I think she might come to help Daddy out soon. Then he won't need you anymore."

Wendy skipped off to join her sisters, leaving Kaycee stunned that the child disliked her so much. A girlfriend in San Francisco? Coming to the ranch?

Kaycee had learned at least one lesson from Brett. There would be no unanswered questions between her and Jon. If he had a girlfriend, so be it, but Kaycee wanted to know up front, not standing at the altar. And why couldn't Wendy have mentioned this little detail earlier, before she'd fallen head over heels for Jon? Letting go today would be so much harder.

A few minutes later, they scrambled onto the bleachers and settled down. Jon put the older girls on either side of the youngsters while he and Kaycee sat together in the middle. Bo climbed onto Jon's lap for a better view and the twins sat on their knees as the action started.

Kaycee forced herself to keep her spirits up. She whooped and yelled with the rest as ropes whistled through the air, calves were thrown and tied, steer wrestlers leapt from horses onto the backs of steers with lethal-looking horns. Dust rose to the ceiling and the smell of steaming animal hide and manure mingled with the aroma of hot dogs, popcorn and cotton candy. The children's faces glowed with a sheen of perspiration and excitement. A deafening din arose every time a cowboy scored or a wildly gyrating bronc sent one flying. When the last event, bull riding, was announced, the fans roared.

Jon leaned forward, his thigh rubbing Kaycee's, making her very aware of his nearness. Bo stood on his daddy's leg to see over the crowd.

"Watch," Jon said when the first bull came out of the chute like a black tornado. "The rider's legs are behind his rope. He's coming off."

About that time, the bull spun hard left and the cowboy went the opposite direction. Spread-eagled on the sawdust. He scrambled away on all fours as a ton of pounding beef bore down on him. Rodeo clowns flung themselves into danger to save the limping cowboy, who made the fence, pulling himself up out of the way. The bull lumbered down the out chute. Rodeo clowns high-fived and ran back to their positions. The next chute opened and unleashed another whirlwind.

Kaycee listened as Jon gave his sons a blow-by-blow of every ride. He never missed a prediction about who would stay for the eight and who would land on his butt. Nothing escaped his keen eye. Kaycee smiled. Must be that male gene that allowed them to see every move on a sporting field, when they couldn't find their own underwear at home.

Afterward, Bo pitched a terrible-twos tantrum before they crossed the parking lot because the rodeo ended and they had to leave. Once in the SUV, the twins began to whine. The girls bickered among themselves. Kaycee thought her head might explode before they'd gone five miles.

She wanted to have Jon alone to question him. Instead she got pandemonium and not even the slimmest chance of a moment's privacy tonight. *Get used to it, if you care about Jon. This is his life. 24-7-365. If you can't hack it, get out now.*

"I liked the girl in the lavender shirt," Michele said, joining the argument going on in the backseat over the barrel racers.

"Shows what you know," Sam retorted. "She might

have a pretty shirt, but she couldn't ride. She came in last. You're so lame."

Michele began to sob, so Kaycee put her arm around the girl.

"Cut it out, Samantha," Jon said sharply. "All of you. I want to hear quiet time back there."

Bo continued to wail.

"What about Bo?" Tyler pouted. "How come he gets to cry?"

"He doesn't know any better. Find his blanket under the seat and give it to him."

Tyler grudgingly handed over the blanket. Bo stuck his thumb in his mouth while he nimbly manipulated the satin border with the fingers of his other hand. Gradually he snuffled himself to sleep, then one after another the other children drifted off. Michele's head lolled against Kaycee, who draped her arm around the sleeping child and laid her head back to enjoy the silence.

"You're quiet," Jon said after a while.

The name Bailey was burning Kaycee's lips, but she didn't dare mention it here. "Don't want to wake anybody."

"Good idea."

At the clinic, Jon walked her to the side door. He kissed her good-night, once, twice, then dawdled.

"The kids had a good time regardless of how they acted on the way home," he said. "Thanks for suggesting it."

"I'm glad they enjoyed it."

"I have an appointment set up with Mrs. Hawthorn

at her office in Bozeman on Monday. Is that good for you?"

"Sure. If you still need me to go." Kaycee bit her tongue as Jon looked down at her curiously.

"Why wouldn't I?"

Kaycee shrugged. "Just making sure."

"Okay." Jon sounded confused. "Well, I do need you there. I'll pick you up around eight."

"Why don't we meet at her office. I might have to go in another direction afterward," Kaycee said. She didn't know what her schedule for Monday would be, or how her relationship with Jon might be altered by this Bailey woman.

"Is something wrong?" Jon said.

Kaycee hesitated.

"What?" Jon asked.

"I know you're worried about Wendy already and I hate to hit you with this right now, but I need to know something."

"Uh-oh, what now?"

"Wendy really has a problem with me seeing you."

"I know. She and I talked about it a little. She'll come to terms with Alison's death sooner or later."

"Wendy told me today—"

"Daddy!" Michele called from the car window. "Sam's picking on me again. Make her leave me alone."

"In a minute, Michele," Jon called, turning back to Kaycee. "What?"

From the Suburban, Kaycee heard the escalating argument between the girls. "I think you'd better go. We'll talk about this tomorrow."

"I'll call you when I get home."

"No, it's late. I need to get to bed. I promise it will keep."

Jon leaned in to kiss her.

"Shut up, Sam!" Michele screamed, opening the door to get out of the vehicle. "Daddy!"

Through tight lips, he said, "Sorry. Guess I'd better take care of this. I'll call you tomorrow." He turned and strode toward the car, catching Michele by the arm as she ran up to him. Whatever he said to her, the little girl fell instantly silent. Jon barked an order and Michele crawled back into the car, exchanging places with Sam, who would have the fun of sitting next to an irate Jon all the way home. Kaycee smiled grimly.

Good luck, Sam.

EARLY SUNDAY MORNING, Kaycee's phone rang. It was Jon on the other end.

"Good morning," she answered, smiling. "How are things with you this morning?"

"Quiet. Very quiet," he said.

"I was glad not to be in Sam's seat last night."

"She wasn't too happy to be there, either. The girls are all punished today. Restricted to their rooms. A few extra chores."

"All of them?"

"Turns out Rachel was egging them on more than trying to stop the fight. Wendy was about to go scot-free when she smarted off to me, and I wasn't in the mood."

"What about?"

Jon fell silent for a long moment, then said, "Doesn't

matter. Just some of this silliness she's been coming up with lately."

"About you and me?"

"Yep."

"Jon, maybe we should—"

"She'll get over it," Jon said in a voice that wouldn't bear argument. "Now, what were you going to ask me last night?"

Kaycee didn't want to get Wendy in more trouble. "It was nothing. We can talk about it some other time."

"No. Now. You were concerned about it last night. Something Wendy said. What was it?"

"Jon, really, it can wait. I probably misunderstood her anyway." Not likely. The name Bailey and the image of a woman who supposedly looked a lot like Jon's late wife had whirled around her head all night long, disturbing her waking and sleeping hours.

"Kaycee, you can tell me what she said to you or I can take it up with her."

The lesser of the two evils would be talking to Jon about it now and trying to minimize the situation.

"I think she was just trying to find another way to discourage me from marrying you. You have to tell her the truth, Jon."

"What is the truth, Kaycee?"

Jon hit her with the question, straight out, that Kaycee had been avoiding. He asked for honesty and that was what she wanted from him. But before she could make that decision, she needed to know.

"I have to ask a question before I can give you an answer," she said.

"You're talking in riddles."

"Not really. Are you sure none of the kids are listening?"

"They're confined to their rooms. No phones in there. Go ahead."

Kaycee took a deep breath. "Wendy told me that you have another girlfriend."

"What?" His voice shot up a couple of notches. "That's nonsense."

"Said her name is Bailey. According to Wendy, you don't need me anymore since she's coming to help you out."

The silence on the other end scared Kaycee. Was it true, this girlfriend rumor? But why hadn't he told her? After their date Friday night, their relationship had changed—at least for Kaycee. She'd thought Jon felt it, too. As the silence dragged out, a sinking sensation swirled through Kaycee's midsection. She must have been wrong.

Finally Jon said, "Just what I need. A sucker punch from my own daughter. I'll have another talk with her. I don't have another girlfriend."

"Who's Bailey?"

"Bailey is Alison's cousin from San Francisco."

"Oh." That didn't do anything to alleviate Kaycee's misgivings. "Is she coming out here to help you?" .

"No. Bailey is not coming here, I guarantee that. Nobody in San Francisco is going to help me right now."

"I want you to understand, Jon, I've been hurt once before. I don't intend to be hurt again. I'd rather know right now if you're interested in somebody else."

"I wouldn't do that to you. Trust me. I'm not interested in anybody else. Especially not Bailey."

Trust me. Weren't those the exact words Brett had used?

"Why would Wendy think she's your girlfriend, then? She said you'd dated her since Alison died."

"I did not date her," Jon said adamantly. "Marjorie and Hal invited Bailey to dinner one night that time I took the kids out there after Alison died. The four of us went to a restaurant. Maybe that's what she's talking about. I heard Bailey hung around a lot while they were visiting, supposedly helping Marjorie out."

Kaycee mulled his explanation. He seemed sincere. So had Brett. Right up until he dumped her. Kaycee wondered if this might prove to be worse than the crack-up she'd suffered in South Carolina.

"The truth is, the kids love Bailey, but I don't have any use for her."

Kaycee said nothing in spite of the uncomfortable hesitation she heard on Jon's end of the line.

"Not good enough, huh?"

"Shaky," she admitted.

"Okay, okay. Let me figure out how to put this. She…um…I don't know how to say this except the way it was. She spent a couple of weeks out here every summer when Alison was alive. They were close to the same age and grew up together. Alison and the kids were crazy about her. But a few years ago, Bailey did her best to seduce me."

"You're kidding? As close as you say she was to

Alison?" Bad enough the boss's daughter, but your own cousin!

"I don't know what she was thinking. She'd gotten mixed up with a wild crowd in L.A. and I suspect she was doing some drugs. Anyway, I sure didn't go after her."

"And did she succeed?"

"Too damn close. Alison and I were having some problems, things going wrong on the ranch, her parents interfering again…Bo was going through a colicky stage that kept us up nights on end. Ill tempers, hurtful words. Bailey gave me the old 'poor mistreated husband, I understand, let me make it better' routine and I was more than a little susceptible. I almost made a stupid mistake. So you can rest assured, she is not invited to the ranch, no matter what Wendy says."

"Did Alison know?"

"Yes. I told her. Bailey never came back after that summer. I assume Alison didn't invite her, but I didn't ask."

"I see."

"I'm telling you the truth, Kaycee. Not only am I not seeing Bailey, I don't even like her."

When she didn't comment, Jon said, "Come on, don't blame me for something I haven't done. I've had enough of that from Hal and the damned social worker. I won't hurt you the way Brett did. I promise. I…I need you."

Kaycee pictured him on the other end of the phone, waiting for her answer. Jon…the man who had kissed her breathless in the moonlight. She had to trust again. She couldn't go through life holding every man responsible for what Brett had done.

"I need you, too."

Jon's relief was palpable. A sense of hope awoke in Kaycee.

"Are you coming to church today?" he asked.

"I'm going to the early service. I have a couple of calls in the afternoon."

"Oh." He sounded disappointed, but she couldn't change her plans now. "We can't get there by then. I guess I'll see you tomorrow at Mrs. Hawthorn's office."

"I'll be there."

CHAPTER ELEVEN

KAYCEE WAITED OUTSIDE the building that housed the county offices of Child and Family Services. A few minutes before his appointment, Jon drove up. He looked good in a navy sports jacket, light blue shirt and khakis. She might never get used to seeing cowboy boots with dress clothes, but Jon wore them well. He seemed nervous, but he smiled when he saw her.

"Morning," he said, giving her a light kiss on the lips.

"Are you ready?"

"Ready to get this over."

He escorted her into the building. They were admitted almost immediately to Mrs. Hawthorn's office, where she waited behind her desk. They declined her offer of coffee and took seats across from her.

"Mr. Rider, Dr. Calloway," she said, "I appreciate you coming in."

Jon nodded. "I want to resolve this so my family can get back to normal."

Mrs. Hawthorn pushed her glasses up on her nose and perused her paperwork.

"I was impressed with your new housekeeper. She seems capable of handling the children. I hope you manage to keep her."

"I'm going to do my best."

"Good. That satisfies the child neglect charge. And I've checked your references who, I'm glad to say, were more than happy to vouch for you. You seem to have an excellent reputation in the community."

"Mrs. Hawthorn, you and I both know that report didn't come from Lobo. It came from California. My in-laws don't like the children living in Montana. They want them to grow up in San Francisco, but there's no justification in letting Hal Arant disrupt our lives trying to get custody."

Mrs. Hawthorn nodded thoughtfully. "At least this case can be closed, since you have supervision for the children and seem to have a plan for the future with Dr. Calloway."

"Closed today?"

"No, but soon, I hope. I have to staff it with my supervisor first. You know, procedure, red tape. I have to go by the book. I'll notify you."

Jon looked thoroughly disgusted, but he held his tongue. After a few more minutes, Mrs. Hawthorn dismissed them.

Outside, standing between their trucks, Jon said, "I don't like this. Her not closing out that report."

"She said it was just a technicality."

Jon pursed his lips and gave a slight shake of his head. "I don't know. Maybe. I don't trust Hal and just don't know what he might have up his sleeve."

"There's nothing you can do about it at this point."

"That's true," he said. He lifted her chin and gave her a brief kiss. "What's on your plate today? Can you come out to the ranch?"

"Later this afternoon."

"I'm going to get on home, then. I'm far enough behind as it is."

MIDAFTERNOON AND Kaycee still hadn't shown. Jon ran the back of a leather-gloved hand across his forehead, partially to flick away the sweat, but mostly out of frustration. In his other hand was a broken strand of wire from the fence separating a bull from a pasture full of heifers. The same bull that stomped the fence had caused the problems with his first-year heifers this past calving season. That bull was on the next truck to the stockyard.

He worked for another half hour repairing the section of fence and was pulling off his gloves when he heard the approach of an automobile. He threw the gloves into his toolbox and set the toolbox down in the barn as he passed through and out the front.

Instead of Kaycee's truck, the family Suburban pulled up in front of the house and the girls piled out. Michele, Rachel and Sam shouted a greeting to Jon before releasing the young boys from their car seats. The twins made a dart for the barn, but Rachel ordered them back and herded them into the house. Wendy climbed down last and waited for Rosie to get out from the driver's side. Rosie held out her hand and Wendy took it, the look on her small face warning Jon more trouble was afoot.

"What?" he said, as the two stopped in front of him.

Rosie gave Wendy a nudge and said, "Go ahead. You need to tell him, not me."

Wendy tuned up to cry, but she managed to say, "I got…in trouble at school today, Daddy."

Jon raised his eyebrows. Wendy, his shy, good little girl?

"How?"

"I...I cheated—"

"You cheated!" Jon barely kept himself from blowing up. "How did you cheat?"

"On a test." Tears streamed down the child's face.

Rosie cleared her throat. "I'm sure she—"

"Go get the children a snack," Jon ordered sharply, his eyes locked on Wendy.

Rosie pursed her lips indignantly and lifted her chin. *Uh-oh.* Jon knew he couldn't afford to lose her.

He took a deep breath and said carefully, "Please. I want to talk to Wendy alone. We'll be inside in a few minutes."

"Yes, sir," Rosie said, her body stiff as she walked away.

"Come in the barn," he told Wendy and stalked away leaving her to follow. His kids didn't cheat. He and Alison had drilled the importance of honor and character into them from the time they could understand.

"I'm sorry, Daddy," she said, as she dogged his footsteps inside. "I'm so sorry. I won't do it again, I promise."

"No, I want to know why you did it this time." Jon towered over her tiny form. "You cheated on a test?"

"Yes, sir. Because I couldn't remember what Rachel told me last night when she helped me study. I didn't know how to do the problem. And...and...I didn't want a bad grade. So I looked at Bobby's paper. And the teacher saw me. And...and...you—" Wendy looked stricken, as if the world was coming to an end "—you have to go see her and the principal tomorrow morning."

Jon heaved an aggravated sigh and looked heavenward. "That's all I need right now," he muttered. "You know you're going to be punished for this, don't you?"

"Yes, sir," she said, wiping her eyes with her hands. "I won't do it again. It's just been so hard to think lately and—"

The sound of tires on gravel caught their attention and they looked out the wide barn doors as Kaycee's truck pulled up. Suddenly, the weight on Jon's shoulders seemed lighter.

"We'll talk about this later," he told Wendy.

The child narrowed her eyes as Kaycee got out, then she looked up at Jon defiantly. "I don't care what you do to me," she said. "And I might cheat again. I hate you!" Before Jon could stop her, she darted past him and ran out.

"Wendy!" he roared, taking off after her, but she disappeared around the barn and was gone.

"What was that all about?" Kaycee asked, meeting him just outside the doorway.

"My good girl's gone bad," he said, managing to muster a wry smile. "She cheated on a test today."

"Oh, Jon. Did she say why?"

"Said she couldn't remember what she studied with Rachel last night and that she couldn't think lately."

Kaycee frowned. "Poor little thing."

"Don't be 'poor little thinging' her. She can't act out just because life's tough right now. I don't mind pouting or sulking, but I won't stand for this kind of misbehavior. Besides that, I have to waste time going to the school tomorrow for a meeting."

"Are you going to punish her?"

"Yes. Probably take away those damned Harry Potter books she loves so well. Let her get some of that magic mess out of her head."

Kaycee's expression told him she didn't agree.

"Have you thought about getting counseling for her?" she asked.

"Counseling? Like a shrink?"

"More like a child psychologist."

"Hell, no. My kids don't need a shrink."

"Jon, your kids have been through as much trauma as you have and—"

"And I don't need a shrink and neither do they."

She held up her hands. "Okay, just a suggestion. They're your kids."

He gave a curt nod. Exactly, they were his kids. Except Kaycee's disapproval stung. Alison would have been giving him the same look, he suspected. She'd been the disciplinarian and he'd backed her up. Since she died, he'd had to learn to temper his tendency to overreact to every stunt the kids pulled. But today was the first time one of them had done something this serious.

"Okay, all right. I'll think about what you said," he conceded. "I'll talk to her tonight."

"Good," Kaycee said, wrapping her arms around his waist.

Jon looked down into Kaycee's understanding eyes, took in her soft smiling lips. Those lips that so willingly kissed his that night by the river…. The tension gradually released its hold on his muscles as she reached up and kissed him now. He was beginning to feel better. Much better. The need that hit him when her hand brushed his jeans made him wince.

"Let's go for a ride," he said.

"Where?"

"Up in the mountains. Anywhere. I need to get away from here before I suffocate. You do ride?"

"Yes, of course. Mostly English, but I've ridden Western."

"Did you own a horse?"

"No. I was raised around them, but never had one of my own."

"Did you want one?"

"Oh sure, from the time I was a child. I always hoped there'd be a pony for Christmas, but my folks really couldn't afford the upkeep. Especially in a town where horses are big business. Not much cheap around there."

Jon tucked that snippet of information back for the future. He wouldn't let another Christmas go by without putting that pony in a stocking for her, or maybe the barn. A smile twitched on his lips, as he thought about which horse he wanted to give her.

Not knowing Kaycee's riding ability, Jon saddled a calm bay mare as they talked. He put a saddle and hackamore on Happy, found a hat for Kaycee in the tack room and led the horses from the barn. He tightened the girth on Kaycee's mare, stalling to see if she wanted a boost. Instead, to Jon's admiration, she took the reins from him and swung into the saddle like a pro. Jon did the same. Side by side, they rode out of the barnyard onto the wide track leading up the mountain.

"We're bringing the remuda horses down from the upper pastures next week. Why don't you come out and watch? Usually pretty funny seeing my cowhands dumped on their butt."

"What about you? Do you get dumped, too?"

"Me? Never. I'm a bull rider. A bronc's like a rocking horse to me." Jon laughed in his teasing way. "Generally I don't do the bronc busting. I've got a couple of young hands for that. If I get broken up, who's going to take care of my kids?"

"I'd love to come. Any particular time?"

"We start early Monday, around daybreak, bring the horses down in two or three roundups, then work with them all week. Then the men get the weekend off to go into town. Rosie, Clint's daughter Claire and the girls make food—and this year the twins get to choose their first colt to raise. It's a lot of work, but fun, too. Come whatever day you want to."

"Okay, I'll try to make it Monday."

His mind drifted back to Wendy and his stress level began to rise again. He turned to Kaycee to divert his thoughts. And divert them she did. Just looking at her face held up to the sun, her slender neck arched back, sent stinging needles of electricity through him. She'd changed from the business suit she'd worn that morning into stonewashed jeans that fit her like a dream, a crisp striped cotton shirt and a light jacket.

Jon didn't really care what clothes she wore, though. All he wanted was to get her out of them. The swaying movement of her butt in the saddle in cadence with the mare's stride ignited his blood. He fought to control the urge to tackle her out of the saddle and make love to her in the middle of the road. Maybe not such a good idea. This was the main thoroughfare between the upper and lower ranges.

He urged Happy beside the mare again, to get his attention off her backside and maintain a semblance of control.

"Jon," Kaycee said thoughtfully. "I want to hear more about your life with Alison."

Why did she have to bring up Alison today of all days? The last thing he needed hovering over him was his wife's memory and the guilt he felt over her death.

"What do you want to know?" he asked reluctantly.

Kaycee shrugged. "How did you meet?"

He glanced at Kaycee, so different from Alison in every way. Their romance, if it grew, would be based on a maturity that he had yet to attain when he fell in love with Alison at first sight.

"She was in law school and hating every minute of it when we met."

"You went to law school?"

Jon grunted. "Me? No. I'd already graduated in Animal Science and was following the California rodeo circuit that winter. One night I was spending the money I'd just won at a local hangout near her college. Alison was celebrating acing her midterms. That was it…. Her next break, she followed me around the circuit. We dated less than a year. After my dad died and I moved back here, she told her parents she wanted to marry me.

Her dad went ballistic, making noises about sending her to another college—maybe in Europe. One weekend, I picked her up from her dorm and we got married in Reno on the way back."

"I can imagine her parents' reaction to that."

"'Bout what you'd expect. As far as Hal was concerned I brainwashed her, seduced her and kidnapped her. He accused me of keeping her barefoot and pregnant, but she wanted the kids as much as I did."

"That's her in the painting in the den?"

"Yes, she painted that the year before Bo was born.... It's the only painting we have at home. She didn't want even that one in the house, but it was my favorite and she finally gave in."

"I didn't realize she was an artist. Where are the other paintings?"

"Up there." Jon indicated the trail leading farther up the mountain. "She turned a line shack in the high meadow into a studio. She was really good, but... Her father undermined her confidence and she wouldn't show her work anywhere. Wouldn't even hang it at home, where her father might see it and criticize her. He thinks the one over the fireplace is a professional portrait."

"That's sad. What about the children? Do they know?"

"Sure. We used to take them to the studio for overnight stays until they got too old to enjoy being cooped up there. All but Wendy. She never got tired of it. Turns out she's a pretty good little artist herself."

"Who watched the other kids while Alison was away?"

"We always had help after the second baby came. An extravagance on a ranch some would say, but she gave up a lot of luxury when she chose to come live here with me. Being able to give her that freedom meant a lot to me. And I generally stayed pretty close to the house when she was gone. It's only a couple hours ride."

Kaycee imagined Alison behind an easel putting the vivid colors of the mountains on canvas, with Wendy close by, her nose stuck in one of her favorite books. Kaycee couldn't draw a straight line. "I'd love to see her work sometime,"

Jon reined Happy in and Kaycee's mare stopped, too. The low meadow where they'd had the picnic was spread out before them, a riotous display of wildflowers dancing in the breeze. Jon crossed his arms on the saddle horn and leaned toward her pensively.

"Maybe someday. Nobody's been inside since she died. She's buried farther up the mountain because… That was her favorite place on earth." He kicked a leg over the saddle, slid to the ground and held Kaycee's mare for her to dismount.

Taking her hand in his, he brought it to his lips. "Let's walk."

He held on to her hand, strolling slowly through the tall grasses, bending now and then to pick a flower for her until she had a fragrant nosegay.

"Remind me to take some of these back to Rosie," he said. "I got on her bad side this afternoon."

Bees hummed around them in the warm air while early butterflies flitted from flower to flower, adding moving color to the kaleidoscope.

At the crest of the meadow, Jon pulled her up onto a broad outcropping of granite rimrock. In the distance, a breathtaking palette of azure, aquamarine and misty gray painted the snowcapped mountains. Far below, a broad stream meandered through the valley, flashing silver in the sun. Kaycee pulled her knees to her chest, breathing in the mingled sweet and spicy scents of the wildflowers in her hand and the clean mountain air.

Jon pointed down the valley. Crossing the stream, a whitetail buck and his does stopped to drink. The buck lifted his head, scenting the air in their direction. On some unseen signal, the deer bounded into the nearby underbrush and disappeared.

Kaycee was acutely aware of how close Jon was, of the scrape of his boot heel as he stretched out full length on the warm rock. He reached up and gently drew Kaycee across his chest until her eyes were inches from his, their lips barely touching, his breath warm on her face. He feathered the curls back from her face.

"You are so beautiful, Kaycee. I meant what I said the other night." He gently nibbled her lower lip. "I don't want to call off our engagement. I want to make it real."

She felt the vibration of his voice, the staccato beating of his heart against her breast. A few layers of clothing was all that separated them.

"What about the kids? Wendy? I'm not like Alison. What if they never accept me?"

With a hand behind her head, he pulled her closer. "They will. We can work out the rough spots. I need you."

She didn't resist as his mouth covered hers, lips soft and warm. He pulled her shirt out of her jeans then slid his hands underneath it, caressing her bare skin before he got up to take off his heavy coat and lay it across the rock. He lowered her on top of it, his fingers deftly unsnapping her blouse, then her jeans, his lips following the trail of his hands downward until she lay naked beneath him. His murmured endearments thrilled her, and he drove her almost mad before rolling back to unfasten his own jeans. Then it was her turn to explore the man who had become her nightly dream.

By the time they came together, she knew why Alison had made so many babies with Jon. Lean and muscled, every inch of him exuded raw power honed from hard work and exposure to the sun and wind. He had an instinctive awareness of what she wanted, what she needed and how to give it to her.

Kaycee offered him her body.

They ground against each other until Jon's skin burned. Her legs locked around his waist and he splayed his hands across her firm buttocks to keep the rough rock from cutting into her flesh through the coat. The pent-up need of the past months exploded from him in a physical and emotional rush.

Afterward, he didn't pull away for a long time, reveling in her heat, resting his head on her shoulder, running his hands idly along the soft undersides of her arms flung wide, her body open and vulnerable. When he finally shifted to the side, Kaycee's hand followed, her touch igniting his desire again.

He pulled her on top and she eased down on him.

This time he slowed the pace considerably, prolonging the sensation, his fingers playing in her long, sun-kissed hair. He never wanted to break this connection as she rocked against him, her strong hands spread across his chest. As his breath stopped, he closed his eyes and came again with a shattering force. How would he be able to stand his lonely bed without her beside him?

She stirred and he felt the cold air settling around them.

"We need to get back," he said.

She trailed her fingers downward along the hairline of his belly. "It's a very long time until tomorrow."

Jon slicked his hair back then dried off before stepping out of the shower. All he could think about was Kaycee and the unbelievable way she'd loved him this afternoon. He refrained from calling her, although he wanted to hear her voice. That would only make him ache for her more, and he was already walking around in a permanent state of semi-arousal. He hadn't felt like this since he was a reckless, twenty-year-old, testosterone-intoxicated bull rider. But he wanted more than sex from Kaycee. He wanted another life companion. A soul mate. He wanted her to love him like he loved her.

He hung his towel on the rack, pulled on a pair of boxers and went to bed, but he tossed and turned, reliving every moment in the meadow with Kaycee. Was this the way he would spend his nights until he could convince her to marry him?

And how soon would that be? She seemed to like long engagements. He didn't. He'd homed in on Alison within a half hour of meeting her and proposed a few months later. Kaycee, however, had spent five years with Brett before they decided to marry. Five years? No way. Somehow he was going to shorten Miss Kaycee's waiting period.

Then, again, there was the possibility he'd gotten her pregnant. He'd been kicking himself all night about that. Maybe she was on the pill, but he didn't know. And frankly, it had been so long since he'd had to worry about protection that he wasn't prepared, hadn't even given it a thought until afterward. Personally, he didn't care. Another baby, Kaycee's baby, would be fine by him. But she had her career and he had no idea if she wanted children so soon—or ever. After dealing with his seven, she might not want any more.

So many things they needed to talk about. So much he wanted to know about her. He fell asleep looking forward to tomorrow for the first time since Alison died.

WENDY LAY CURLED UP in Michele's bed with her back touching her sister's. She tried not to make any noise as she cried, but Michele heard her anyway.

"Stop crying and go to sleep or you'll have to go back to your own bed."

"Daddy doesn't love me anymore," Wendy sobbed.

"Dodo, of course he does."

"He said he was going to talk to me tonight. I wanted to try to explain."

"You can't explain cheating to Daddy and you know it. You'll just have to take your lumps and not do something like that again."

"He didn't come punish me."

"He's probably thinking up something really bad." When Wendy sobbed harder, Michele turned over and slung an arm over her sister. "I was just kidding. He forgot, that's all. Or he's waiting to talk to your teacher before he decides what to do."

"He doesn't even care anymore. All he cares about is Dr. Kaycee. When she came, he forgot all about me. He loves her now, not us."

"You're nuts, Wendy. Go to sleep."

CHAPTER TWELVE

THE NEXT MORNING, Jon drove Wendy to school for the meeting with her teacher, Mrs. Carson. She sat in glum silence for the entire ride, despite Jon's attempts to draw her out. At school, he watched her through the glass pane in the door of the principal's office, sitting straight-backed in a hard chair in the waiting area, her feet dangling, her face set.

"I'm not making excuses for her. Cheating's not tolerated in our family and she will be disciplined for this," Jon told the two educators. "But she's been having issues I wasn't aware of over the death of her mother. I thought we were all getting past that, but apparently Wendy had an idea her mother might come back."

"She does have a vivid imagination," Mrs. Carson agreed. "And I've noticed the past few weeks, she's been more distracted than usual. She's had difficulty retaining what we go over in class and her homework isn't always complete."

Jon shook his head. "I didn't realize that. I've been… there have been extended family problems I've had to deal with lately. I'll pay more attention to her."

"Fine. I'm sure she'll be okay. She's very conscientious about her work. Perhaps a few sessions with the school counselor would help."

Jon nodded acquiescence, recalling Kaycee's similar suggestion about counseling. "I appreciate you working with me."

"She's such a precious little girl," Mrs. Carson said. "I want to see her back to her old self."

"So do I."

"I'm going to have to give her a zero on this paper, however."

"I understand."

"I hope she will."

They called Wendy in and told her. She stood dry-eyed until she was excused to go to class, then walked stiffly from the room without a glance in Jon's direction. He took his leave and exited the school, wondering what the hell could happen next.

His gaze drifted in the direction of Kaycee's clinic, not five minutes away. Why not? He'd dreamed about her last night and awakened to find he was helplessly twisted in sweaty sheets, clutching Alison's pillow. He wanted to feel Kaycee's touch, reestablish proof that what had happened between them yesterday was no dream.

He caught up with her as she was loading her truck. She waved as he parked beside her and got out.

"Going somewhere?" he asked, disappointed.

She made a face. "As always. I've got calls from Belgrade to Big Timber today. The vet over there who stood in for me the day of the rodeo doesn't waste time calling in favors. Except he asked me to cover for him the rest of the week. How did the meeting go?"

Jon shrugged. "Wendy's not speaking to me today. She got a zero on the test, but she never uttered a word—to complain or defend herself. Just stood there, then went back to class."

Kaycee raised her eyebrows. "Sounds like a problem might be brewing. You'd better pay close attention to her."

"I will," Jon said, unable to keep a touch of defensiveness out of his voice. After all he'd been raising these kids on his own for a while now.

She slipped her arms around his waist underneath his jacket and looked up at him. "I know you will. I didn't mean anything by that."

He relaxed a little. He was just too damned touchy lately.

"I was hoping we could have a cup of coffee," Jon said, leaning down to brush her lips with his, not caring what Little Lobo thought about him today.

"I'm sorry, I really can't. I'm already running late for my first appointment and if I get too far behind, I'll never catch up. Maybe tomorrow?"

Jon shook his head. "I can't come in tomorrow. Too far behind myself."

Her warm hands gently rubbed his back, subtly pulling them closer together until their warmth and scents mingled inside Jon's jacket. She smiled at the physical effect her closeness had on him, then pulled away, leaving a cold space between them that Jon didn't like at all.

"I see I'm starting something I can't finish right now," she said, "and I promised not to tease you. I have to get on the road."

Jon gave a curt nod. He wasn't happy and she noticed.

"I'm really sorry. But, listen, why don't I rent a couple of movies Friday and bring them out. We'll pop popcorn and I'll get a couple of Disney movies for the kids, then something for us to watch after they're in bed."

A night surrounded by the kids wasn't exactly what he had in mind, but maybe it would give Wendy a chance to get to know Kaycee better.

"Okay," Jon said. With a final lingering kiss he released her and opened the door to her truck.

"Be careful on the road," he said.

THE NEXT COUPLE OF DAYS flew by for Kaycee because of the sheer workload from the other vet's practice. If Daniel agreed to join her practice, she wouldn't be obligated to ask favors to get time off. That meant more time to spend with Jon and the children.

Friday morning on her way out of town, she stopped by the video store and chose four movies. Three kids' picks and an action flick with a little romance in it.

As had happened every day that week, the day's appointments stretched longer than they should have. By late afternoon, Kaycee was thirty miles on the other side of Little Lobo from the Rider ranch on her way to an emergency that Sarah had phoned in to her. She'd had to turn around and head back into the mountains where a dead zone left her with no cell phone service. She had asked Sarah to phone Jon to tell him there was no way she would make it to the ranch on time. At best she'd be over an hour late.

When she arrived at the small mountain spread, the rancher met her at the truck, rushing her into the barn where a prize quarter horse brood mare was trying to foal without success. Kaycee knew the night was shot. This mare was not going to drop that foal without a lot of help. With a sinking feeling, she realized she wouldn't be spending even a shortened evening with Jon and the kids.

"Do you have a phone I can use?" she asked the farmer. "I need to make a quick phone call before we get started here. My cell phone's dead up here."

"Sure, in the house."

He showed her into the kitchen and introduced her to his wife at the sink finishing the dinner dishes. She smiled and said hello, as Kaycee dialed Jon's number. Busy. She tried the clinic number and got the answering machine. Glancing at her watch, she realized it was dinner hour at the café. Sarah might be tied up with customers. Kaycee made a mental note to look into a full-time answering service. Sarah was a great friend and did her best, but the café was her priority.

Frustrated, she dialed Jon again. Still busy. One last call to Sarah. This time her friend answered.

"Little Lobo Veterinary Hospital. May I help you?"

"Sarah, thank goodness," Kaycee said. She could hear the hubbub in the café. "I know you're busy, but I'm going to be tied up here most of the night. I need you to call Jon again and tell him where I am and that I'll call him in the morning, okay? His line was busy when I tried, but I need to you to keep trying."

"Sure, I'll tell him, but he wasn't too happy with my first call. Anything else?"

"No, just make sure you get in touch with him so he knows why I'm not there."

"I will. Gotta go."

Sarah disconnected. Kaycee set the phone in its cradle and turned to the rancher.

"Thanks. Let's get back to your mare."

BY NINE O'CLOCK, the children were in bed and Jon had been to the back door a dozen times, thinking he heard Kaycee's truck pull up, vacillating between anger and concern. For the umpteenth time, he punched the off button on the phone when he got her cell phone service's recorded message instead of her voice mail. Nobody had answered at the clinic when he called earlier. Pacing the house from end to end, he finally dropped into the lounger in the great room with the cordless phone in his lap.

Something must have happened to her. She'd run off the road into a ravine and wouldn't be found until morning. She'd fallen asleep at the wheel and crashed into a tree. He squeezed his eyes tight to block out that horrific vision and forced himself to be rational. She probably got stuck working late because she took on that other vet's practice for the week. She'd call any minute. This worrying and waiting—he wasn't used to it and he didn't like it one bit.

Finally he drifted off to sleep in the chair, only to be jolted awake when the phone rang. Alarmed, he fumbled for the phone.

"Hello?"

"Jon, this is Sarah. I'm sorry—"

"What's wrong?" Jon's stomach twisted viciously. "What time is it? Where's Kaycee?"

"I'm sorry, Jon, I was supposed to call you hours ago. It's around eleven. She's tied up on a call in the mountains and…"

The immediate relief left Jon weak, but in the next moment, anger got the better of him. Whatever Sarah had just said was lost to him.

"When is she coming back?"

"I don't know. She called around six, but things were a madhouse here. I tried to call you, but couldn't get through. Then I totally forgot in the rush. I'm really sorry. I know you were worried about her."

"Yeah. Thanks for calling, Sarah. Do me a favor. Leave her a message to call me tonight as soon as she gets home, whatever time that might be."

"Jon, don't be mad at Kaycee. It was my fault for forgetting."

"It's not anybody's fault." Jon hung up.

Kaycee called a few hours later.

"Sarah left a message to call you tonight. I was going to wait until morning so I wouldn't wake you," Kaycee said.

"I wasn't in bed."

"Why not? It's two in the morning—"

"Exactly. And you're just getting home."

"Yes. Long, long day."

She sounded exhausted and Jon knew he should leave the lecture until tomorrow, but he felt as tired as she sounded.

"I'm awfully sorry about tonight," she said. "Couldn't be helped."

"You could have at least called earlier."

"I tried as soon as I saw I wasn't going to make it. But the line was busy, then—"

"Nobody's been on the phone here tonight."

"Well, it was busy when I phoned at six. Didn't Sarah call you?"

"Yeah, at eleven o'clock."

"It was an emergency foaling," she said.

"The kids were really disappointed. They'd looked forward to this for the past two days."

"Don't make me feel guiltier than I already do. I said I'm sorry. I'll try to make it up to them."

"It's just hard to explain to the kids why you didn't show up, when I didn't know myself."

"You know what, Jon? This conversation is counter-productive. I'm tired and dirty and I'm going to shower and go to bed. If you want to make an issue of this, we can argue tomorrow."

Jon heard the frustration in her voice, but he was equally upset by the realization that he wouldn't be able to keep her safely tucked away on the ranch. He didn't like the idea that tonight's episode might play out again and again.

How would he live like this—always worrying whether she was safe? Or frustrated because she put her job first? Alison had never put anything ahead of him and the kids.

"Fine, I'll try to catch up with you sometime tomorrow—unless you're too busy," he said and hung up.

KAYCEE TOOK A HOT SHOWER, washed her hair and let the soothing water run over her body. The clean, crisp sheets felt wonderful after four long days of double duty. She wouldn't be doing that again anytime soon.

She lay in bed a long while, staring at the moonlight striating her ceiling through the slatted blinds. Jon's reproach replayed in her mind. Surely he understood she had no choice tonight. This roller-coaster ride was killing her. She needed to believe that he wouldn't hold her career against her. But that wasn't how it sounded.

She couldn't be the partner he wanted. And she didn't like the idea of trying and failing, especially when seven young lives would be affected. He was accustomed to a full-time, doting wife who could immediately turn her attention to his needs or the kids' problems. She loved the kids, but had worked too hard and enjoyed her career too much to give it up.

She turned onto her side and curled up, the old fear creeping back into her heart.

CHAPTER THIRTEEN

SATURDAY TURNED OUT to be a miserable day for Jon. Friday night's events left a bad feeling in his gut and he couldn't decide if he needed to apologize or Kaycee did.

Instead of brooding over it, he went looking for work requiring a hammer and a lot of pounding. He repaired fence lines until sunset, sat with his mind a million miles away while the children read to one another, then went to bed for a restless night's sleep.

Sunday he sent the kids to Sunday school and church with Rosie and Clint then rode up the mountains on Happy to check on the herd they'd be bringing down tomorrow. He stayed away from the ranch as long as he could and got back after Rosie had cleared the dinner dishes away. While he showered, she filled a plate for him and warmed it. He picked at the food without interest. He hadn't been hungry for two days now.

"You need to eat something," Rosie said. The flowers from the meadow sat in a vase on the counter, having done their job of soothing Rosie's ruffled feathers. Apparently the flowers he sent Kaycee from the florist in Little Lobo hadn't worked the same magic on her.

"Kaycee wasn't in church today," Rosie said, wiping

down the counters and stove. "The kids looked for her, but her truck wasn't at the clinic, either."

Jon shrugged. "So."

"Thought you might like to know."

"I'm not her keeper."

"Hmph," Rosie said. "Guess I'll get the boys bathed. But in case you want to know, she called this afternoon. Wanted you to call her back."

Jon pushed the plate away and picked up the phone, then changed his mind. Finding the Sunday newspaper still folded on the counter, he took it into the den. A few minutes later, a well-scrubbed Zach and Tyler ran downstairs and settled at Jon's feet to play with their toy cars while he stared at the paper without seeing the words.

He'd been in a bad mood for days now, short-tempered with everybody and everything, trying to work Kaycee off his mind and sweat her out of his body. But every pounding blow of hammer on nail, every long hour in the saddle, had been penance for hurting her feelings and still he felt guilty.

"Daddy," Zach asked, drawing Jon out of his reverie. "Is Dr. Kaycee coming to see us pick our colts tomorrow?"

"She said she was, but that was last week, so I don't know. She might have to tend to sick animals and not be able to make it."

"Yeah, she said she was bringing movies and she didn't. I hope she'll come tomorrow though."

Jon lifted a shoulder in a weak shrug. "I hope so, too."

"Did she stop liking us?" Tyler asked.

Across the room, Wendy lifted her head from her book.

"No, I'm sure she still likes you. She's just busy. I told you from the beginning she had a hard job and not much time for a family."

"I want her to come again," Zach persisted. "I don't care if she forgot the movies. I like her a lot."

"Me, too," Jon muttered.

"Tyler. Zach. Bedtime," Rosie called from the bottom of the stairs. "Let's go."

"You're coming to say good-night later, aren't you, Daddy?" Tyler asked.

Jon nodded. "Before you go to sleep. Like every night."

"If you talk to Dr. Kaycee, tell her to please come," Zach said, driving the stake deeper into Jon's heart. "Tell her we all still like her."

When the twins left the room, Wendy crawled into his lap.

"Not mad with me anymore?" Jon asked, snuggling her.

"No. I'm sorry I cheated."

"Don't do it anymore. If you need help with your homework, come find me. Okay?"

"Okay." She yawned and wrapped her arms around his chest. "I like it when the house is quiet like this, Daddy. Just you and us kids. If I can't have Mama back, I wish things would stay just like they are."

"You mean without Kaycee?"

Wendy nodded. "We're not real important to her, are we, Daddy? Else she would have come Friday night and she'd be here for the boys tomorrow. Wouldn't she? She doesn't really love us. Not like Mama did."

The words hit like a blow. Could a child see what Jon couldn't. Was he thinking with the wrong part of his body lately? Maybe Wendy was right. Maybe Kaycee didn't care and maybe they were better off without her. But it felt so damned wrong, it made him sick to even think about it.

"Get ready for bed, Wendy. I'll be there in a few minutes."

When she was gone, Jon picked up the phone beside his chair and dialed Kaycee's number.

"Hello?"

"Kaycee, I…I don't know what to say. The other night, I didn't mean—" His stumbling met with silence. "I just called to see if you're still coming tomorrow."

"I don't think I should commit. If something comes up, I wouldn't want to disappoint the kids again."

Jon's muscles went limp, as if all the strength had drained out of his body. "It will break the twins' hearts if you're not here to see them pick out their first colts. Tonight, they wanted to know why you don't like us anymore. At least do this one last thing for them."

Jon waited. Finally, he heard her whisper.

"All right. For the boys." She hung up.

Jon held the phone against his ear a long time. Finally he disconnected and leaned over, his elbows on his knees, head in his hands. *Bull riders don't cry.* His father's mantra. But Jon had learned the hard way that sometimes they do. He hadn't cried since Alison died. But he did now.

KAYCEE ARRIVED at the ranch early Monday morning after a sleepless night. As she stepped down from her truck, she could hear pandemonium in the distance. The thunder of hooves grew louder, intermingled with whoops and yips from the half-dozen cowboys herding them along. Rachel and Sam hung over the top of a high wooden fence on the other side of the barn. Kaycee climbed up next to them.

"Dr. Kaycee, you made it! They're bringing in the first herd now," Rachel said. "Daddy told us there'll probably be three roundups today."

"Where's Wendy and Michele?"

"Wendy's in the house with Rosie watching Bo," Sam explained. "I don't know where Michele is. She and Wendy had a fight this morning and she's been sulking."

"What did they argue about?" Kaycee asked.

Rachel and Sam exchanged a look then Rachel shrugged. "You know kids, it's always something."

Kaycee noticed that the fence where she and the girls hung was actually a gate that blocked access to the yard around the ranch house. Other gates and fences created a network of pens. One gate had been swung open to form a large chute that fed into the corral behind the barn.

Kaycee's searching gaze found Jon riding Happy hard on the fringe of the drove, lariat circling overhead as he urged the strays back into the herd. She dreaded coming face-to-face with him.

The horses churned through the passageway, stirring

up clouds of dust as they poured into the corral. There must have been fifty of them, all sizes and colors. Edgy and nervous, the animals milled around trying to find a way out of the enclosure. Clint rode up on a burly black quarter horse and closed the gate.

Jon stopped next to Kaycee and the girls, towering over them on Happy, his hat pulled low over his eyes, his face ruddy from the sun and wind. He sat his horse with a natural ease. Dust-covered and windblown, he looked rugged and fit in his suede work chaps. A bright bandanna that had been tied around his face against the dust now rode high on his neck.

"Thank you for coming."

"You're welcome," she said, her words catching in her throat.

His eyes caught hers and she saw a flare of desire she hadn't expected.

"I want to talk when we break to eat," he said, then rode off.

Confused, she stared after him.

"Each cowboy's got a dozen or so horses he'll train all year," Rachel began. Kaycee tried to concentrate on what the child was saying. "They'll start roping them off one at a time. The bronc-busters work with the unbroken two-year-olds, the cowboys take the rest. They halter break the young foals, get the remuda horses gentled enough to start working again. Keep some of the youngsters for breeding, sell the rest."

"Full day," Kaycee commented.

"This is just the first herd of the day," Sam said. "There are more up the valley, waiting. Mama always said Daddy raised cattle for profit and horses for fun. That's why we have so many horses."

A couple of hours later, the horses had been separated into adjacent pens and the main corral stood empty. The cowboys began to cut yearlings from the herd and move them into the enclosure. When fifteen head of the best colts and fillies milled there, the gate was shut. Jon brought the twins in with him. One of them looked her way and waved, punched the other in the ribs and he waved, too. Kaycee could see the excitement on the boys' faces and the difficulty they had keeping their exuberance in check, but from so far away, she couldn't tell them apart. She was glad she came.

At a safe distance, the cowhands paraded one foal at a time before the boys. Tyler squealed when a high-stepping Appaloosa pranced by. Jon had the cowhand move the colt into a small holding pen. Zach pointed out a pretty brown-and-white paint. That one, too, was penned.

Kaycee was about to climb down from the fence when Sam caught her by the arm. "Wait. Daddy's coming over."

Kaycee had done her duty by the twins and now she just needed to escape. She bit her lip and waited.

"I want to talk before you leave," Jon said again. "At least stay for lunch. The kids would love it."

"I don't think—"

"Did you see, Dr. Kaycee?" Zach cried, clambering up the fence. "Did you see my horse?"

Tyler climbed through the fence to her side. "Did you see mine, too?"

"I did. Good choices. Both of you."

Tyler grabbed her hand. "Come sit with us to eat. I want to tell you how I'm going to train my horse."

Lunch was served under the canopy of wide-spreading cottonwood trees along the stream meandering behind the house. The large corral was empty, the gate open for the next herd. Kaycee took her plate and settled between the twins at one of the long plank tables that had been set up in the shade and tried to concentrate on their prattle. Rachel sat beside Tyler. After the twins gobbled their food, they talked Clint into taking them to look at their colts again.

Rachel moved closer to Kaycee when they were gone. "You and Daddy aren't getting married anymore, are you?"

"You know we never made any real plans to marry, don't you? The social worker caught us by surprise and we said some things we shouldn't have," Kaycee said, not wanting to cause any disturbance in the already stressed family. "Your dad and I haven't known each other very long. It takes a while to know somebody enough to marry them."

"But we'd begun to think it was going to work out after you had a date. Like a fairy tale. Love at first sight and that sort of thing. All of us wanted Daddy to marry you. Well, except Wendy, but she's just confused. You'd be good for him. That's what's the matter with Michele. She and Wendy tore each other up this morning arguing about Daddy marrying again."

"I don't want y'all doing that. You're a wonderful family the way you are, and your daddy will find the right woman to be your mother. I'm just not sure it's me.

Like Friday, when I couldn't keep my promise. I let you down and I feel bad about that. There would be other times when I wouldn't be there for you and that's not fair. It's not the kind of mother you're used to."

"We all know you're a vet. That's so cool. It won't be like it was with Mama, but it wouldn't be with anybody else, either. I'm old enough to take care of the boys when you were tied up somewhere. And now we have Rosie. Besides, heck, Mom used to spend the day away, and we managed fine."

Kaycee put her arm around the young girl's shoulder, her heart so constricted she thought it might quit beating. "I'm sorry, darling," she whispered, planting a light kiss on the top of her head. "I wish it could have worked out. But I don't think I'd be the kind of wife your daddy really…wants."

"You're wrong," Rachel said, her voice husky. "Daddy's not acting right lately. I saw him crying last night when he thought nobody was around." Rachel watched her father for a long minute. "I know he loves you."

Across the way, Rosie began to clear the tables. Rachel rose to go help her. "Please talk to him."

Kaycee pushed the food around on her plate. She hazarded a glance his way and found him watching her. He crossed the lawn and took her by the elbow. "Come with me."

She didn't argue, but followed him away from the others, out of earshot. He cleared his throat and readjusted his hat higher on his head. "Listen, about Friday night. I was just…the kids…"

"You wouldn't even listen when I tried to explain."

"I know. I was mad. But when you didn't call and didn't show—"

"I tried to call," Kaycee insisted. "My cell didn't work in the mountains. The mare was in difficulty and I didn't have a second chance to use the phone in the house. By the time I got back in the truck, I was too tired to do anything but drive. Besides I thought Sarah had called you right after I talked to her. I assumed you were in bed until I got home and heard your message."

"I don't like you on the road like that in the middle of the night. Something could happen."

"It's part of my job."

"Well, that part of the job might need to go by the wayside."

Kaycee frowned. "Are you telling me how to do my work?"

"I'm telling you that if we're going to make it, there's going to have to be some compromise. I've got kids that would be depending on you and I won't have them neglected because you're somewhere—"

"Just wait a minute, Jon. We're not married. I'm not those kids' mother and if I were—"

Jon tried to interrupt, but Kaycee poked her finger in his chest and backed him up a step. "And if I were, they would have to understand that sometimes I wouldn't be there. They might have to learn that sometimes responsibility carries a price. And sometimes adjustments have to be made on their part as well as mine."

"No," Jon snapped. "Family comes first. Alison would never—"

"Don't throw Alison up to me," Kaycee said in a fury. "I wouldn't be the same kind of mother and we wouldn't have the same kind of marriage. I'm not some pampered girl who wants nothing more than to sweep and dust and bake cookies. I love helping animals, I worked my butt off to pay my way through vet school and I've worked even harder to save the money to start my own practice. I have no intention of giving that up now or after I marry. I might make some concessions, but I'm not Alison and I never will be."

"You got that damned right," Jon said hotly. He turned on his heel and called the men back to work.

Rosie and the girls stared until Kaycee looked their way, then they hurriedly began to clear the remains of the meal from the tables. Steaming, Kaycee wanted to escape to her truck and leave, but she refused to let Jon see her run. Instead, she began to stack plates and gather crumpled napkins.

The twins and Bo played close by, the hectic corral being off-limits to them without an adult. Kaycee kept her eyes averted from the children, knowing she'd cry if she let herself think about not being part of their lives. Some of this was her fault. She'd warned herself not to get involved with Jon and his problems, that she'd get hurt. Sometimes it's hell to be right, she thought, gathering a stack of dirty dishes to take inside. Rosie followed with bulging bags of trash.

"Come on, boys, in the house for a while," Rosie called.

"Awww," Tyler complained. "They'll be back with the next herd any minute. And I want to see my horse again. Let us stay here."

"No. There's nobody to watch you. I want you inside. Come on, I don't have time to argue."

"Bo?" Kaycee called, expecting to see the little fellow toddling along with the twins. "Where's Bo?" she asked Tyler.

Tyler shrugged.

"Rachel, where's Bo?" Rosie shouted.

Rachel looked anxiously around. "He was right here just a second ago."

Kaycee scanned the area. A tiny butt disappeared under the gate. "Over there, in the corral!" Kaycee jerked her head in that direction.

"Bo!" Rosie cried. "Come back here!"

"Lookee, the horses!" Bo yelled. "Here come the horses!"

The earth shook from the oncoming herd. Kaycee dropped the dishes, running for the fence, Rosie on her heels.

"Bo!" Kaycee screamed. "Get out of there. Come here!"

Kaycee saw Jon jerk around in the paddock of young horses. In the middle of the chute, Bo waved his hands gleefully at the wild stampede pounding nearer every second.

Jon dropped the halter he'd been holding and raced for the chute, yelling to Bo. The thunder of forty thousand pounds of horseflesh bearing down drowned his cries. Jon's boot hit the fence halfway up, his hands caught the top rail. He vaulted over and snatched Bo up on the run, trying to make it to Kaycee's side of the fence.

Kaycee flung a leg over the top reaching for the toddler. Urged on by the wild whoops of the riders, the first wave of horses filled the chute like a tsunami with Jon still several yards away from her. With a look of despair, he yelled and waved his free arm as he ran, trying to turn the animals back. Kaycee shouted and waved, too. Powerful muscles reacted violently. The surprised horses stumbled, shied, but they were driven on from behind.

"Get the baby!" Jon yelled, striving toward Kaycee's outstretched arms. "Take Bo!"

One horse flung itself into the air to avoid them. Its haunch caught Jon's shoulder, knocking him off balance. Instinctively the other horses followed the leader.

"Take Bo!" he cried, staggering a few steps closer before another horse shouldered him. His face contorted as he went to his knees with Bo in his arms. Trapped, Jon used his body to shield the toddler as he scrambled for the bottom of the fence. Then father and son disappeared into a maelstrom of flailing hooves.

CHAPTER FOURTEEN

"JON!"

Kaycee screamed for help as she leapt down on the outside of the chute. She flattened herself on the ground, peering under the fence. Jon shoved Bo toward her. Kaycee grabbed the shrieking, dust-covered toddler by the arm and dragged him roughly through the narrow opening between the ground and the bottom rung. She hugged Bo to her, her eyes riveted on Jon, knowing he had no chance of escape.

He pressed his body hard against the fence and threw his arms over his head as the horses swept in, flinging lather and dirt. Eyes wild, mouths gaping, they crashed against the fences trying to dodge the man on the ground. There were too many horses, the chute too narrow. She heard the thud of hooves glancing off Jon's body, heard a muffled cry, then the frenzied animals churned the hard ground into dust and she lost sight of him.

A cowhand ran toward Clint, trying to stop the drive. A couple of bronc-busters managed to get beyond Jon and turn back the last of the horses. On horseback behind the herd, Clint yelled at them, not understanding what had happened. The two cowboys pushed the outer gate closed. One of the ranch hands hazed the rest of the horses into the corral and slammed that gate, leaving the chute clear.

"You hurting me. You hurting me!" Bo cried.

Realizing she was crushing the child to her in her distress, Kaycee pushed up from the ground, looking around frantically for help.

"Somebody come take Bo," she yelled. She heard Rosie behind her, urging Sam to get the screaming twins away. Bo was squirming to get loose as Kaycee quickly handed him to Rosie.

Clint caught the fence from the saddle and flung himself over into the chute when he realized what had happened. Kaycee was a step behind him. She knelt beside Jon's prostrate form on the ground. Bright blood mingled with dirt in his matted hair.

The girls had run out of the house at the commotion.

"Is it Daddy?" Wendy shrieked, peering through the rungs. "Oh, no! Please, no!"

Rachel caught the hysterical child and pulled her back.

Jon tried to push up from the ground, looked at Kaycee with a dazed expression for a brief moment then collapsed, eyes closed.

"Oh, dear God, Jon," Kaycee whispered, struggling to clear her mind and recall what little emergency first-aid training she'd had years ago. She fixed animals, not people. ABCs. Airway. Breathing. Cardio. She checked. He was breathing, his airway was clear. Surprisingly strong pulse at the major points.

"Call 911, Clint," she said quickly. "Tell them we need EMS and a helicopter to the trauma center in Bozeman."

Clint pulled out a cell phone and dialed. The other men gathered around, watching in uneasy silence as Kaycee continued to check for injuries.

One of the young cowboys squatted beside Jon. "Want me to turn him over for you, ma'am?"

"No," Kaycee said, pushing his hands away. "Don't move him. He could have a spinal injury. Get clean towels and water." Then she said to the other cowboy stooping beside her, "Find a blanket, something to cover him."

The men ran for the house. She touched the deep gash on the back of Jon's head, feeling gently for a skull fracture. The cut felt superficial, though it bled profusely. Blood saturated his hair and shirt, soaked into the sand beneath his head and in the vicinity of his hip, as well. Through his ripped shirt she could see an ugly abrasion just above the belt. His legs had been partially protected by the fence and looked okay. Hopefully no broken bones there, but she wasn't as optimistic about his back. His rib cage barely rose and fell with his shallow, rapid breathing. Kaycee fought down her panic. She didn't know how to help him, other than keep him still in case of spinal injury. She had to stay calm, keep everybody else calm until help arrived.

Fear pumped through her as the seconds passed and he didn't move. She took a clean, dry towel and pressed it gingerly to the back of his head, trying to stem the bleeding.

"Hold this," she told the nearest cowboy. "Not too much pressure in case he's got a skull fracture I didn't feel. Please don't die, Jon," she whispered, hovering over him as she checked his pulse and respiration again. "I swear we'll work it out. Just live."

"I've got 911 on the phone," Clint said. "They want to know if he's conscious."

Kaycee shook her head, taking the phone from Clint to speak to the operator herself. "I've got a male, mid-thirties, blunt force trauma. He was awake for a few moments but he's unresponsive now. His airway is clear, respiration shallow with a rate of twenty-four. Some visible contusions and a deep scalp laceration. Pulse is good in all extremities. We need EMS and life flight to a trauma center." Quickly she gave directions to the ranch and handed the phone to Clint so he could explain the situation to the operator.

No sound, no movement from Jon. Kaycee felt carefully along his body for unseen injury, but found nothing that she could recognize as life-threatening. He was too still.

The young cowboy came back with blankets and helped spread them over Jon, then stepped back. None of the men said a word.

The time ticked by, the waiting interminable. "Where's that chopper?" Kaycee muttered, knowing that every minute that passed lessened his chances of survival.

"Bo. Where's Bo?"

Kaycee could barely hear Jon's voice, but her heart leapt at the sound.

"Is Bo hurt bad?" Jon rasped.

Kaycee looked to Clint for an answer. "How's Bo?"

Clint nodded slightly. "He's okay. Rosie's got him." Into the phone, Clint said, "He's talking."

"Bo's all right, Jon. Where are you hurting?"

"My back, head," Jon mumbled. "All over. Is Bo hurt?"

"Tell them he said his back and head hurt."

"Bo's all right," Kaycee told Jon.

Jon winced. "I'm hurting bad. Need to get up and walk it off."

"No, don't move, Jon," she said urgently, keeping his head still. "You're going to be okay. Just don't move at all."

"Where's Bo? Is he hurt?"

Kaycee blew out a soft breath and glanced at Clint. "He keeps asking the same questions."

Clint told the dispatcher then turned back to Kaycee. "The woman says just keep answering him. He's probably got a concussion. She says see if he knows what month, what day it is."

Kaycee nodded. "Jon, do you know what month it is?"

"No."

"What day of the week is it?"

"Not sure," he murmured.

Clint knelt at Jon's head. "You're going to be all right," he said. "You've been bucked off worse than this."

"Don't think so," Jon whispered. "Is Bo okay?"

Rosie motioned to Clint from the gate. Clint spoke

to her for a moment then came back to squat at Jon's side. "Looks like Bo's arm's hurt, is all. Doesn't appear to be any worse than that."

"I want to get up," he said, struggling to push himself over.

Clint laid a huge hand on Jon's shoulder. "Not yet," he said gruffly. "You just be still 'til we can get help out here."

He made no effort to move any part of his body other than his arms. Was he paralyzed? The possibility left Kaycee weak. Earlier in the day on horseback, he'd appeared so strong and in his element. *Please, God, let him be all right.*

Fear gnawed at her as minutes crept by. Jon asked again and again about Bo, unable to remember what she told him. He appeared to be weakening fast. Listening to his low groans, she hoped it was pain keeping him still, not paralysis.

After what seemed like an eternity, distant sirens split the air. A few minutes later, a Lobo fire truck and a paramedic unit crunched to a stop in the parking area, followed by a county sheriff.

Firemen and emergency medical techs converged on the wounded man, one of them cutting off Jon's clothing with practiced efficiency. The paramedic did a quick triage, then fitted a cervical collar around his neck. The med techs turned Jon onto a backboard and strapped him down, immobilizing him in spite of his protests.

"Get a blanket on him, keep him warm. We're going to load and go as soon as the chopper's down."

The paramedic gave clipped orders as the techs

worked in a rush of ordered chaos, pressing an oxygen mask to Jon's face, taking vitals. One inserted an IV. Jon struggled briefly, then gave in and let them do whatever they wanted. Or he might have passed out again. From where she stood, out of the way, Kaycee couldn't tell.

The chopper set down at a distance, its blades beating the air. They lifted the stretcher and rushed for it.

"We've got a child who needs to be checked out, too," Kaycee said to one of the ambulance medics who was gathering equipment, as Rosie brought Bo over, cradled in her arms. "He wasn't trampled, but his father fell on top of him to protect him and his arm is hurt."

The medics took Bo and laid him on the stretcher. He quickly examined the child as Kaycee explained in more detail what happened.

"I'm not finding anything serious," the man said, "but he needs to go in, just in case this arm's broken."

Bo began to wail as the medic took him toward the ambulance.

"You go with them, Kaycee," Rosie said. "Bo likes you and I need to stay here with the others."

"Is that okay?" Kaycee asked the medic.

"Are you his mother?"

"Not yet, but he'll be scared by himself," Kaycee said, realizing that in her heart he *was* like her own child.

"Okay, you can ride up front."

"I'll find Jon's wallet for his insurance card and follow you to the hospital," Clint said.

The girls huddled together, Rachel and Sam each with a twin on her hip. They were all watching with hollow, frightened eyes. Wendy and Michele hugged each other, crying. Michele broke away and ran to Kaycee. "He's not dead is he, Dr. Kaycee?"

Kaycee hugged her. "No, darling, he's not dead."

"Don't let my Daddy die. Please, please, Dr. Kaycee. You saved Dusty. Don't let Daddy die."

How could she promise this child something she had no power to deliver? "I'll call you as soon as I know something."

She handed Michele into Rosie's care and climbed into the front seat of the ambulance as Bo was loaded into the back. She closed the door as the blades of the nearby helicopter picked up momentum, flinging dirt and debris in all directions. Sucking back a sob, she heard the steady *whomp-whomp-whomp* of the chopper as it lifted off with Jon inside.

Wearily, Kaycee closed her eyes, listening to the static of the ambulance radio and the muffled road noise as the ambulance picked up speed.

Why hadn't they watched Bo closer? None of this had to happen. And what would these children do if Jon died?

SMALL FINGERS tentatively dialed the phone in Jon's office. Waiting for an answer, Wendy stared anxiously at the locked door. If the others caught her, she'd be in trouble, but she had to talk to somebody and everybody in the house was too preoccupied.

"Hello?" The familiar voice on the other end calmed her a little. Her mother's voice, even if it wasn't her mother.

"Gram?"

"Yes, precious. I'm surprised you called two nights in a row."

"Gram…"

"Wendy, dear, what's wrong? Have you been crying? Are you all right?" Gram's voice grew faint as she said, "Hal, pick up on the other line."

There was a click and the deep voice of her grandfather asked, "Who is it?"

"Me, Grampa. Daddy and Bo went to the hospital," she blurted out. "I'm so scared."

"Hospital? Is Bo hurt?" Gram asked.

"Yes. Rosie thinks his arm's broken. Daddy did it when he—"

"Your father broke Bo's arm? That son of—"

"Hal!" Gram snapped. "Watch what you say. Darling, tell us what happened."

"He didn't mean to. Bo ran out in front of the horses and Daddy—"

"I knew something like this was going to happen sooner or later on that damned ranch. I told you, Marjorie. We never should have left those kids with him this long."

"We'll talk about it later. Hush. Dear, listen. Don't be afraid. We'll fly out and get you."

"No, I don't want that. Don't do that—"

"Don't cry anymore," Gram said. "We won't let anything happen to you. Is that new housekeeper Rosie there? I'd like to speak to her."

"She's here, but she can't come to the phone. I have to go. Please don't call back for Rosie. I'll get in trouble."

Wendy hung up, wishing she hadn't phoned. If the others found out, they'd yell at her and she was already in enough trouble. Cautiously, she opened the office door. Her sisters and Rosie sat in the kitchen at the end of the hall, talking in low, worried voices, but she didn't go closer to listen.

She wished she could pretend nothing had happened. But, what if Daddy died? What would they do then? She missed her mother so much. How would she live without her father, too?

Her stomach churned and she thought she might throw up. Tears started to burn behind her eyes again. She tiptoed upstairs to her bedroom and crawled into bed with her clothes on. With the covers pulled over her head, she clutched a pillow to her chest and curled up in a tight ball. Squeezing her eyes shut, she choked back sobs and tried to block out the terrible memory of her daddy lying on the ground, still as death.

JON LAY ON THE emergency room bed, motionless, barely breathing. It flat out hurt too badly to move any part of his body. He knew where he was, he just didn't know how he got there. His eyes felt like they were full of grit. Looking up at the bright light overhead spiked his already brutal headache, so he kept his eyes shut and ran through the short list of bulls that could have put him here.

The only one that had ever come close was old Redeye. But he couldn't remember pulling Redeye's number today. Couldn't remember even being in the arena. He seemed to remember Bo had been riding the bull. Impossible. The frenzied beep of the heart-rate monitor brought a doctor to the bedside stat.

"Mr. Rider, can you open your eyes?"

Yep, if I wanted to. The thought of the excruciating light overhead kept them closed.

"Can you hear me? Move your right hand if you hear me."

That's a little easier. Jon lifted his right hand.

"Good. Can you say something?"

"Leave me alone." He'd endured all the agonizing poking, prodding, turning, X-raying, CAT scanning, disinfecting and stitching in relative silence. Now he just wanted to go home and sleep off the pain.

"Open your eyes."

"Hurts. Too much light."

Jon heard the flip of a switch.

"Overhead light's out. Open your eyes."

Jon squinted up at the doctor leaning over him.

"You're a lucky man, Mr. Rider."

"I don't feel lucky."

"Probably not, but after the trampling you suffered, it's a miracle you're alive. I'm Dr. Robbins."

Jon nodded slightly.

"Here's the good part—your head CT was negative for any bleeding or swelling in the brain, the X-rays showed no broken bones, but given the bruises on your back and legs, you're going to be sore for quite a while. There was no sign of injury to your kidneys or internal organs."

"Okay, what's the bad part?"

"You've got a concussion that we're going to need

to monitor overnight, and I want to repeat another CT tomorrow."

He paused to take Jon's pulse.

"No matter what," Dr. Robbins finally said, "I wouldn't recommend any exertion until you're symptom free. That means no headaches, no memory or eyesight problems. No dizziness."

"How long's that going to take?" Jon asked, hoping he'd be back to full speed in a day or so.

"Could be several days to weeks. You need to be followed by your doctor because concussions can lead to long-term problems. Do you understand what I'm saying, Mr. Rider?"

"Hell, no. Are you writing it down?"

The doctor grunted. "It'll all be on your discharge papers. If any symptoms get worse—disorientation, vomiting, progressive headaches, blurred vision, seizures or anything else unusual—you need to be seen immediately."

"So I can go home now?"

"Ah, no, like I just said, not today. We'll see how you're feeling tomorrow. Do you have somebody at home to help you?"

"Yeah, sure. I don't remember what happened. What bull stomped me?"

"I understood it was a herd of horses, not a bull." The doctor was busy writing in Jon's chart.

Bo! The stampede flashed through Jon's fractured mind. Bo laughing and waving at the horses—about to be run down. Jon couldn't remember anything else. Did he get there in time?

"My son," Jon said, struggling to get up. "My son, Bo?" The pain felt like a red-hot dagger through his back. He cursed as the doctor grasped his shoulders and eased him down on the bed.

"You're not ready for that yet. I'm going to transfer you to a room for the night. How bad's the pain?"

"Bad," Jon admitted, trying to catch his breath. "Really bad."

"I'll order something for pain and muscle spasms."

"My son, Bo. Where is he? Is he…?" Jon was afraid to ask the question he most needed answered.

"The little boy who came in by ambulance? He's fine. Had a buckle fracture of the left radius." The doctor tapped his lower arm. "An orthopedist was on call and set it, let him choose a cast."

"Can I see him?"

The doctor hesitated then said, "I don't mind you seeing him, but I don't think you want him to see you right now. He's already upset, and you've looked better, I'm sure."

Jon gingerly touched his swollen, scraped face and nodded. "You're probably right. Does he have to stay the night, too?"

"No. He can go home when his arm is set. You'll have to sign the paperwork to release him."

"Who's with him?"

"A Mr. Ford. I believe he said he was your ranch foreman. Do you want to release the child to his care? You said you have somebody at home to watch him?"

"My housekeeper, Rosie. I'll release him to Clint."

Jon relaxed. Clint would take care of Bo. But where

was Kaycee? She must have had better things to do than make sure he and Bo were all right.

BO TOOK IN the stranger who held him. His eyes welled up and his lower lip trembled. He twisted around toward Kaycee and Clint, holding out his good arm and curling his fingers for them to come get him.

"I go home. I go home."

"It's going to be okay, Bo. Let the nurse finish your cast," Kaycee said, putting her arm around his small, hunched shoulders.

A trooper, he'd hardly grimaced when the doctor set his arm. More than Kaycee could say for herself and Clint, watching. Kaycee treated animals for a variety of injuries on a regular basis, but seeing the bone bulging the skin on that tiny arm and hearing the grinding pop when it went into place turned her stomach. As one nurse worked on a sling, another called Kaycee and Clint to the side.

"No, no, no, no!" Bo cried, wiggling to get to Kaycee. "I go home. I wanna go home. I want my daddy."

"We're not going away, Bo," Kaycee assured him. "I'll be right here where you can see me."

Bo's eyes were riveted on her.

The nurse looked at the chart. "Bo told us that his daddy broke his arm," she said, looking from Kaycee to Clint. "Do either of you know what happened?"

Clint nodded as Kaycee said, "Yes, we were both there."

"Would you tell me how Mr. Rider broke his son's arm?"

"You make it sound like he did it on purpose," Clint barked. "Didn't happen that way, no, ma'am."

"I didn't mean to imply that. I'm just going by what the child said. I need to know the circumstances."

Kaycee described the accident then added, "It wasn't Jon's fault the boy got into the corral. Jon was in another area working with horses. Bo was playing with his brothers well away from the corrals and there were at least four adults right there, watching the children. He just slipped away in the blink of an eye. If Jon hadn't gotten to him, the child would have been seriously injured."

After a more detailed interrogation to fill out her paperwork, the nurse said, "Well, from your statements, I see no need to involve Child Protection Services. It's amazing how fast children this age can get in trouble."

"Yes, frightening is more like it," Kaycee said, wondering if her own heartbeat would ever slow to normal again. "Do you know how Jon is doing? I'm really worried that we haven't heard anything."

"I'll go check on him. In the meantime, I'll turn this in so Bo can be released."

"Thanks." Exhausted but relieved, Clint turned to Kaycee. "I thought for a minute she was going to call that woman again and try to take Bo."

"Me, too. As soon as you can, get him back to Rosie."

Kaycee kissed Bo on the forehead and brushed his hair back from his face. "Your daddy's going to sleep at the hospital tonight, but Uncle Clint's going to take you home so you can play with Tyler and Zach."

An hour later, Clint left the hospital with Bo while

the emergency room receptionist directed Kaycee to a consultation room. A few minutes later the doctor came in, introduced himself and gave her the details of Jon's condition. When she heard there was no paralysis or critical injury, Kaycee clamped her hands to her mouth to keep from shouting.

"He may be released tomorrow, depending on how he's feeling. Right now, he's sedated. When he gets home, he needs to stay in bed a few days. No need to aggravate the concussion or those bruised back muscles. I sent orders for pain medicine and a muscle relaxant to the pharmacy in case his back seizes on him at home."

The doctor told her the floor where Jon would be.

"He should be in his room by now."

Kaycee called Clint and told him the good news.

"I'm going to stay the night," she said.

"I'll be back up there first thing in the morning," Clint promised.

When she approached Jon's bedside, his eyes were closed, his breathing strong and steady. But his handsome face was marred by scrapes and bruises. Above the loosely tied hospital gown, she could see a massive black bruise that spread across his neck and disappeared over his shoulder. Kaycee swallowed hard. That looked painful and there had to be worse ones on his back.

"Jon," she called softly, touching his hand, careful not to disturb the IV drip.

He opened his eyes briefly then closed them again.

"How do you feel?"

"Like I was trampled." His voice was slurred. He

tried to lift his head, but dropped back onto the pillow. "They doped me up. Can't stay awake." He forced his eyes open again. "Told me Bo's got a broken arm," he mumbled. "Get Wendy to draw a picture on his cast." He took a deep breath. "Won't let me go home until…" His voice trailed off as he dozed.

Kaycee brushed the back of her hand gently across his stubbled jaw, avoiding the deep scrapes on the side of his face then kissed his lips lightly. She went out to dial the ranch. Rosie answered on the first ring.

"How's Jon?" she asked immediately.

"He's going to be okay," Kaycee said. "Clint's on the way home with Bo."

"Oh, thank heavens. Hold on."

Kaycee heard her talking to the children, relaying her message, then their excited voices in the background.

"How are they holding up?" Kaycee asked when Rosie came back.

"They're better now," she said. "I had some pretty scared kids on my hands. I was worried, too. When can he come home?"

"Hopefully tomorrow. I'm going to stay the night here. Clint said he'd come back in the morning."

"Take care, Kaycee," Rosie said, "and thanks. 'Bye."

Kaycee's stomach growled. With Jon sleeping soundly, she went to find the hospital cafeteria.

THE WORLD CAME BACK to Jon in small snatches. Bits of foggy memory. A dimly lit room. Aches in every muscle. Warm bedcovers. Opening his eyes a fraction more, he took in the IV stand beside the bed, the tube attached to a needle in his left arm, a dark TV suspended from the ceiling.

He shifted in bed and pain shot through his back and neck. When he tried to lift his head, it felt like he'd been hit by a jackhammer. He lay back until everything subsided to a dull ache. Not good. He didn't particularly want to be drugged again, but he'd like to be able to move.

A chair in the corner of the room was empty. Somehow that miffed him, but he seemed to recall yelling at Kaycee that she'd never be Alison, so he didn't see why he should expect her to be there, and hopefully Clint had taken Bo home. Somehow he knew that Bo had a broken arm; that his own injuries were painful but not critical. He couldn't recall who told him. He'd really been out of it. And with a pounding headache and constant dizziness, he still couldn't think clearly.

He had to go to the bathroom, but getting there alone was going to be tricky, if not impossible. He located the call-bell near his hand and pressed it. A voice came over the intercom. Barely able to raise his own voice above a scratchy whisper, he managed to make the nurse understand what he needed.

A burly male nurse showed up within minutes.

"My name's Alfred," he said. "How you feelin'?"

"Help me to the bathroom," Jon muttered.

"Nah. Let's not go running around just yet. I got a bedpan or a urinal here, whichever you need."

Just great. But judging from Alfred's expression, it was the only game in town.

When Jon finished, Alfred took the urinal to the bathroom, washed his hands and came back. "Want to watch some TV?"

"No, but I'm thirsty," Jon said. "And hungry."

"I'll see what I can do."

"What time is it? What day?"

"Monday night. About nine-thirty. I'll bring you a drink and see what I can rustle up for you to eat."

Through the open door, Jon listened drowsily to hospital sounds in the hall outside his room. Carts rolling, stopping, rolling again. Nurses chatting together as they worked. Reminded him of the constant activity at his house and made him want to go home. Now.

Alfred returned in a few minutes with a food tray, followed by a female nurse who took vitals and asked personal questions.

"When can I get out of here?" Jon asked.

"I don't know," she said. "The doctors usually make rounds about nine in the morning and five at night, so you've missed him tonight. You're probably better off here for a while longer anyway. When that pain medicine wears off, you're going to want more."

He couldn't argue. Every minute the discomfort was increasing and even now all he wanted to do was drift off again to escape the pain.

The nurse obliged with more medication in his IV and by the time he finished half of the bland hospital fare, Jon was feeling the euphoric, doping effect. When they took the tray away, he sank back into the pillow and fell asleep.

CHAPTER FIFTEEN

"OH, MY DARLINGS! My sweet darlings."

Wendy jerked her head up in surprise from the plate of food she'd been picking at before going to school. An older, beautifully dressed version of her mother stood in the doorway of the kitchen. Behind her, their grandfather looked angry and Wendy's heart began to pound. What were they doing here?

"Gram! Grampa!"

A general outcry ensued as the children scrambled to hug their grandparents. Wendy held back, knowing her call had triggered their visit. Rosie eyed them warily from the stove where she was cooking Bo's oatmeal.

"I am so glad to see you," Marjorie cooed, embracing each child in turn, and showering them with kisses. She plucked Bo from his high chair. "Oh, my precious baby Bo, look at your pretty cast."

Bo grinned. "Broke," he said proudly. "I didn't cry." He pointed to a drawing of a smiley face on the top.

"Who drew that?" Marjorie asked.

Bo pointed to where she sat. "Wennie."

"Wendy did a good job. Does your arm hurt, baby?"

"Nuh-uh." Bo shook his head, then squirmed and

pointed to his high chair, where Rosie had just set a bowl of warm cereal. "I want to eat."

Marjorie set him back in his seat and adjusted the lapels of her jacket. Rosie shooed the rest of the children back to the island to finish their meal.

"Come here, Wendy, darling, and give Gram a hug."

Reluctantly, Wendy crossed the room and hugged her. Now that Gram was here, her voice didn't sound so much like her mom's, Wendy realized. And her mother wasn't ever coming back. And her daddy was going to hate her for what she'd done. He might make her go live with Gram and Grampa. Or give her to that social worker. She choked back a sob as she pulled away and ran back to her place at the island.

"Everybody hurry. We have to get going." Rosie sounded anxious, and Wendy knew her mistake was going to affect her, too. If only she could take back all those phone calls.

"You must be Rosie." Marjorie held out a slender, ring-bedecked hand.

Rosie's large, work-worn hand took the soft, fragile one briefly, her expression pleasant, but not what Wendy would call welcoming.

"I'm Marjorie Arant, the children's grandmother. And this is their grandfather, Hal."

"Nice to meet you," Rosie said.

"Rosie, would you make me a cup of tea?" Marjorie asked, walking around, peering into the hall and den. "We spent the night in Bozeman, and the hotel service was atrocious. No hot tea, no—"

"Marjorie, dear," Hal said sternly, "stop complaining." He turned to Rosie. "Would you mind leaving the room for a few minutes? My wife and I would like to talk to the children."

"I don't know that Mr. Rider would—"

"Jon's not here and I'm their grandfather. Now if you don't mind…"

"But I do mind," Rosie said firmly. "I don't work for you. I work for Mr. Rider, and these children are in my care. Say whatever you have to say, but I'm staying."

Wendy saw the same relief in her older sisters that she felt. Rosie would take care of them until Dad got home. Hal's chest rose and fell in aggravation, but Rosie crossed her arms and he didn't challenge her. Instead he turned to them.

"Children, your Gram and I have been worried about you lately."

"Why?" Michele asked.

"Young lady, haven't you been taught not to interrupt adults?" Hal reprimanded.

Michele's eyes grew moist, but she clamped her lips together and didn't cry. Wendy froze, afraid to move. She'd never heard her grandfather talk like that to any of them.

"You've been here without adult supervision, without food in the house. Now your father's injured and may take a long time to recover…and we're just lucky Bo wasn't hurt worse."

"I thought Daddy was okay," Zach ventured in a small voice.

Before Hal could jump down the boy's throat for interrupting, Marjorie said, "He will be, but we don't know how long before he's completely recovered." Then she whispered in Hal's ear, "Don't frighten them."

"Sure, he's going to be fine in time. But, Gram and I want you to come live with us in San Francisco while he's recuperating."

"What's recoop'rating?" Tyler whispered to Sam.

"Getting well," Sam whispered back, her eyes on Hal as if she might get punished. "Shh."

"I'm not going to San Francisco," Michele announced.

"Well, young lady, you'll have to, if we agree it's best for you."

"My daddy's not going to agree to that. He's already told us," Michele said, undeterred, narrowing her eyes. Wendy looked at Michele in amazement. She'd never have that much courage.

"I'm sure your father will understand that it's the best thing for you," Hal said. "And that's what's important."

Rosie began to herd them off the bar stools. "Come on kids," she said, "we need to be heading for the school bus. If we miss it, I'll have to drive you all the way into Little Lobo."

Hal glared at her. "They're not going to school today."

"Sure they are. They don't need to miss school. You can visit with them this afternoon."

"As soon as I contact that social worker and get temporary custody, we'll be flying back to San Francisco. There's no reason for me to have to go to the trouble of pulling them out of school."

"I can't believe Mr. Rider has agreed to this," Rosie said.

Ignoring Rosie, he turned his attention back to the wide-eyed youngsters. "Now I want you all to go upstairs and pack your favorite clothes and toys to take along. I'll buy you whatever else you need when you're settled at our house."

Wendy's heard pounded so hard she could hardly hear what he said. But Rosie looked awfully worried and her Grampa was getting more angry by the minute. From the pale, anxious looks on the faces of the older girls, Wendy knew they were as scared as she was.

"Let's go," Rosie said quickly, giving Hal a look that could·kill. "We'll talk about this upstairs."

Behind them Wendy heard Marjorie say, "Hal, maybe you were too abrupt with them. I'm not sure they understand."

"Marjorie, we have to get them away from here before something else happens. I'm going to force that damn social worker to give me custody today before Jon gets out of the hospital, even if I have to pull strings."

Wendy began to tremble. She forced herself to put one foot after the other until she was up the stairs and in Rachel and Sam's room with the others. She slumped onto Sam's bed, trying hard to hide her fright.

"Do we have to do what he says?" Rachel asked. "I don't want to go to California. I want to see Dad."

"I know. Don't worry," Rosie said. "Just do what your grandfather says for now, so he won't get angry."

Rachel dropped onto her bed, her face thoughtful, then her forehead furrowed and she looked around. "Which one of you has been calling Gram and Grampa telling our business?"

Michele and Sam straightened and stared at their sister. Wendy quickly did the same, so not to be singled out.

"What do you mean?" Sam said. "Dad said not to call them right now."

"I know that," Rachel said. "But somebody has, 'cause Grampa knew everything that's going on in our house. About the housekeeper quitting. About us not having food in the refrigerator that one time. That's why the social worker was out here. And now Grampa knew about Bo and Daddy getting hurt the same day it happened. Who's the blabbermouth?"

"Not me," Michele said. "I don't know their number."

Sam and Wendy both shook their heads. Wendy wanted to confess and have somebody tell her everything would be okay. But she knew that wasn't going to happen. She'd done too many bad things. First she'd cheated, now she lied. And even before that, she betrayed her daddy by calling Gram and Grampa when he said not to. And somehow, she wasn't quite sure why, she felt responsible for Daddy and Bo getting hurt today.

Her sisters would hate her if they had to live with Gram and Grampa. None of them really had fun out there, even though their grandparents showered them with clothes and gifts and took them to museums and fancy resorts and restaurants.

And how would she ever face her father again? He could never love her again after this. When had she become so bad?

Looking in Rachel's eyes, she dared not confess. She sat very still and wished she could disappear.

"Couldn't be you, Rosie. The social worker came before you did. Wouldn't be Uncle Clint. He hates Gram and Grampa," Rachel said. "Got to be one of you girls and when I find out who, you're going to be in some kind of trouble."

Rosie patted Rachel on the knee. "Everything's going to work out all right. I'm going to find out what's going on."

Rachel nodded, but without much confidence. "Rosie, call Dad. He needs to come home."

"I don't know if he can," Rosie said. "But I'll think of something, don't worry. I'm not going to stand by and let anybody take you away."

After Rosie left, Wendy slipped out of the room as soon as she could without being obvious and crept along the hall. Downstairs she heard loud arguing. Nobody would ever forgive her.

STILL GROGGY, but coming out from under the latest dose of drugs, Jon turned onto his left side with great effort. At least that side wasn't wracked with pain. He'd refused another shot when the nurse offered it a few minutes ago. Glancing at the clock on the wall, he realized the girls were in school by now.

Nobody was in the room with him and there was no sign anybody was coming back. He'd dreamed about Alison. And Kaycee. And his kids. A worrisome dream where everybody kept eluding him, disappearing and reappearing. He wanted to know the children were okay.

The phone sat just out of reach on the bedside table, but Jon was slowly working up the gumption to reach for it and call home.

As if to torture him, the damn thing rang before he was ready to move. He waited a couple of rings, hoping somebody might materialize and answer it for him, but nobody came. Finally, with a groan, he shoved over enough to get his fingers on the receiver.

"Hello?" he mumbled.

"Daddy?"

The tremor in Wendy's voice chased the lingering grogginess away. "What's the matter, sweetie? How did you get this number?"

"Rosie wrote it on the pad in your office. Daddy, are you going to be sick a long time?"

"No, I should be home by tonight. Why?"

Wendy snuffled as if she'd been crying.

"Wendy, what's wrong?"

"Oh, Daddy, I did something really, really bad and…and—" she began to sob "—and now Grampa is going to make us go to San Francisco and live with them. We don't want to, Daddy. We really don't."

Jon pushed himself up, the adrenaline that shot through him a far more powerful painkiller than morphine.

"Is he there now?"

"Yes, sir." Wendy was crying so hard, Jon could barely understand her. "Grampa told us to pack our favorite clothes and stuff. That the social worker is coming today to let him take us home with him. Nobody wants to go with them. Daddy, I'm so sorry. It's all my fault."

"No, sweetie, it's not your fault. Is Rosie—"

"I have to go before they find me. I want my mom so bad. I just want to talk to her," Wendy whispered into the phone, her voice desperate and haunting. "Daddy, please don't hate me. I'm so sorry. I love you."

"Wendy. Wendy, don't hang—"

The line went dead. A cold sweat broke out on Jon's forehead as he swung his feet over the side of the bed to sit up. He held his aching ribs for a minute until he could catch his breath. It took a minute for him to focus enough to figure out which number to dial first.

"Answer the damn phone," he muttered as it rang. On the second ring Rosie answered.

"Rosie, what's going on? Is Hal there?"

"Jon? Where are you calling from?"

"From the damn hospital. I asked you a question. Is Hal there?"

The hesitation on the other end gave the answer. He could hear Rosie's agitated breathing, but he still got no response.

"Rosie!"

Finally, she said, "I wanted to get in the other room, away from him."

"Wendy called here scared to death. She said her grandparents are at the house. When did they get there?"

"Maybe an hour ago. Right after Clint left. Mr. Arant says he's planning to take the children to San Francisco today. He says he's pulling strings."

The thunder of Jon's heart reverberated through his body as he tried to think. Sweat trickled down his sides. "Where did Clint go?"

"Clint's on the way to the hospital."

"Call the sheriff, Rosie. Get him out there."

"I already did. He's on his way."

"Tell him I've got custody and Hal cannot take the children off the property. Tell him I'm getting a restraining order against Hal. I'll be home as soon as Clint gets here. Rosie, look on my desk. Find my lawyer's private number. His card should be there somewhere."

He waited impatiently for what seemed to be forever, before Rosie came back with it. He hung up, repeating the number over and over until he could dial it. His brain wasn't working right, but fortunately, he'd remembered correctly. When his lawyer answered, he explained the situation as best he could.

"This is kidnapping, Frank, pure and simple. I want a restraining order against him. My housekeeper is calling the sheriff out there."

"A restraining order will take time, Jon. But they can't legally take your children without a judge's order and that's not going to happen without going to court."

"What if Hal forces them to go? Like right now, before the sheriff gets there."

"Kidnapping. A whole other matter. Let me make some calls, see what kind of pull your father-in-law's got around here. How can I reach you?"

"I don't have my cell phone. Call my foreman. I'll be with him in a few minutes." Jon gave him Clint's number, hung up and dialed Clint himself.

When Clint answered, Jon said, "Where are you?"

"On my way to the hospital. Have you been released?"

"Hell, yes, I'm released. I'm releasing myself."

"Jon, what's the matter. You don't sound—"

"Hal's at the ranch. He came after you left," Jon said. "How far away are you?"

"Another half hour maybe."

"Are you bringing me clothes?"

"Yeah, I got some clothes, but—"

"Just hurry." Jon hung up, miserable and anxious. He needed Kaycee.

What had he been thinking to run her off? All those hateful things he said came from a place of fear and frustration, but could he make her understand that? If she ever spoke to him again.

Alfred, the nurse, opened the door. "Mr. Rider, are you all right? I thought I heard you talking in here."

Breathing hard, Jon gripped the edge of the bed. "I'm fine," he said through clenched teeth.

"You need pain medicine?"

Jon waved him off. "I don't need anything." When Alfred was out of sight, Jon peeled off the tape and slid the IV needle out, pressing the sheet against his skin until the bleeding stopped. Fighting the pain, he shuffled to the bathroom, holding on to the bed, then the wall for support.

The man in the mirror was not impressive. His unkempt hair stuck out in all directions; sunburned face scraped and bruised. His right shoulder was black and he could turn enough to see other bruises chasing one another down his back underneath the open-backed hospital gown. Gingerly, he touched the sutured gash on his head, the cause of this demon headache. But, Jon told himself ruefully as he tried to plaster down the unruly hair, a good hat pulled low enough could hide a multitude of faults.

Alone in the sterile, unnaturally bright bathroom, he leaned on the sink, sick to his stomach. What the hell could that Hawthorn woman be thinking, turning those children over to a man like Hal?

"Forgive me, Alison," he whispered. "I didn't mean to let you down."

Turning the cold water on full force, he threw double handfuls on his face until he felt better. As he dried off, he heard somebody come in the room.

"Jon?" Kaycee said, opening the bathroom door. She sucked in a breath. "What are you doing up?"

"Kaycee?" Jon said in surprise. "You came back."

"I haven't been anywhere except to get breakfast and pick up your prescriptions. You've just been asleep. As you should be now." She reached for his arm. "Come on, let's get you back to bed. Where's your IV?"

He grabbed her and hugged her, in spite of the pain the movement caused. "No, you don't understand. I thought I'd run you off yesterday. I was sure you hated my guts."

"I don't scare that easily. But you didn't have to get yourself pounded into the dirt to get out of an argument, you know," Kaycee said, drawing back gently. "We're going to take up the issue again when you're better. Now you need to get back to bed."

"I'm going home."

"You can't leave in this condition," she said, eyeing him head to toe. "You can barely stand."

"Hal and Marjorie are at the ranch threatening to take the children back to San Francisco today. Clint's on his way to pick me up."

Kaycee shook her head. "I don't think Mrs. Hawthorn will let them. She knows what Hal's been doing."

"Bo was hurt," Jon said. "Hal might be able to sway her."

"It was an accident."

"Maybe you trust the legal system, but I'm not taking any chances. Anybody who tries to take my children off that ranch will have to go through me."

"You're not thinking straight, Jon. You could make things worse."

He turned a deaf ear to her as Clint came through the door with an overnight bag in his hand.

"Finally," Jon said.

"Huh," Clint retorted, "I just about got a ticket getting here as it was."

"Help me get dressed," Jon said, easing into the chair in the corner.

Sensible man that Clint was, he brought a pair of relaxed-fit jeans and a soft flannel shirt. Kaycee politely turned away while Clint helped him dress, ignoring his occasional groan. He wanted another dose of that pain-killer they'd shot into him all night, but didn't intend to chance falling asleep.

"At least see a doctor before you leave here," Kaycee said when he was dressed and standing.

"I don't have time. Where's your truck, Clint?"

"In the out-patient area. I brought the Suburban. Thought it would be more comfortable."

As Jon limped past the nurses' station assisted by Kaycee and Clint, Alfred came around the desk and blocked their way, taking Jon by the upper arm. "Where do you think you're going, Mr. Rider?"

"I just released myself." Jon pulled his arm free and staggered backward. Clint and Kaycee braced him. Damn, he hated debility. "You can't keep me here against my will."

"No, but I don't want you to leave before you're ready."

"Same thing I said," Kaycee agreed.

"Let me get a doctor," Alfred said.

"I'm going home."

"At least sign an AMA form since you're leaving against medical advice. Won't take me but a minute to fill one out," Alfred added. "We can't be responsible if you leave like this."

"You're off the hook." Jon moved around him and continued down the hall.

Alfred grabbed a wheelchair from the corner. "Well, I'm not going to let you drop dead in my hall." He insisted Jon get in the chair and wheeled him to the patient loading area.

On the way home, Jon slumped in the front seat of the SUV, his fists pressed hard against his pounding temples. The least bump in the road drove fiery pain through his back and chest. By the time he endured the long ride to the ranch, Jon figured he'd be wishing he were back in that hospital bed. He closed his eyes. He couldn't think anymore. He just wanted this headache to go away. Wanted his children safe. Wanted things to be the way they used to be.

Thank God he had Kaycee by his side again, even if she thought it was temporarily. He needed her strength and good sense right now. When all this was over, he was going to make amends to her. And work through their problems. Somehow. Because, just like his kids, he was never going to let her get away from him.

CHAPTER SIXTEEN

ENTERING THE HOUSE through the back door, Jon immediately noticed the unnatural silence. Like in the days after Alison's death. Quiet like he'd never wanted to hear again. Were his kids already gone?

"Rosie?" he called out anxiously, limping into the kitchen.

From somewhere in the house he heard, "I think I hear Daddy." Within a matter of seconds, five scared kids surrounded him and Kaycee, trying to hug them both at the same time and firing questions like nails into Jon's head. He kept hearing Wendy's name again and again in the hubbub. Glancing around, he missed her at once.

"Hey, guys, settle down. I'm home. Everything's going to be okay now. Where's Wendy?"

Kaycee gently moved the youngsters back a few feet. "Your dad's kind of sore right now. Give him a little room."

Rosie was right behind the children, her face a mask of concern.

"Where's Wendy?" Jon repeated.

"We've got a bad situation, Mr. Rider. Wendy's

missing. We're pretty sure she took Dusty and ran away."

"That doesn't make sense. She never rides," Jon said, dread running through his veins like ice water. "When did you miss her?"

"Just a few minutes ago. She went to her room earlier and we thought that's where she was," Rachel said.

"Who's looking for her?"

"The sheriff was here, and he and Mr. Arant sent all the hands out right away," Rosie said. "Then the sheriff called into his office to form a larger search party, but he said it might take a few hours to get organized."

"Hal's gone looking for her?"

"He insisted. He's very upset."

"As well he should be," Jon said, "since he's the one who caused all this."

Marjorie appeared in the doorway, her face pale.

"I'm so sorry, Jon," she said, then covered her mouth.

"It's a little late for that now. My child's run away because you and Hal frightened her so badly."

"What do you mean? We didn't cause her—"

"Yes, you did. Threatening to take them back to California today. That's exactly why she ran away."

"We thought we were doing what's best for them. I know Hal will find her."

"Hal couldn't find his way out of hell. If something happens to Wendy…" Jon couldn't finish. He didn't know what he might be tempted to do if anything happened to Wendy.

"I'm so very sorry, Jon," she whispered. "We never meant this."

Jon stared at her for a long minute, seeing the shadow of Alison in her face. Finally, he said, "We'll find her." He turned to Clint. "Call the neighbors and see if you can get more men out there…. Do you girls have any idea where she might be? I want you to think hard. Did Wendy say anything about running away or where she might be hiding?"

"No," Rachel said. "The only thing is I fussed at all the girls because I know one of them has been calling Grampa and telling him everything that's going on here. I said whoever was doing it was going to be in a lot of trouble. I think now, maybe it was Wendy."

Marjorie gasped. Jon shot her a look. "Is that true? Has she been calling you?"

Marjorie nodded weakly. "Jon, you don't understand how hard it was for me, for Hal and me, to be cut off from our grandchildren. I wanted to know how they were doing, so I called one day and got Wendy. I gave her our phone number and asked her to call me every week and tell me how they were doing because… because I knew you wouldn't let me talk to them if you answered."

Jon shook his head in frustration. He'd never seen those calls because he'd set up unlimited long distance for Alison to talk to her parents whenever she wanted. The long distance calls weren't listed on his bills. "So that's how Hal knew every step I made? Wendy told you and you told him."

"Yes," she said. "Yes. I told Hal. I had no idea he'd called that social worker until we were on the plane here this morning. I didn't mean to bring this on you, Jon. I only wanted to stay in contact with the children. I love them. I never wanted to hurt any of you. Please believe me."

Jon nodded slowly. "I believe you, but…Rosie, put some bottled water and jerky in a pack and send it out to the barn with one of the girls. And put a lot of aspirin in there."

"What are you thinking, Jon?" Kaycee said. "You can't ride."

"I have to. Wendy's—"

"Not on your life," Clint said. "You're not going anywhere. I'll ride out looking for her."

"If you figure I'm sitting here while Wendy's missing, you're crazy. Saddle Happy for me and quit wasting time."

"Be reasonable, Jon. We'll be looking for two people when you pass out and fall off the damn horse."

"He's right, Jon," Kaycee said, turning him around to face her. "You're in no condition to be out of the hospital, much less on a horse."

Fighting his pain and anxiety, Jon wavered as dizziness swept over him.

Clint jumped on his weakness. "You see, you wouldn't get out of the barnyard. You go to bed, take one of those pain pills. I'll find Wendy, I swear." Clint gave Kaycee a conspiratorial nod. "Get him some medicine, Dr. Calloway. See that he stays here."

Kaycee took Jon by the arm. "I will. Come on, Jon. You know you can't ride. Clint will find her."

Jon knew a losing battle when he saw it. He allowed Kaycee to lead him to his bedroom. Rosie brought a glass of water and turned down the bedcovers while Kaycee gave him a couple of pills.

"Take those and try to rest," she said.

Jon put his hand to his mouth then took a gulp of water and laid down on the bed in his clothes. "I'm going to rest for a few minutes and I'll be up. Kaycee, call Frank and tell him what's going on. Rosie can give you his number."

"Okay, I'll be back shortly."

Jon heard Kaycee say as she closed the bedroom door, "I sure hope Wendy's back when he wakes."

Jon closed his eyes for a moment to let the splitting headache subside. He slipped his hand into his pocket and deposited the pain pills he hadn't swallowed—he might need them later. Then he waited for the voices to recede outside his door.

Why would Wendy take Dusty? She was afraid of horses, always rode double behind Alison if she had to ride. Hadn't been on a horse since her mother died…

He pushed up from the bed with a frown, his phone conversation with Wendy echoing through his head. *I want my mom so bad. I just want to talk to her.*

He knew where she was. And probably nobody would think to ride that far looking for her.

Jon made his way to his closet and found an old pair of boots, ignoring the pain bending over caused as he put them on. He eased himself out through the sliding doors that led from his bedroom to the patio, then across the yard to the barn, staying clear of the windows along the back of the house. He wanted to be gone before anybody missed him. Once outside, he noticed for the first time the towering bank of clouds coming fast and low over the farthest peaks. *God.* He'd been concerned about the danger of mountain lions and wolves, but those clouds were a bad omen.

Gaining the safety of the tack room in the stallion barn without attracting attention, he leaned against the wall to recover. Forcing himself to move, he gingerly pulled on a heavy riding coat, checked for gloves in the pocket, then took the smallest jacket for Wendy. He lifted a loaded rifle from a high rack out of reach of the kids, then tested a flashlight and electric lantern from the cabinet and set them on the bench. Even if he found Wendy before the impending storm brought on early nightfall, they would never make it home by dark.

Saddling Happy was an ordeal, but the horse seemed to sense Jon's struggle and stood quietly while Jon tightened the cinch. He strapped the lantern to the pommel and tucked the flashlight and small jacket into the saddlebag, then slid the rifle into the scabbard on the side of the saddle. Glad that nobody was there to see him, Jon used the mounting block in the corner to haul himself onto Happy's back. It took a couple of attempts. He rode out of the barn toward the high meadow.

As soon as the big horse broke into a canter, Jon hunched over and grabbed his side. Grudgingly, he pulled Happy to a brisk walk to keep from falling out of the saddle.

He'd gone less than a mile when one of the dogs overtook him and he heard the fast approach of horse's hooves. Expecting Clint or one of his hands, he didn't look around. The second dog bounded past as the lone rider caught up to him.

"What do you think you're doing?" Kaycee said angrily. "Trying to kill yourself?"

"Go back," he ordered.

"Not unless you do." She reined her mare in step beside him. "Jon! Stop."

He shook his head and nudged Happy on. "How did you know where I was?"

"Sam saw you ride off. She told me you took the trail to the high meadow where Alison's buried. Is that where you think Wendy is?"

"Yep. Or maybe the line shack where Alison used to paint."

"Then let me call Clint or somebody to go after her."

Jon twisted toward her in the saddle, waited for the pain in his ribs to subside. "Listen to me, Kaycee, I'm not turning back. You can call Clint. Tell him to follow me up there. I'll be okay."

"I'm not going back, either. But I will call Clint." She tried her cell phone, but couldn't get service.

"Forgot to mention, cell phones don't work well up in the mountains," Jon said. "You'll have to go back to the ranch to call him."

"You're acting just like a man. You'd fall off that horse before admitting you need help."

Jon grunted.

"How far is it to this line shack?"

"At this rate, well over two hours."

Jon stopped to yell for Wendy. He got no response, and moved on. He scanned the landscape as he rode, searching for any sign that Wendy had been that way. Anxious to go faster, but knowing he couldn't take it, he called for her again and again, as did Kaycee. The temperature dropped rapidly as they moved higher. Lowering clouds scudded overhead. The dogs ranged out, but didn't herald a scent.

Soon snow swirled in flurries, powdering the ground and the shoulders of their coats. After almost an hour of steady uphill riding with no sign of Wendy in any direction, Jon stopped to rest for a few minutes and regroup. They shared a bottle of water Kaycee pulled from her saddlebag. Before starting off again, they called out for Wendy, but their words were blown back at them by the wind racing through the passes and down the trail. As Jon suspected, no searchers had ventured this way.

The dogs leapt ahead out of sight on the narrowing trail. Wet snow fell faster, peppering their faces, clinging to their eyebrows and lashes. Jon didn't know how much longer he could stay in the saddle. The cold numbed his body, but couldn't deaden the pain or stave off the weariness that settled in every bone, every muscle. Dizzy and jerking with cold by the time they reached the line shack, his heart sank. No signs of life.

"Wendy?" he called.

No answer. There was only one other place Wendy might be.

"Kaycee, go make sure Wendy's not inside. I doubt it's locked."

Kaycee came out of the cabin shaking her head, her wide eyes dark with worry. "Where could she be?"

"At her mother's grave, I hope," Jon said. "Stay here and try to get a fire going inside. She'll be freezing."

Jon felt the last of his energy leaching away. He leaned on the saddle horn, not sure he could go another step.

Kaycee laid her hand on his thigh. "This is it for you, Jon. Get down and go inside. Tell me where the cemetery is and I'll find her."

"You'll never find it in this storm."

"You can't go alone. If you fall off I won't know how to find you, either."

Past argument, Jon nodded wearily and nudged Happy toward the last place he knew to look for his little girl.

CHAPTER SEVENTEEN

JON TURNED HAPPY up the mountain toward the small family cemetery where Alison was buried, and prayed.

He allowed the horse to pick his way along as the trail became steep and rocky. Up here, the wind howled through sparse, weather-beaten trees and snow blanketed everything. Their voices were torn from their throats and smothered by the wind. The snow swirled and eddied like a fast running stream, almost blinding in its stinging intensity. Jon pulled his collar up around his face and pulled his hat down to shield his eyes. Even in gloves, his fingers felt like sticks of ice.

"Wendy!" he and Kaycee cried periodically as they rode slowly along, trying to find their way.

The dogs ranged off the trail, stub tails twitching. Suddenly, Happy pricked his ears and nickered. Above the howling wind, Jon heard a faint answering whinny. Reining Happy in that direction, Jon called for Wendy.

Finally, he heard the blessed words, "Daddy! Over here, Daddy. Over here. Come get me!"

In a stand of fir trees, Dusty hunkered against the wind. Wendy clung to Dusty's neck, her body pressed close to the warm horse.

She jumped off and ran toward them. Kaycee leapt down from her mare and met Wendy halfway, scooping her up with unconcealed joy and hugging her like Jon wanted to do. Wendy wriggled away and ran to Happy, tugging at Jon's pants leg. "Take me up with you, Daddy. Please."

Jon reached back, pulled her jacket from the saddle-bag and handed it to Kaycee. "I think there are gloves in the pocket," he said.

Kaycee helped her into the jacket, then hugged her again. "We were so worried about you. Come on, let's all go get warm."

"I thought I could make it back to the cabin but the snow started and I couldn't see," Wendy said, more to Jon than Kaycee.

"Help her up," Jon said.

Kaycee boosted Wendy into the saddle in front of Jon. Cold and scared, the girl shook uncontrollably and her teeth chattered as she settled against him. Jon unfastened his own coat and wrapped it around her, holding her close to his chest with one arm. Grabbing Dusty's reins, Kaycee mounted, starting down the mountain ahead of them. Jon took a moment to say a silent prayer of thanks before reining Happy around behind Kaycee's mare.

"I'm so sorry, Daddy," Wendy said, beginning to cry.

Jon tightened his grip reassuringly and leaned his head down next to hers. "Don't cry, sweetie. Every-thing's okay now."

Wendy jerked in a couple of hard breaths. "Do you know what I did? Do you hate me?"

"I could never hate you, Wendy. None of you kids."

"I caused all the trouble, though," she confessed. "I sneaked and called Gram. I told her all about the housekeeper leaving and about Dr. Kaycee and…and…Rachel said that's what made the social worker come."

Jon hugged Wendy, nestling her head against his chest. "What's going on between your Grampa and me started a long time ago, before I married your mother. You didn't cause it."

"Why doesn't Grampa like you?"

"I'm not sure you'd understand. We'll talk about it when we get warm."

Wendy's jacket hood and Jon's coat were thick with snow when they finally reached the cabin. Wendy's small body was the only warmth he felt—he'd long ago lost feeling in his hands and feet.

Kaycee dismounted and, reaching up, took Wendy from Jon's arms, kissing the top of the child's head. Kaycee looked up with tears in her eyes and smiled at Jon as she set the youngster on her feet in the snow. He nodded and smiled back.

Kaycee caught Jon by the arm as he dismounted. His knees gave way and he almost sank to the ground. "Jon, let's get you inside."

"We take care of the horses first," he said. "Wendy, come help."

Wendy led Dusty to the lean-to stable next to the cabin. The three of them worked together to quickly bed down the horses, loosening the cinches and removing their headgear. Jon turned Happy loose in one section of the enclosure and the mares in another.

"Scoop some snow in a bucket, Wendy. We can melt it for them to drink later."

"Hurry inside. I'll do that," Kaycee urged, taking the bucket, and handing Wendy the electric lantern. "You've both been out in the cold too long."

Wendy caught Jon's hand with both of hers and pulled him up the two steps to the porch. Kaycee scooped the bucket full of snow and bounded after them. Within minutes she had a fire going in the fireplace.

Aching all over from exposure and injury, Jon slumped onto a bench beside the hearth. He glanced around the room. He hadn't been inside since Alison died. Paintings covered the walls and were stacked along the floor. He could still visualize her at work at her easel. Sometimes he'd surprise her when she came alone to paint, bringing her something special to eat or a handful of wildflowers. He could barely look at the rough-hewn bed in the corner, so bittersweet the memories. Probably a couple of his children were conceived on that lumpy mattress that right now looked as inviting as a feather bed.

Ever vigilant, Kaycee recognized his fatigue. She turned down the covers. "Go to bed, Jon. I brought your medicine."

"Not yet," he said. "We have some things to talk about, all three of us. Sit down here, Wendy." He patted the bench next to him.

Wendy glanced furtively at Kaycee then looked at him with dread in her expression.

The snow in the bucket had melted, so Kaycee took

the handle and said, "I'll water the horses while you talk."

"No, this involves all of us. Pull up a chair."

Wendy looked stricken, but Kaycee sat a short distance away. Jon looked from one to the other, his gaze lingering on Kaycee. "Okay, Wendy, I'm going to let you talk first. I want to know about you calling your grandparents. How long has this been going on and how did it start?"

She stared at her feet. "I want to talk to you alone, Daddy."

"No. What you did caused us all a lot of worry. Running away today put a lot of people in danger, including Dr. Kaycee. Now answer my question."

Resigned, Wendy tried to hold back tears. "Gram called one day…a few months ago…and I answered. She asked me if I would call her every week and tell her how we were doing."

"I asked you kids not to call them until I could work out my problems with your grandfather. Why did you disobey me?"

Wendy looked up with shimmering eyes. "Daddy, it's just that…well…Gram sounded just like Mama on the phone and I wanted to talk to Mama so bad. When I called Gram, I could make believe Mama was still alive, just away visiting, and someday she'd come home."

Wendy snuffled and Jon pulled out his handkerchief for her. He put his arm around the child and drew her closer. "Wendy, I'd give anything, do anything, to bring your mother back. But she's gone and we can't change that." He lifted her chin so she looked up at him. "There have been lots of times when I felt like I was responsible for her death because I was driving. But we can't dwell on things like that. We have to go on with our lives. Do you understand that?"

Wendy nodded slightly.

"I have to ask you an important question and I want you to be honest. Do you want to go live with Gram and Grampa?" Jon asked, the words constricting his throat. If she said yes, he didn't know what he'd do.

"No. Oh, please, no. I want to live here with you and everybody else. But, we all love Gram, too. And Grampa—except today he scared us talking about us having to live in San Francisco. I just wish we could still see them sometimes like we used to and nobody fight over it."

Jon blinked hard. He'd been so immersed in his own war with the Arants that he hadn't seen the toll it took on his children. "Grown-ups make mistakes, too, sweetie. I was trying to protect you, to keep your grampa from taking you away from me. But maybe I…went about it the wrong way."

"I didn't mean to make trouble, Daddy."

"It's been a hard year for all of us, including your grandparents. But running away like you did today isn't the solution. You put yourself and a lot of other people in danger. There are searchers still out looking for you because we can't tell them you're safe."

"I was scared nobody would ever love me again. Except Mom. I went to her grave and sat there a long time, then it started snowing really hard and I couldn't see the trail anymore. I didn't know what to do, except stay close to her."

"You did the right thing. If you'd wandered off we couldn't have found you."

Wendy wrapped her arms around him. Jon caught his breath as pain shot through his rib cage.

"You need to rest, Jon," Kaycee said, rising to help him.

He motioned her back to her chair. "No, we're not done yet. Now it's my turn to talk."

CHAPTER EIGHTEEN

KAYCEE WATCHED JON with concern. That he was managing to stay upright was a miracle. But from the determined look on his face, there would be no point in arguing with him. She eased back down into her seat, waiting to hear what he had to say.

He was quiet a long time, hugging Wendy. Finally he took her by the shoulders and held her at arm's length, studying her face. "I understand you have a problem with me wanting to marry Kaycee."

Wendy's eyes grew wide and she pulled back.

"Jon, don't…" Kaycee said.

"I want everything out in the open. Secrets only hurt people. You did tell Dr. Kaycee that Aunt Bailey is my girlfriend, didn't you?"

Wendy's face fell and she shot a reproachful look toward Kaycee.

"Did you think she wouldn't tell me?" Jon said. "If you make up something like that, you have to be prepared to face the consequences. Do you understand that the only reason Kaycee came into our lives was because Grampa called the social worker and we got caught in that silly predicament about us being engaged?"

Wendy nodded. "I guess. But, I didn't want another—"

"Another mother. I know."

"And…and she didn't keep her word Friday. She never came with the movies."

"Because she was helping a mare foal and the mare or the baby might have died if she hadn't stayed to help."

"Oh."

"She said she tried to call, but the line was busy."

Wendy sucked in a soft breath. "When I was talking to Gram?"

"You called Gram that night?"

"I…when Dr. Kaycee didn't come, I didn't want a mother like that. I wanted to hear Gram's voice and pretend I still had Mom."

Kaycee listened, her lips drawn tight.

"I was angry with her, too, Wendy. I thought just about the same thing you did. I said some unfair things to Kaycee that hurt her feelings."

"You did?"

"Yes. Things I wish I'd never said. Things I can't take back." Jon wouldn't look Kaycee's way, but Wendy did.

"What did you say to her?"

"That she would never be like your mother, for one thing. And I said that she wouldn't be the right kind of mother for my children."

"You did?"

Jon nodded. "Isn't that what you think? That she wouldn't be a good mother?"

Wendy screwed her face up and thought. "I don't know. My sisters think she'd be great. I didn't ever say she wouldn't be a *good* mother, just that I didn't want another mother than the one I had."

"How can she be a good mother when she's got such a busy job?" Jon asked. "There would be lots of times when she wouldn't be around when you needed something. Times when she promised to do something with you and was called on an emergency. That never happened with your mom."

Kaycee fought back tears.

"I know, but that was different," Wendy said. "Lots of my friends' moms work. Besides, Mom hasn't been around for a long time and we got by."

"Well, I know, but if Dr. Kaycee said she was going to be your mother and then couldn't do all the things Mom used to do... I just didn't think it would work. If we married, it would just be too different from before. That's basically what I told her."

Wendy frowned. "You told her that?"

"You said Sunday night, you liked it with just us if you couldn't have your real mom back. Didn't you?"

"Yes, but I...I...Rachel and Michele say you and Dr. Kaycee are in love. Are you?" she asked earnestly.

The corner of Jon's mouth twitched. "I can't answer for Dr. Kaycee, but yes, I'm in love with her."

Kaycee's lips parted in surprise at the frank admission. Jon sneaked a glance at her.

"But I really hurt her feelings and I doubt she loves me anymore."

Wendy stared up at him in silence for what seemed

like minutes. "But if you love her, won't you be unhappy without her?"

Jon nodded. "Yes, I'll be very unhappy without her. I think I could adjust to her being a different kind of wife. Could you adjust to a different kind of mom?"

Wendy smiled. "Maybe you'd better ask her if she still loves you."

"Maybe I'd better." They both looked Kaycee's way.

Kaycee couldn't hold back the pent-up tears. "It really wouldn't be the same," she said. "I could never take your mother's place, Wendy. I wouldn't even try. But we could make our own kind of family. Do you want that?"

"Do you love Daddy?" Wendy asked with a child's frankness. "And us?"

Kaycee tried to wipe away the continuing stream of tears. Jon waited.

Wendy slid from the bench and ran to her. "I'm so sorry, Dr. Kaycee. Please still love him. I don't want him to be unhappy anymore."

"I do. I love every one of you with all my heart."

Wendy flung her arms around Kaycee's neck. "We'll be a good family."

"Yes, we will be," Kaycee said, gazing over the child's head into Jon's intense blue eyes. "Let's start by making your father go to bed. He's really tired and needs to sleep."

"I'll take you up on that now," Jon said, rising unsteadily and limping to the bed.

Kaycee sent Wendy to water the horses. While the child was gone, she helped Jon take off his damp clothing down to his underwear and pulled the covers over him, then gave him the painkiller and muscle relaxant, according to the directions.

Jon dozed off almost immediately. Kaycee sat on the edge of the bed until he began to snore softly, her gaze roaming the walls, covered with Alison's artwork. After a moment, she realized Wendy was watching her. The child smiled and she smiled back.

Kaycee got up from the bed, careful not to rouse Jon and walked slowly around the room, studying each painting.

"Your mother painted all these?"

"Except those three. They're mine."

"Really?" Kaycee said, admiring the portraits of the ranch dogs. "Very nice."

"My mom was a good artist."

"I see that. Tell me about these."

Gradually, Wendy opened up as she described her mother's work.

"What's under here?" Kaycee asked, reaching for the cloth covering an easel.

"Mom's last painting. The one we were working on when she…died."

Kaycee stepped back, but Wendy pulled the cloth off. It was a portrait of Jon in a rodeo arena, riding a massive, red bull. Alison had transferred all the raw power of the contorting, wrenching bull—and the poignant courage of the solitary man harnessing that power with only a one-handed hold on a rope girth— to the canvas in bold color and strong, confident strokes.

"That's Redeye, my daddy's favorite bull. The last

one he rode before him and Mama got married. Daddy said that bull always knew him and was the only one that ever caught him after he got bucked off. Daddy's got a scar on his back from the horns."

Wendy touched the painting reverently. "I painted this part." Her finger brushed Jon's brilliant blue shirt and matching chaps. She looked up at Kaycee. "Do you like it?"

Kaycee nodded and hugged the child. "It's wonderful."

"It's not quite finished." Wendy pointed to a section where the paint faded to pale, color-washed canvas.

"Then you'll have to finish it."

Wendy shook her head. "I don't think I'm good enough without Mama to show me how."

"I think you are," Kaycee said.

"Really?"

"Really," Kaycee said. "Come sit with me and tell me more about your mother."

Wendy hesitated then took Kaycee's hand. The cabin was warm and quiet as they curled up in a blanket, and Wendy told her about life at the ranch and how much she missed her mother. Just before she fell asleep, she gazed up at Kaycee and touched her face.

"Thank you for coming after me, Dr. Kaycee. And for loving Daddy."

As the child's breathing grew even and soft, Kaycee kept vigil in the cabin. And somehow she knew that Alison had passed the watch on to her that night.

CHAPTER NINETEEN

KAYCEE OPENED her eyes as the bedsprings creaked slightly. Jon, who had slept peacefully through the night, sat up with difficulty, the bedclothes around his waist. The sight of his broad, muscled chest—albeit now horribly bruised—took her back to the warmth of the rock in the meadow.

"Good morning, beautiful," he said in a low voice, smiling at the sight of Wendy cradled in her arms. "Do you still love me this morning?"

Kaycee nodded.

"That's all I need to know."

"How do you feel?" she asked.

"Wicked headache. But stronger."

Wendy stirred. "Daddy!" she cried, scrambling out of the blankets to run to him.

Jon kissed her face. "How do you feel? Catch a cold out in all that weather yesterday?"

Wendy shook her head. "Nope, I feel fine. I showed Dr. Kaycee all the paintings Mama and I did. She thinks we should take some of them home and make a gallery in Mom's memory. Can we, Daddy? Can we do that?"

Jon gave Kaycee a grateful smile. "I like that idea.

We'll all come one day and let everybody choose which ones to take." Jon pulled the blanket gingerly around his shoulders. "It's cold in here."

Kaycee brought him his dry clothes and helped him slide his arms into his shirt sleeves. He made them both turn away while he managed the jeans by himself. As he eased up from the bed, his expression became pained, but he didn't complain.

"I'm going outside for a few minutes. Be back."

He went out the door with the dogs on his heels. After a while, Kaycee heard the horses milling around in the lean-to next door. He came back in a few minutes with a few pieces of firewood.

"Blizzard's passed," he said. "Somebody ought to be up here after us in a few hours."

Kaycee took the wood from him, placing the logs on the fire irons above the glowing embers. A fire blazed in a matter of minutes.

Midafternoon, Clint and the sheriff's rescue party reached the cabin on snowmobiles. Jon couldn't recall seeing Clint cry since the day Claire was born, but he had to wipe his eyes when Jon and Wendy came out to greet them. Kaycee, Wendy and Jon hitched a ride home on the snowmobiles, while Clint rode Happy, leading the mares on a slow, careful journey along the tracks tramped down by the snow-mobile runners.

The lights from the ranch house windows glowed in the early dusk. Jon had never been so glad to see anything as when his kids spilled onto the porch at the sound of the snowmobiles outside. The kids rallied around Wendy as they pulled her up the steps, bombarding her with questions.

Everybody was exhausted. Those who had weathered the storm on the mountain, those who had searched until they had to give up and everyone at home who'd waited anxiously through the night. After a hot meal from Rosie, Jon sent the children upstairs and summoned Hal into his office.

Keep your cool. Some way or other, he was going to find common ground with his father-in-law. Jon closed the door behind them. Hal pulled a chair opposite the massive oak desk that had been in Jon's family for generations. Knowing that more than one deal had been struck over this desk, Jon took his seat and contemplated his father-in-law's stern expression. Hal was a man who liked to drive hard bargains, who had made his wealth that way. Stubborn, sharp, with the staying power of a pit bull.

"Where do we begin, Hal? We almost lost Wendy yesterday because of this animosity between us."

Hal's face tightened. "Are you saying that was my fault?"

"You played a part. We were damned lucky to get her back unharmed. We can't do anything about what's gone on in the past. But these dangerous games with my family are about to stop."

"Bottom line, Jon, I want my grandchildren safe and raised right. I don't think you can do that out here in the middle of nowhere. Certainly not without their mother to help. I think they would be better off with Marjorie and me."

"There is no way in hell I'm going to give you my kids. You know that. Have you asked them what they want? They don't want to live with you. Especially after you betrayed Wendy."

"What do you mean? We never betrayed that child. She called us and told us she was scared—"

"Wendy's nine years old. She's timid and gets scared easily. Do you know why she was really calling Marjorie? Because Marjorie sounds like Alison on the phone. She pretended she was talking to her mother."

"Her mother? I…we just wanted to be sure they were cared for. Fed. Supervised. We wanted to be sure they were safe."

"Safe? She could have died in that blizzard, Hal."

Hal was silent.

"If you're really concerned about the children, do what's best for them. Let us go on with our lives."

"You're planning to marry that woman vet?"

"Yes, I intend to marry her."

"Wendy doesn't like her."

"Wendy didn't like her because she wanted her mother to come back. Now she understands that's impossible."

Hal pursed his lips and frowned. "You've got it all figured out, haven't you? Marry again, and keep Marjorie and me from ever seeing our grandchildren?"

"No, not at all. In fact, Kaycee believes the children need you in their lives. Honestly, I do, too. They love you. But they need to be here, where they were born, where they knew their mother. Here with me. I love them better than anybody on earth can love them. Do you love them enough to forget about revenge?"

Hal sat glowering at Jon, and another time Jon would have said to hell with it and sent him packing. There was too much at stake today. Jon slowly got up and limped to the window, his sore leg stiff from sitting. "Let's end these hard feelings between us. I wish we'd done it while Alison was alive, but we have to do it now. If you'll stop trying to take the kids away, I promise I'll let you and Marjorie see them on a regular basis. There's no other way, Hal. We've got to call a truce for their sake."

Jon turned back to face the other man, who was sitting like stone in his chair.

"We all lost a part of us when Alison died," Jon said quietly. "Nothing's going to change that. I want to marry Kaycee and start a new life. She loves the kids and they love her."

Hal rubbed a hand over his jaw, and stared at Jon. Finally he pushed up from the chair.

"I'll talk to Marjorie," he said gruffly, turned and left the room.

When Jon came into the kitchen, all the children were gathered around the island, listening to Wendy embellish her ordeal in the blizzard. Kaycee slipped to his side and they stood arm in arm, listening. Jon leaned down to kiss Kaycee lightly on the lips. When he looked up, Hal stood in the doorway. He stepped into the kitchen, followed by Marjorie. The kids grew quiet, all eyes riveted on the tall, stern man now standing in the center of the room.

"Marjorie and I have had a talk. We only want what's best for you. Most of all, we want you in our lives."

Jon's heart sank. What more could he do to appease the man?

"But, I—we don't think the children would be happy living with us. This is where they belong."

The kids went wild. Rachel and Sam jumped from their stools, dancing and hugging. Wendy ran to her grandmother. Marjorie stooped to join her in a frenzy of hugging and kissing. Yipping and yelling, the twins raced around the room.

Michele grabbed Jon and pulled him down. "I love you, Daddy. You kept your promise."

"Your grampa had a lot to do with that. Why don't you thank him?"

Michele flew around the counter. Surprised, Hal caught her as she jumped into his arms. She clung to his neck and kissed him on the cheek.

"Thanks, Grampa! We love you!"

Hal quickly flicked his thumb under his eyes. *Iron man melts,* Jon thought with a measure of satisfaction.

"It's the right thing to do," he said to Hal.

"I know." Still holding Michele with one arm, Hal took the hand Jon offered.

"Children," Marjorie said, "I have something to tell you."

They gathered round her, eager to hear. "Your grandfather and I are going to find a house in Bozeman so we can live close to you part of the year. You can come visit us there as often as you want."

The kids liked the idea. So did Jon. He'd have an easier time letting them stay in Bozeman than San Francisco until he was satisfied Hal could be trusted. He smiled and gave his mother-in-law a hug.

"Thanks, Marjorie."

She pulled him down to her level, kissed him on the cheek, and whispered, "I'm sorry it took so long. And now introduce us properly to your Kaycee."

A FEW MINUTES LATER, Jon caught Kaycee by the arm and they slipped away from the chaos. In the shadowy barn, he took Kaycee in his arms.

"You know, I've been giving the situation some thought," he said slowly. "And I've concluded I'm going to need a vet on retainer this year."

"You told me you never need to call a vet."

"I said I never used to need one," he corrected. "Until I found out just how indispensable they are. The wages aren't much. Room and board."

"Room and board?"

Jon put his fingers on her lips. "But the benefits are excellent."

"And what might that be?" Kaycee noted the laughter in his eyes.

"Hugs and an overwhelming number of kisses from eight people who love you."

Her heart pounded, her skin tingled where his fingers touched. "Jon, I don't want to give up my career."

"I don't want you to, either. I don't know how I'm going to stand the worry of you out all hours of the night, but I guess I'll manage."

"I've been giving that some thought. First thing, I'm going to get a more reliable answering service than poor harried Sarah, so you can find me when you need me—most of the time, anyway. And as soon as Daniel graduates, he's going to join me."

"Wendy had a point last night. We've learned how to take care of ourselves since Alison died. I think we're going to be just fine."

Kaycee smiled through her tears. "I think we are, too."

Jon touched his lips to her forehead, the tip of her nose, her lips. He entwined his fingers in her hair as he pressed his mouth to hers and kissed her until her knees went weak and she clung to his broad shoulders just to remain standing. He lowered his forehead to hers.

"And someday, we could make some babies of our own, you and me. I really like making babies, in case you haven't noticed."

"I have noticed. And you're very good at it."

Jon grinned, but Kaycee's uncertainty must have showed when she pulled back.

"What's wrong? If you don't want any more babies, I can live with that, too," Jon said quickly.

"No, it's not that. But our relationship—it's been so unorthodox. I mean I'm not sure when it became real."

Jon ran his thumb slowly across her bottom lip, his face inching closer to hers as he spoke. "Oh, for me, about the time you realized I had seven children, my own private social worker and no food in the house and, instead of running, you invited us to breakfast."

Kaycee smiled. Jon brushed the curls off her forehead with his fingertips. "Time's not what matters."

"You're right," Kaycee whispered. "I love you more than I've ever loved anybody."

"I was hoping you'd say that." Jon dropped carefully to one knee and grimaced.

"Jon, get up. You need to be in bed. Your leg—"

"Shh, the leg will heal and I want this done right. Believe me, as soon as I take care of this business, I'm going to take that pain medication and sleep a week." He caught her hand in both of his. "Katherine Calloway, I love you with all my heart. I want to spend my life with you. Will you marry me—and my children?"

Jon's face blurred. With her free hand, she wiped her eyes.

"That's a proper proposal," he pointed out. "And I'm not under the influence of drugs or anything else right now. And the sooner you say 'yes,' the sooner I can rest."

"Yes, I'll marry you—and your children."

"She said 'yes!'" Michele screamed from the doorway.

Kaycee looked around in surprise as a swarm of kids bolted down the aisle. From the doorway, Rosie, Clint, Marjorie and Hal clapped their approval.

Jon slowly got up. "Well I hope you meant it. Things are going be this way from now on."

Kaycee laughed, her eyes sweeping the excited children jumping around them. "I meant it. I love it!"

The kids gave a cheer.

"You kids scram. All the way to the house," Jon said with a broad grin. "Now!"

"We love you, Dr. Kaycee," Michele cried, as they ran out of the barn. "Hurry and marry Daddy! We want you to live here."

Wendy lingered. Shyly she went up to Kaycee and hugged her around the waist. "You're going to be a great mom," she said, then took off after her siblings.

When Rosie and the other adults had herded the kids away, Kaycee caught Jon by the back of the neck, pulling him down. As she nibbled on his lower lip, she murmured, "We'll discuss the room and board later, but right now I want to work on some of those benefits you mentioned. The overwhelming hugs and kisses from eight people who love me. Starting with the father."

"No problem, Doc," he said, between kisses. "That's a salary I'll be happy to pay every day."

Ria Sterling has the gift—or is it a curse?—
of seeing a person's future in his or her
photograph. Unfortunately, when detective
Carrick Jones brings her a missing person's
case, she glimpses his partner's ID—and
sees imminent murder. And when her vision
comes true, Ria becomes the prime suspect.
Carrick isn't convinced this beautiful woman
committed the crime...but does he believe
she has the special powers to solve it?

Look for

Seeing Is Believing

by

Kate Austin

Available October
wherever you buy books.

HN88144

REQUEST YOUR FREE BOOKS!
2 FREE NOVELS PLUS 2 FREE GIFTS!

HARLEQUIN®

Super Romance®

Exciting, emotional, unexpected!

HSR07

74 Seaside Avenue

New York Times Bestselling Author

DEBBIE MACOMBER

Dear Reader:

I'm living a life I couldn't even have dreamed of a few years ago. I'm married to Bobby Polgar now, and we've got this beautiful house with a view of Puget Sound.

Lately something's been worrying Bobby, though. When I asked, he said he was "protecting his queen"—and I got the oddest feeling he wasn't talking about chess but about me. He wouldn't say anything else.

Do you remember Get Nailed, the beauty salon in Cedar Cove? I still work there. I'll tell you about my friend Rachel, and I'll let you in on what I've heard about Linnette McAfee. Come in soon for a manicure and a chat, okay?

Teri (Miller) Polgar

"Those who enjoy good-spirited, gossipy writing will be hooked."
—*Publishers Weekly* on *6 Rainier Drive*

Available the first week of September 2007, wherever paperbacks are sold!
www.MIRABooks.com

MDM2485

HARLEQUIN
Super Romance

COMING NEXT MONTH

#1446 THE BABY GAMBLE • Tara Taylor Quinn
Texas Hold 'Em

Desperate to have a baby, Annie Kincaid turns to the only man she trusts—her ex-husband, Blake Smith—and asks him to father her child. Because when it comes to love, the stakes are high....

#1447 TEMPORARY NANNY • Carrie Weaver

Who would guess that the perfect nanny for a ten-year-old boy is Royce McIntyre? Not Katy Garner, that's for sure. But she has no other choice than to ask her handsome neighbor for help. Never expecting that Royce might be the perfect answer for someone else…

#1448 COUNT ON LOVE • Melinda Curtis
Going Back

Annie Raye's a single mom who's trying to rebuild her life after her ex-husband, a convict, tarnished her reputation. But returning home to Las Vegas makes "going straight" difficult because she's still remembered as a child gambling prodigy. And it doesn't help when Sam Knight costs her a good job. So she sets out to prove the private investigator wrong.

#1449 BECAUSE OF A BOY • Anna DeStefano
Atlanta Heroes

Nurse Kate Rhodes mistakenly believes one of her young charges is being abused by his dad and sets in motion a series of events that jeopardize the lives of the young boy and his father, who are forced to go into hiding. To right her wrong, she must work with Stephen Creighton, the legal advocate who's defending the accused father, and find the pair before it's too late.

#1450 THE BABY DOCTORS • Janice Macdonald

When widowed pediatrician Sarah Benedict returns home after fifteen years in Central America, she wants to set up a practice where traditional and alternative medicine work together. And she hopes to team up with Matthew Cameron, the friend she's loved since she was eight. Loved *and* lost, when he married someone else. Except now he's divorced...and she doesn't like the person he's become.

#1451 WHERE LOVE GROWS • Cynthia Reese

Becca Reynolds has a job to do—investigate the suspicious insurance claims of several farmers. Little does she realize that she "knows" one of the men in question. Could Ryan MacIntosh really be involved? And will she be able to find out before he figures out who she is?